RISK

Roger Granelli

Published by Accent Press Ltd – 2008

ISBN 9781906125103

Printed and bound in the UK

Cover Design by The Design House

The author wishes to acknowledge the award of a Writer's Bursary
from the Academi for the purpose of completing this book.

For Lola, Simone
and my mother Joan

Thanks to Elaine Morgan for all her kind help over the years, and to Judith for the computer wizardry.

James was a long time waking. Invisible hands held him, and he was being shaken. He thought an earthquake was taking place. He'd been in one, once. It had taken three days for his brain to realise the ground was no longer moving under him, a week for it to transmit that message to his legs. Today it took him just a few minutes to know that this was him writhing around, sheets throttled in his hands like so many necks, his unsteady bed made more so by his turning body.

James blinked his eyes in an attempt to still the thoughts that were springing back into action. He'd often tried to deny his existence in a dream but it was no good. It never was.

Light. It streamed in through the window to assault him. He'd forgotten to close the blind, again. It formed dappled patterns in his shabby room, picking out the spare, worn furniture, and making early morning dust dance. He struggled to free himself from the bed, got up shakily and lent against the window-sill. As he rubbed at his eyes and looked out, the dawn landscape was also lit up by the coldest and whitest of light. Brown hillside seemed to be coming to meet him in a featureless landslide, above it a blank sky framed the blind valley in its bare winter coat. James shivered in the T-shirt and shorts he'd had on for three days, put all his despair into one long sigh, and got back into his narrow bed.

James knew he was close to the end of things, one way or another. Each click of the wheel in his head told him this, but it did not want to let him go. Recently he'd found out that some called it *the wheel of misfortune*. He'd been too low to laugh, roulette had been his favourite from the outset, a deadly mistress. Now it lay like a cancer at the heart of his weakness, biting into him steadily. There was a supporting cast, cards, horses, dogs and any sport he could bet on, some of which he'd never even seen played.

James wanted to make this day one when he'd pull

down a curtain between brain and eyes and just exist. He'd sleep a lot, curled up foetus-like in a grey limbo, a forty-seven-year-old man's defence against the world. If he was lucky all might be calm inside for a while.

Just for today I will be unafraid.

This was one of his commandments. For addicts. He knew them by heart now, they had become a kind of religion. James repeated it many times, barely moving his lips, but loud enough to hear. His personal mantra. He mouthed another one.

I will try to think of all that is beautiful in my life.

Tricky. If he could change *is* to *was* it might be more feasible. Today, mantras would be needed. It was twenty-four hours to Pete's funeral and each one would drip away as slowly as possible.

It was hard to believe Pete was gone. James had talked to him a few hours before he disappeared. The man seemed lighter, in mind and body. Almost happy. Even attempting a joke. How many times had James read that in newspapers, the man had no problems, the man had a great family, a great life. The man killed himself. Not that any of these could apply to Pete, but it was still a shock.

Pete had been on the doorstep that first time James checked into the hostel. It was a day that was supposed to mark the start of his return to society, or at least the first faltering steps. It hadn't felt like it. Following instructions, he'd taken a bus to the top of the valley, where mountains merged into a full stop. He walked with his small case alongside boarded-up buildings, spattered with badly-spelt graffiti, passed a few metal-grilled, bunker-like shops, and a scattering of poorly dressed people hunched up against the bitter wind. He'd sucked in the air of general decay, smelt a past that was long gone and a future that was a broken promise and thought *perfect*.

Pete thrust out a tremulous, blue-veined hand and introduced himself, a short, slight, straight up and down man, his face an angry puce road-map of look-at-us bumps and bruises; the life mask of a drunk. Wiry remnants of sandy hair stood up in tufts on his head, like tussocks on a stretch of sand, and liquid eyes seemed pickled in a lifetime of booze. Pete's handshake had been light but genuine, and he'd ushered James inside like he was showing around a prospective buyer. James thought Pete was in his sixties, but found out later that he was a much younger man.

Pete softened that first day with his welcome, at a time when James needed a touch of kindness, any touch of kindness. He reminded James of Stan Laurel, same wistful lost air, same probing of the remainder of his hair, same ability to break into tears easily. Pete's were real. He did self-pity almost as much as he did vodka, they trampled in tandem across what was left of his mind. This didn't bother James for he understood Pete; they were kindred spirits. James knew that when he looked at Pete he was looking at himself, another step down. He didn't want to take that step.

Pete gave him the grand tour of the hostel. Coming from the street and squats, it didn't seem too bad. Four years ago, James would have looked at it with horror, and felt sympathy for its inhabitants. It had four bedrooms, a kitchen, shower-room and toilet and was filled with re-cycled stuff. Geriatric cooker and freezer, Formica kitchen table on thin legs that moved, mis-matched chairs, and evidence everywhere of former tenants. Door handles that tended to fall off splintered doors, chunks gouged from walls, a rank stair carpet, showing the many trails of old beer spills, and other, more suspicious, patches. James's bedroom had a thin single bed, with a dark red quilt that looked like it had been taken from a Gothic coffin. In a corner was an ancient, tall wardrobe, and an equally old Wilton carpet to match the one on the stairs. Someone must have donated it. He did have a good view of the hillside opposite, though, and the room was quite light. It would do.

James came to like Pete, and his hopeless boozy

openness. He became the nearest thing to a friend James had had in years. It came as a surprise to him to realise that he needed one.

Pete was gone, but at least he had a sense of theatre. This man who hated walking – bedroom to kitchen was a trek for him – had almost made it to the top of the hillside, where he chose a solitary tree that cut the skyline like a plea with its out-stretched branches. He dangled there for a few hours before he was spotted. A farmer said he thought it was kids messing about, until he got closer, and his dogs started to whine.

Yesterday, James had gone to see Pete in the undertaker's chapel of rest. He doubted if anyone else would. It was in the next village down, a thirty-minute walk. The weather was suitably dreary, and low clouds accompanied him. They scudded down from the hills and the valley's blind end, black on top, dirty grey belly-up. The type that unloaded very quickly, and within minutes James knew that his shoes no longer kept the water out. Clothes were easy to get from charity shops, shoes a bit more personal. Not that his geriatric anorak was much better. It looked substantial but was a fraud and gave up the ghost after a few minutes of sweeping rain.

His feet began to squelch as he walked alongside the river that cut the valley. Rubbish had covered its banks for generations. Rivers were a convenient dumping ground and James viewed multiple rusting sculptures, parts of cars and motor bikes, fridges, washing machines, and the ubiquitous supermarket trolley, all set off by smaller items of rubbish that had been pushed up by the current into the branches of low-lying trees. It was like the still-life display of an insane artist. Or sane. Not still life, James thought. Stagnant life. The button eyes of a child's doll tracked his progress along the bank. It hung high up in a tree, pink, lost, and seeming somehow human.

By the time James reached his goal his feet were

frozen, and the rest of him was getting ready to follow. He rang the bell at the side of the undertaker's double oak doors. He half expected it to boom out some sort of death knell but it was more a sweet-sounding tinkle, a noise so discreet it was almost lost on the wind.

A fresh-faced kid answered. He was in regulation uniform, white shirt, black trousers, and matching shiny shoes, his neck constrained by the tight black knot of a tie. He looked at James suspiciously, raking him from head to foot with a young but already judicious eye. James asked for Pete.

Family?

Brother, James murmured.

He though the lie was prudent, he might not get in otherwise. He followed the young assistant. This place was cool, as cool as a church. They'd tried to disguise the endgame atmosphere with a delicate fragrance but it only served to confirm what the place was. The air was heavy, and final. Music played faintly in the background, so faint it was hard to make out, but James realised it was Mozart, safe, but too sunny. Almost a denial. Junior undertaker was just out of his teens, but already schooled in that respectful, sugary whisper that went with the job. James doubted that death meant anything more than the big sleep, but that was probably a better place for Pete, or at least a better state. He'd always complained of insomnia.

Here we are, the boy said.

James felt a hand lightly touch his shoulder as he was guided towards a side room where Pete was lying in his state-provided chipboard box. James approached cautiously. Pete had been a fan of horror films, and James half expected him to jump up, shouting out that he wasn't dead at all. He was.

A lot of Pete had been smoothed out, a grey blandness had replaced much of what had marked his face. A lifetime of booze had been diminished, but it couldn't be erased that easily, and faint red streaks came through the touch-up stuff. There was a piece of silky cloth placed discreetly around his neck, like a ruff. Pete was going out with a scarf on, looking like a painted mime artist. He would have thought this very funny. James almost laughed himself. He almost cried too. There was not much difference between the two. He thought of kissing Pete on the cheek, but couldn't do it, so he touched his face gently. It was like touching a candle, waxy and cold. Lifeless. Bye, mate, he whispered.

The rain had stopped when James got back outside but it was colder. He dabbed at his eyes and breathed in deeply, as deeply as his chest would allow. He wondered if his asthma would be bad this winter. The last five years had taken his chest into new territory. It feared the cold and wet. He decided to use precious money on a bus back.

James expunged the dread atmosphere of the chapel, felt much better, and wondered at this. Other peoples' passing had often lightened his mood. He'd never been able to explain it. A few relatives had gone since his fall from grace, and he'd turned up like a shadow at the edge of their funerals, not wanting to embarrass himself or anyone else. There was a sense of relief afterwards, maybe because *he* was still alive, and, despite everything, wanted to go on. Maybe he was just twisted. At the last one he thought his ex-wife recognised him under the hat and scarf, Nina always did have sharp eyes. He stumbled away quickly, cracking his ankle on a corner of a tombstone, and cursing the deceased for going into the ground, and not the flames.

There was a kinder edge to the light. He rubbed a circle in the steamed-up bus window and through it saw the hillside edged with pale colour, its empty spaces picked out by the sun. James was struck by how the terraces advanced up the slopes so far, then stopped, as if they had given up. Larger houses had sprung up on the higher reaches in recent times, the new rich people who looked down.

Walking the hills in his early life, he'd met very few people, and even fewer of his own age. They were down below, where the action was, the work, or lack of it, the joy, pain, and chances of failure and success. James tried to call up one of the commandments.

Just for today I will be happy.

The hardest one of all, but he wanted to do it for Pete. To do it without going into the Hollybush, without a glass of courage in his hand, without dreaming of that one big score, the thousand, million, trillion to one shot he'd never get, the Roulette run he'd never have, and didn't have the money to even try any more.

The rain did not hold off for long. A squall managed to soak him as soon as he got off the bus, even though there was still a trace of sun. Typically devious valley weather. James wanted a warming drink. There were always hurdles to get over, bunkers to avoid. He managed to jump the Hollybush hurdle but Pete had left him the remnants of a bottle of lo-cost whisky, four fingers of rotgut, and into this bunker he sank. James had to drink it. It was a matter of honour. His reward for not going into the pub. Brave thoughts soon vanquished.

Next morning James found a white shirt to put on and used Pete's own black tie, almost garrotting himself with it. He looked like someone he would have avoided on the street years ago, the guy who invariably sits by you on the bus or train, and starts talking as his odour wafts up. At least he wasn't hung-over, and he didn't smell. If Pete had left a full bottle he would have surely drunk it all.

James had managed to get the undertaker's car to pick him up at eleven and had made the alien time. He'd even shaved, or attempted to. It was more a slash and burn of his face. Now, two small pieces of tissue paper were stuck to it, white spots with bloody centres. A target on each cheek. He'd pull them off when out in the open air, it was too cold outside to bleed.

Outside the hostel, James waited a few minutes for the car. The wind cut right through his Oxfam anorak with the twisted zip that didn't work, and his black supermarket trousers were hopelessly inadequate. The wind had found all his fetid hiding places of the last few years; doorways, alleys, and squats. James had woken up to it many times, but had never got used to it, he'd feel that each threatened bone had been coated with ice and that there was no heat left in the world. None at all.

A few people were lost in the Crematorium chapel. They made its cold space seem vast, and the rows of empty pews spoke clearly of Pete's position in the world. Pete had a sister somewhere but she didn't show up. James doubted that there was anyone else, Pete would have mentioned it. It was just him, someone from the police, and Pete's support worker, a girl who looked too young for the job. James had seen her a few times before and nodded to her. Her healthy youth was out of place here, though James noticed that light blue smudges were already appearing under her eyes. Put there by people like Pete, and himself. Maybe she thought she'd failed. James felt like going over to her and telling her not to worry, that this was not about success or failure, just an end. Telling her that people like Pete were bent on self-destruction, and that they couldn't be stopped. That was their one talent, the ability to open all the wrong doors and crash through them. Pete had found the right door this time, the one with lights over it, and his name under them.

They sat uncomfortably in the first pew, almost within touching distance of the coffin. A vicar came in holding a piece of paper, with a few details about the deceased. The man was old, well past retirement age, and his face was as pale as his vestments. All they could get, James thought. The vicar mumbled a few things, tracing his notes with shaking finger, mentioned *the Tragedy of Peter* as if it was a play. He said Pete was *at rest*, then tried to lead the sparse gathering through one thin hymn, which started up when he pressed a button. No organist for Pete.

As he made a few movements with his lips, James remembered the hymn from school. He'd hated it then. The old vicar pressed another button and Pete slid away, on his road to ashes. James felt his eyes moisten. He was amazed that they did, and tried to stop them, but they did not obey. A solitary tear settled on his cheek and he brushed it away quickly, before anyone noticed. He thought the support worker might have, and felt himself redden. Then it was over, and his hand was being shaken by the vicar's cold one. It felt like parchment rustling in his hand. James heard something about *sad loss* and sensed the girl approaching him. He got out quickly. The policeman gave him a lift back.

We'll be in touch, the policeman said. They'll need you for the inquest, probably, keep your nose clean until then.

Just for today I will strengthen my mind.

It was the most useful commandment, the one he was trying to follow. He had them listed on a piece of paper. He had meant to tack it up on the back of his bedroom door, but he hadn't got around to it. They probably had something similar for the drunks, James thought, though Pete had never mentioned anything. Pete had only gone to A.A. meetings a few times. Load of bollocks, he said, after one visit, bit like doctors, and shrinks…and bloody Godsquadders. All trying to get into your head. Pete had been like that. Stubborn. He was his own worst enemy. A stubborn man, a dangling man, now ashes which no one wanted to collect.

James stood outside the hostel for a few minutes. He'd been here for three months. Getting friendly with Pete had made it a kind of home, but now it was barren again. James wondered if this might be a place beyond the last chance saloon for him, like it had been for Pete.

They'd chosen the spot well. Two small terraces had been knocked into one, it was the last building in a tawdry row. The house next door was boarded up, rough corrugated sheets had been nailed over the windows and door, it was a metal shell decorated with graffiti now. Someone sucked, someone stank, and someone loved Liverpool F.C. forever. Someone told everybody to *Fuk Off*. The hostel had been part renovated on the outside, but not the part James lived in. Like himself, it was still waiting for its make-over. His bedroom window was rotting soft wood that invited the elements in.

They'd picked out the most anonymous place they could find. Only mountains reared up in front of it. A natural barrier that was a black mass now as the light faded, the sky above it a leaden grey flecked with red. Like Pete's face. Nothing moved on it in this weather; even the sheep had more sense. This landscape fitted his situation and James welcomed its emptiness. It had a special quality, an unchanging nature that stayed honest. When he'd waxed lyrical about scenery like this, Nina used to call him *miserable*. When things started to sour she added *loner*. He suspected she might have also thought *loser*, but that remained unsaid. James smiled now at her percipience, but it was a thin and bitter smile and he felt it cutting at his face.

Are you goin' in or wha'?

Billy Williams was talking to him. James hadn't seen him coming. Billy was back from his afternoon at the Hollybush. It was giro day, and he would have already drunk a fair part of it, sucking the bottom out of each glass that came to hand. Billy stank of lager and rotten teeth. He was small, almost wizened, a scaled-down version of Pete, with a similar, scabby, red, seamed face, but his eyes were still bright. They still looked forwards.

Pity 'bout Pete, huh? Poor bastard.

I thought you might have come to the send-off.

Nah. Funerals – can' stand 'em. Wha's the point? No disrespect to Pete, like, but when you're gone, you're gone.

They can throw me over a hedge, if they wan'. Lemme go natural, like.

Billy's day was divided up into drinking sessions. It was his whole life. For him there was logic and purpose to it, drink, sleep it off, drink, sleep it off. Nothing much existed outside the pub. How Billy stayed alive was a mystery. He never seemed to eat, certainly not in the hostel.

James could see the Hollybush sign at the corner of the street, and felt its pull himself; it was the magnet, and he the pin. If he went down there now he'd be there until closing time, using Pete as an excuse, though drinking was only part two of his problem. It was useful in taking his thoughts away from gambling. It had begun like that, a panacea for the disappointment of losing, and the guilt of trying to win. For a moment, a hopeless joy surged through James at the thought of having a punt. The joy of release, the chance of winning again, and the charge that came with it, rekindled within him. This was his line of cocaine, his mainline needle, but his had been a slower, more insidious addiction. James took a last look at the mountain before he went inside. He was trying to see this raw slab of land as a guardian, and he needed all the help he could get.

Just for today I will strengthen my mind.

Pete had left a box of his things in James's room. Nothing could say goodbye as eloquently as this pitiful collection. A few books, unread, the black tie that James had worn today, three pounds seventy pence in change, and a small collection of photographs. James arranged these on the bed. None was recent but it was possible to chart Pete's life, to some extent. There were two black and white shots, one of a toddler in a large garden, another on a beach. Someone had written, *Peter, aged seven, at Tenby*, in neat handwriting, on the back. It was hard to equate the smiling, beach-playing boy, with the man they'd just burnt. Pete had a shock of blond hair, too long for a kid, but true sixties style. The rest were later shots. Pete in high school, serious, and squinting at the official school photographer, the hair already turning sandy. There were a few more in his early twenties, a family one with his arms around maybe mother and sister, the sister who never showed up today. In another, Pete was older, pushing forty perhaps. His face was well on its way to ruin in this one, drink had taken its hold and marked him up. He was angry, hand out-stretched, in defiance, or maybe just to shield himself from the intrusion of the lens. Pete had never shared stories. James did not even know if his parents were still alive, probably not, or they would surely have appeared at the crematorium. James had once asked about his past, to be told it was the drink, just drink, as if that explained his whole history, so it was a surprise when he turned over the last photo. Pete was standing outside a church, confetti in his hair, a pretty dark-haired girl on his arm. He looked about twenty five. The police must have found his wife, ex-wife, must have told her, and she hadn't attended. That drew the line under his demise.

James sat near his bedroom window, on what passed for an armchair. The radiator was under the window but it had to contend with the rotten window frame, which leaked copious amounts of draught into the room. They'd promised new windows next year. His thoughts were taken back forty years, to primary school, and wet, interminably long winters, dangerously hot radiators and huddled bunches of kids drying out. Macintoshes smelling of the cold and damp, and starting to steam. *Macintoshes.* Clothes from another time. His time. It didn't seem like forty years. It didn't seem like any time at all.

James twirled a letter around in his hand. It came yesterday, he'd recognised the handwriting on the envelope and didn't want to open it until Pete was sorted. *A letter.* That was also becoming a thing of the past, but so much better than something spewed out of a machine. Give me snail-mail any time, James thought, quite pleased that he had learnt the jargon. One of the support workers had mentioned about getting the hostel a computer, to be met by blank stares and a giggle from Pete. Billy was quite keen. He'd sell it the first chance he got.

The letter was from Clare, his elder daughter. It had followed him around, but had eventually found him. James wished Pete had left more whisky. He ran his tongue around his teeth, trying to tease out an echo of it. In his head he added the money Pete had left to his own meagre stash. Enough to buy a bottle of corner-shop special, the stuff that companies disguised with bizarre Scottish names, sold by a teetotal Sikh. He fought to stop himself leaving the hostel, in search of *Cream of the Lochs*.

James took a deep breath and opened the letter, cutting the top of a finger in his haste. This was a day of cuts, shaving cuts, paper cuts, bits of pain to keep him focused. He sucked the end of the finger, and kept it away from the four pages inside the letter. He hesitated, told himself the pages wouldn't bite, but he had every expectation that they might. Nothing bit deeper than families.

Clare was her mother's girl. Full of clear analysis and practicality, qualities he'd never had. Blind action, wrong moves and crumbling resolve were more his line. James smiled to himself, a wistful purse of the lips. Even now, holding the first letter from the family in ages, he turned it around to himself. He'd become the centre of his world, and the problem at the heart of it.

Clare wrote in a neat, accountant's hand. That was what she was, or on her way to becoming. He couldn't remember if she'd finished all her exams or not. He couldn't remember if she'd even told him. Clare got straight down to it. Her mother had met someone else.

James usually tried to block off thoughts of Nina, they didn't do him much good, but now they flooded back into his brain. Thoughts led to images which led to a rapid freeze-framing of twenty-five years' history. James shut his eyes for a moment. There was pressure behind them which he hoped wouldn't lead to a migraine. He'd been plagued with them recently.

Another man. Of course. Why not? It was normal. It was okay. Best for everyone. They'd been divorced for three years. It was *okay*. Understanding words, but they fell like bitter pills into his guts. It was hard to get his breath, and his eyes watered. Twice in one day. He twisted the pages in his hands and threw them down. James wasn't sure if he was having a panic attack.

Billy was singing in his bedroom. *Whisky in the Jar.* His favourite drunken anthem, sung when all his fantasised Irishness came out on parade, lies took wings, and Billy soared up into the dream he'd created. Usually he passed out with the song on his lips, but this time he was having one of his 'turns'. Things were being thrown around. Something heavy crashed against the adjoining wall, it was as if Billy was acting out what was in James's own head. When Billy was like this Pete had calmed him down, communicating with Billy in their own whisky patois, the secret language of *drunken*. Pete wasn't here any more, and maybe this was Billy's show of grief, the nearest he could get to it.

Outside the rain was coming down hard. James watched it collide with the window and run down onto the sill, forming tiny pools on its rutted surface. The streetlight outside the window was coming on. It glowed pink, then red, then gradually turned to its orange strength. At first he'd hated it so close to the window, like a searchlight marking him out, but he'd grown used to it. When it came on it signalled he'd got through another day, but there was yet another night to endure. It was the sign of his new world, a world gradually shrinking down to nothing.

The noises in the next room stopped and James thought of checking on Billy, but the man might start up again and there was no one else in the hostel. A newcomer had been expected, now Pete was gone there might be two.

James got up from his chair, pushing some of its padding back in as he did so, and retrieved the letter. He'd scrunched up the pages but had not destroyed them. He smoothed them out and tried to control his breathing.

Adrian, that was the man's name. *Adrian.* He sounded like a scout leader, a hairdresser, a gay minister, a librarian who lived with his mother. Maybe even an angel. James looked down at his stomach turning to paunch, eyed the fraying ends of his trousers and ran a hand over the wear of his face. He'd always looked younger than he was, when he turned forty Nina said he could pass for thirty. Not any more. A youth that lasted too long had turned on him viciously; now he looked *older* than he was. Like Pete had. Like Billy did. Nina would be thinking security, safety, and compensation for a marriage gone wrong. She'd be thinking about hitting fifty. James read on.

Clare *had* finished her exams and was working for a local company. Adrian was there too. He was the financial director. The man was her boss. This got better and better. Adrian had a place in the Vale. Yes, of course he did. Not that Nina ever had a thing about money, but she'd had to get used to stretching it out, making it go further when he lost the ability to provide much. By the time he was dropped by the teaching agencies, all his energies were taken up with betting, his mind never left that small casino in Cardiff, and the many betting offices that lead like tributaries towards it. Then the adjacent pubs. At first drink crushed out guilt, re-fuelled hope, but need turned to addiction and he was snared and could not stop. Dared not stop. Then there was nothing to stop for, for he'd lost everything that had been dear to him.

James wondered how much of her past Nina would tell this man. *Yes, Adrian, none of us could understand it. No one on either side of the family has ever gambled – I doubt if James's father would have known how – and he kept it secret for so long – until it was too late.* Adrian nodding sympathetically, making comforting noises as he thinks of the future.

Zoe was doing well in college, Clare told him. His descent and fall had been harder for his youngest daughter. At least Clare had left school by the time things got bad. Zoe was Greek for a zest for life, and she had lived up to it. Dizzying heights, great depths, with no grey worlds between. Zoe hadn't talked to him or made any communication since the divorce, that was their mutual punishment. James doubted that she'd like a step-Dad. Zoe would have got used to having her mother to herself by now. She'll make your life hell – Ade, James thought.

I finished with Russ a few months ago, Clare wrote, *we just sort of fizzled out.*

James tried to remember who Russ was, but it was hard. His head was still full of Pete. He wished he'd found him, then he'd have one clear, awful image, not the many variants that scudded through his mind. He saw him from every angle, the distant, gently swaying spot, so far away it could be an errant branch, then up close, close enough to hear the slight creak of the tree's limbs, and see the distorted blackened face, protruding tongue and wet trousers. He missed Pete, a man even more hopeless than himself he'd only known for a few short months. Someone he might once have given a few coins to on the street, or tried to avoid.

Clare talked about a world from which James had excluded himself, and it was getting harder to picture it. Especially today. Hanged men, the flames of damnation and the need for a drink occupied the front seats of his thoughts, but Adrian was in the balcony. Looking down. Clare wanted to make contact. *I'd like to see you, Dad. Will you phone this number?* It was the last thing she wrote.

James's hands were shaking when he put the letter down. A shake that came on more often now and was harder to control. The thought of Clare appearing at the hostel was unnerving, but she didn't know where he was. He hoped she didn't. In the morning that woman from social services would be around. Checking up. Tragic events got them agitated.

He needed a drink. It had started to challenge the need for a bet and was more achievable. James was far removed from the places of his first ruin, his old haunts were hard to get to now, even if he had the money, but drink could always be had. His legs wanted him to go to the corner shop, grab up the bottle of rubbish Scotch, wince under the cheery grin of the shopkeeper and skulk off with his prize like a thief in the night. Just about making it back to the hostel before he tore off the top.

James heard Billy go out again. He'd napped for a while, now he was ready for the night shift. For a moment James was envious of him. Billy didn't want to *get better,* or change in any way. In his eyes he'd done it right, no wife, no kids, no one but himself to hurt. Billy thought he was an individual, in the warped logic of the loner-drunk he was a warrior prince, courtesy of the state.

When he'd still read, James had come across a copy of Patrick Hamilton's *Hangover Square*, a well-thumbed out-of-print edition he found on a market bookstall. Now he could relate to George, the main character, hapless lover and drunk, his life as stale as the book smelt. Hamilton got it right about the stagnation of lives gone sour. James knew, he was living amidst the proof. He was part of it.

Self-disgust, laced with self-pity and tinged with anger, began to brew up into a vile concoction, Pete's death, Clare's letter, were bringing it to the fore. Only when he got really drunk could James stop beating himself up. Just the self-pity was left then, and a maudlin re-working of the past. He tried to hang on to his commandments.

Just for today I will be unafraid.

James wasn't sure if he imagined the thunder at first.

17

He thought it might be another marker in his descent, maybe a sign of the ultimate crack-up. No, it *was* thunder. Black clouds were heaving up over the mountain ridge, beating out the last of the light, and scouring the streets with sheets of rain. James got up and stood by the window. He'd always been fascinated by a good storm.

A few lightning streaks came down onto the ridge, yellow fingers pointed out the place of Pete's last stand. For a moment, the landscape was lit up by a cool white light, framed in his mind for ever. This is for you, mate, James thought, your own, personal send off. Soon small rivers washed the gutters. Within minutes each drain had its own trash-world, paper, plastic and polystyrene piled up into soggy pyramids on metal grills, topped by dog crap. All the rubbish being washed, but not washed away. James put Clare's letter back in its envelope and carefully placed it in one of the few books he had. A racing guide, two years out of date.

James left the window and went to bed. It was all he could think to do. At least he'd coped with Pete's meagre send-off and had resisted the booze.

Just for today I will be strong.

*

Maybe my life is starting to go ahead again. Nina Read – survivor. Survivor of all James threw at me in our last five years together. The girls are getting sorted and I'm watching Adrian put my suitcase in his car. Mine's quite large for a short trip away but it looks lost in the space of that boot. Adrian's almost lost in it too. It's not that he's particularly short, just slight. A bare minimum of flesh over his bones. A boy's body. I should be glad, that's much better than a middle-aged man who looks like he's six months pregnant, perhaps what I should be expecting, at my age. This trip to Scotland is my birthday present from him, my fiftieth birthday present, from a new man. *A new man*. I say it to myself quietly, and tease the novelty of the phrase around with my tongue. I'm glad I'm spending my fiftieth away, it's not a milestone I care to advertise. It's hard to believe I have half a century of memories, but I'm not so depressed about it as I thought. There's no point, I can't change it. No one can.

I still feel self-conscious about the Mercedes though, an echo of James, perhaps. God knows I had enough of his opinions and judgments over the years. If James ever succeeded at anything it was shouting the odds. He was a champion at that. Even when he knew he was wrong he'd still be right. I was saturated in planet James for more than twenty years, and as old friends drifted away I became his captive audience of one. If I close my eyes, I can hear him now, his voice getting higher and higher, his face redder, chasing the tail of each thought around in his head as he'd return from school full of frustration and rage. Full of hate at the end. I learnt how to build up a wall against this. Treating him like a child who demands attention, and letting his rants pass over my head. This did not bother him. By this time James only required me to receive, not respond.

Maybe this trip is making me edgy. I can picture James's face if he had Adrian's car in his sights. His old socialism would rear up like a banshee, a rather thin banshee, the cloak for all that pent-up jealousy. How the banshee wailed in our last year together, when the supply work dried up and James was home most of the time. He'd become too loose a cannon and was no longer wanted. He'd even started to turn up at schools not entirely sober. At nine in the morning. He must have thought the bottle he kept in the glove compartment of his car was invisible. When I got home James would already be there, spitting barbs at falling standards and hopeless kids, and how beneath him the job was. Sounding like people he would have hated just a few short years ago. The girls upstairs hearing every word. I had no idea at the time that this was being fuelled by his crazy gambling, but I did know something was badly wrong, and that he was so much better than this. Always edgy, restless, but at least connecting with the girls, being the type of father they thought cool.

Are you ready?

Adrian is impatient to go. He looks so well turned out and enthusiastic, his socks matching the colour of his corduroy trousers. The same weight since college, he tells me. Adrian has never lived with anyone. That might be a problem. I bite a lip and tell myself to stop being negative. Be a little selfish. What does Zoe say? *Seize the moment.* She hasn't said much about Adrian yet, neither has Clare, apart from he's okay to work for. I'm worried about Zoe's reaction. She does simmering silences very well and I'm waiting for the eruption that will inevitably come. Adrian is a sea change for us all.

Go on, mum, he's waiting, Zoe shouts down from her bedroom window.

She's home for the weekend, taking advantage of my absence, no doubt. She's happier than I've seen her for a time, there's probably a new boyfriend around. Zoe hasn't spoken to her father for years, and she's not yet twenty. She's stubborn, to the point of masochism. Just like Dad.

For a moment I see James in college. I can still remember the feeling when he asked me out, or at least my body can. Floating on cloud nine, the envy of all the girls on the third floor. My toy boy. Two years younger than me. I see him twenty years later, looking older than he should, disappointment set on his features, skin tighter, eyes that never looked interested any more, that never focused on me for more than a few seconds before they flitted away.

He's been such a bloody fool. Two gorgeous daughters who idolised him should have been enough. I was never sure why he seemed to be permanently disappointed. He'd had vague notions about being a writer, musician, photographer, any damn thing that involved dreams, and not much action, but he didn't give any of it much more than lip service. This didn't stop him coming on as if he was a mixture of Tolstoy, Dylan and Cartier-Bresson, however. All he had to show for it was a few poems in local magazines, a short story once, and third prize in the local paper for one of his moody black and white shots of trees. It had all fizzled out by the time he was thirty. James wanted people to clap, but no one did.

I still think it was all to do with James's childhood. It must be, but he'd always clammed up about his early life. Despite pontificating about everything else under the sun, he never opened up much about his family and had kept contact with his parents to a minimum. I was surprised when he told me he had any. The girls had hardly seen their grandparents on his side, and then they were gone, dead before sixty. Distance, that's what James did best, but rifts have a habit of growing into chasms.

I can't believe it, I'm about to go away for my first weekend with a new man, and, after three years, James still won't get out of my bloody head. Clare tells me she's written to him. Whether he gets the letter is another matter. God knows where he's holed up now.

Come on, Nina! I want to get off to an early start.

Alright.

Adrian's all precision and timing, a lifetime's competence. On our third date he talked about his collection of old clocks. He is so proud of the things. Went on about them like they were his kids. Perhaps they are. Certainly they're symbols of the order in his life, which I think he's needed. Routine is important for the lonely. Adrian is *nice*. I can't think of a better word and I need nice right now, at least I think I do. I lived more than twenty years with a man who could go from magnificent to disastrous without changing gear, and disaster eventually won. Adrian could never reach either point. I shouldn't be comparing, it's not fair on anyone but it's inevitable. Adrian has been the first since James. *Nice.* Such a bland word, and if I want it, need it, I wonder why it seems to lie like a warning somewhere in the back of my mind.

I'm getting used to the car's leather seats. Bit like sitting on a moving sofa.

Close to the border now, be passing through Gretna in another 20 minutes, Adrian says, attempting a wink. I've allowed for the traffic.

This man is quiet. It's the first thing he's said in ten minutes. We've been driving for half a day with one services stop. In this time James would have talked a good book's worth. Even a moment's silence was a challenge to him. I must try to put James out of my head for the rest of this long weekend. He is the past. Adrian might be the future.

I can't believe we're driving to Scotland. Flying to Paris and spending the weekend in cosy bars would have been more to my liking, the chance to speak French outside of the classroom again, but this is Adrian's surprise. Driving me all this way seems to be important to him, it's better to see a long journey unfold, he says. Even in this comfortable car, my back doesn't agree. Anyway, Paris is for lovers.

*

James lay with his hands behind his head, and stared at the uneven ceiling, its network of cracks, imperfections and evidence of former smokers. The rain hammered on the roof, keeping good time. He wished that the roof could vanish and the rain cleanse him of all his sins and wrong moves. Light faded and the room darkened. James had rituals at night, many ways to tackle his insomnia, none of them very effective. Lately, he'd taken to mouthing his commandments, they were as good or useless as anything else. He felt the tremor on his lips, and willed them to do their work. This time he almost did drop off, but, like most nights, he had to settle for the limbo of half sleep.

He was in the casino. In his dream it was a kind place, full of promise. The promise of happiness, fulfilment, the promise of winning, a rosy future delivered up to him by the well manicured hands of a beautiful girl. At first he'd noticed the table girls as much as any other man, which was why they were there, before gambling became a vice, then an illness, which killed his libido as thoroughly as a castration.

He was winning. At Roulette. He had control of the wheel. It was his, and he could make it fall on black, on red, on any number. Everyone else stopped playing and gathered round. The floor manager was nervously phoning upstairs. There was enough in the pot to retire on. He was glad he wasn't in Vegas, where he might not be able to hang on to the money long enough to get it to the bank. His back was being clapped. He had the money. He held his future in his hands.

James was going home. The family home. Opening the bag and watching its contents cascade down. Blue, green and brown heaven. Buying back love from Nina and the girls. James almost woke with this last thought, even in a dream, its shallowness jarred. Someone was calling him. He thought it was Nina and reached out as he woke up. There was a noise outside. A milk bottle smashed.

Oi, Jimmy, Jimmy Read, lemme in, for fucksake. I'm drownin' out here. Los' my key, an' I.

James went down, the dream slipping away instantly. He let Billy in, which was more a case of catching him as he fell through the door.

Ta, butt. Warra night, eh? Cats an' dogs, or wha'? You should 'ave come down the 'Bush. Give ol' Pete a proper send off.

James sniffed Billy's breath with a sigh. It was the same when he first gave up smoking. Deliberately standing next to someone who had a cigarette on, enjoying the tantalising smoke. He helped Billy up the stairs and put him belly down on the bed in his room.

Thanks, son. You're a diamond. Eh, it was a great night.

It's always a great night for you, Bill. Get some sleep, and don't crash about in the night.

Course not.

But he would, fumbling his way to the toilet like a wayward rhino. Sometimes he made it, sometimes he didn't. James lingered by Pete's door for a moment, then went back to his room, to start the ritual all over again.

He got the dream back. It turned darker. It usually did. Nina was throwing the money back at him. It's too late, she yelled. Who do you think you are? Then a new image. Adrian was there. Trying to calm things down. Walking towards James with out-stretched, placating arms. A man sensibly dressed. A man in control. James was fighting the sheets, twisting and pulling at them. His body knew this routine well and he woke in a sweat that the chill in the room instantly attacked, making him feel clammy, unhealthy. James sat up and licked the outside of his lips, tasted the salt, and wondered what Billy might have in his room.

The door yielded to his touch. Billy hadn't moved much. He'd burrowed into his bed, snoring and muttering to himself. The room smelt like a brewery. James looked around, at the markers of Billy's life. From the light of the passageway he could see empty bottles scattered about on the floor like glass mines, supported by cans of all varieties. All drinks were Billy's favourites. There were more on the windowsill, some under the bed, one nestled in a shoe, and a few lined up neatly on a table, standing to attention in sad pride. It reminded him of his old undergraduate flat, when boozing trophies had been displayed with student bravado. That wasn't the case here. These were the necessities of Billy's life. A few cans had been crushed into the sticky carpet and, amongst them, one not opened. James entered the room and sank down by it as if giving thanks. One you must have missed, Bill, he murmured. It was a can of cheap cider, nine per cent brain rot and one of the few drinks James had never bothered with, but it was nectar tonight. He flipped its ring-pull before he got back to his own room.

The storm had eased, replaced by a steady, insistent rain. James watched the road gleam orange, as he drank the naturally chilled drink, trying not to down it in one, trying to make it last as long as he could, which wasn't that long. Two short swallows, as he teased the sweet liquid around his mouth and into his throat, then one big draught until the can was drained. Not long enough, but the cold can on his lips was calming, and the cider took hold quickly. He held out a hand in front of him and saw that its fingers had stopped dancing.

Although an addicted gambler, James didn't think he was an alcoholic, not yet, but he was getting close. The cider's rapid hit to his brain told him this. If Billy had woken up and tried to grab the can back James wasn't sure what would have happened. Maybe that *was* a definition for addiction. A desire that distorted life until violence became an answer, until it became necessary, and vital.

In his guts the cider was picking a fight with the whisky he'd drunk earlier. James realised he hadn't eaten since breakfast. He abandoned the idea of sleep and went downstairs to the communal kitchen. Communal made it sound spacious but it was not much bigger than a typical terrace kitchen, just room enough for a table and four chairs, fridge and cooker. Each man had a section of the fridge, not that Billy ever kept anything in it. Pete had left a few eggs, which James took. He scrambled them up into a pan and ate them from it standing up. The food almost brought the cider back up but when he sat down he felt better. He had some greasy ballast in him, something to counterbalance the last few days. They had been impressively grim days, even by the standards of the hostel, and its inhabitants. This was a snack on Pete, James thought, the nearest thing to the Last Supper he could get.

It was almost three in the morning, and the milkman was delivering outside. James hummed the old Sinatra song to himself and thought about dying breeds. A few people here still got their milk this way, including himself. It was at the mercy of birds, and any early morning thief, but it still reminded James of better times. Using milk from a bottle, a glass bottle, must make him some sort of dinosaur. He went to the front door, and picked up two bottles. Intact. He opened one and drank, smelling the wet pavement on its glass.

James let the rain drift against his face, thinking it might cool his thoughts, but they were in full flow now, as stubborn as he was. He used to think his stubborn streak was a sign of strength, but that had long since been proved wrong. It was more fatuous vanity. Stubborn for him meant not being able to change, and when things started to fall apart, he hadn't been able to change that either. He'd gone with this downward flow, as his marriage failed, and his kids despaired, as if he was a spectator, and it had nothing at all to do with him. James thought of the girls, when they were young, when everything was moving forward with happy efficiency, marriage, children, job. God was in his heaven, and the meaner world lay elsewhere. He went back upstairs, accompanied by Billy's snores, a steady, snuffled sound that came through his bedroom wall stealthily.

*

Adrian has booked us into a small hotel on the seafront at

Oban. It's cold, wind-swept, with very few people about, but the weather seems to suit him. Bracing, he calls it. I could never see this man sprawled on a beach.

I'm a bit of a Scotsophile, Adrian said. Is that a word? Been coming up here for years. Wait 'til we drive through Glencoe tomorrow. Magnificent scenery, especially if the weather perks up. Do you know the history?

A little.

Yes, something to do with treachery and butchery, I think to myself. What men do.

I'll fill you in on the details as we go, Adrian says.

This is a boy's trip. I don't think Adrian is selfish, in fact I'm sure he's not, just unaware, like most people who've been on their own for a long time. This is the only kind of break he knows. I'll have to teach him other kinds.

Adrian was engaged once. I was surprised when he told me this. She broke it off a few weeks before the big day. That was years ago and I think I'm the first chance he's taken since. I've told Clare how we met, but not Zoe. I don't think she's ready to know that Mum went to a singles night with a teacher friend and came back with Adrian. Clare's been quite supportive, Zoe would yuk-yuk and pretend to go into paroxysms of shock-horror. Maybe not just pretend. She'd think me desperate but I don't think I am. Practical is the word I'd like to use and I'm setting my sights at a realistic level. That's what practical is.

Come on, Nina, there's time for a walk along the front.

This man has energy, in an understated kind of way. I sense that it needs to be released. *Adrian* needs to be released, from his ledgers and financial reports, his formal, rule-laden world. Like I needed to be released from five days a week in the classroom, when all energy and innovation has been siphoned from me years ago. I'm doing supply now, following James, not so satisfying, not so much money, but also not so demanding. Problems can be left at school gates and it's time to be a little selfish in my life. Give myself more time. There was never enough before, and what was left after the girls James demanded. At fifty, I know how very precious it is.

It's almost dark, but there's still a touch of afterglow in the sky, a dirty light yellow at the edge of brooding clouds. Quite moody. Adrian takes my arm as we walk heads down into the wind. I can sense his pride, and it does wonders for my confidence. We're up here for three days. Time enough to tell a lot about where I'm going with this.

There's a great little B and B near Glencoe, Adrian tells me, I've pre-booked it. Not many are open this time of year, but I've stayed there before, in my walking days.

Do you walk much now?

Work gets in the way a lot, since they made me finance director, and, well, it did get a bit tiresome, always on my own. That's why I went to that singles thing. Took me six months to pluck up the courage. It was worth it, though, wasn't it? I still can't believe my luck, meeting someone like you.

With anyone else this would have sounded tacky, but I don't think Adrian does tacky. I doubt if he's thrown a girl a line in his life. There's an unformed element about him that's attractive. It's rare in a man and I think I've come up with the polar opposite of James, even if it is by accident. Better not think about it too much though. Seize the moment.

I like Oban. There's an out-of-season feel here which is quite wistful. Rows of pleasure boats are moored at the quayside, brightly-coloured dashes on a grey sea, their masts clinking in the wind as they wait for summer. It's fresh but bitter. By the time we get back to the hotel I'm scoured and frozen through. I'm half expecting Basil Fawlty to appear. It's that type of place, it even has a stag's head on the foyer wall, but this one stares out at me straight and true, and we are fawned over by competent staff. They don't have much to do, so they treat us as if we're young

28

honeymooners.

The meal is quite pleasant, in an old-style way. Solid British winter fare. Lamb casserole, which used to be called stew when I was a girl. I've begun eating meat again. After ten meat-free years it's a big step and I should feel guilty but I don't, not really. Maybe it's to do with new beginnings, fresh starts. It was James's idea in the first place. He was good at talking up vegetarianism, then being a carnivore in secret. A good metaphor for him, that. Meant well, did poorly. He *did* mean well. I must not lose sight of that, if only for the girls' sake. I had to search for the good in James, but it was there. Grown-up life was not something his weird parents prepared him for, it was left to me, to be wife, mother and play-mate. An impossible trinity once the girls came along.

I polish off a formidable treacle sponge smothered in custard, and accept the Cointreau that Adrian offers. I'll have to watch my weight if this keeps up.

It's morning and the weather's perked up quite a bit. A wide sky saturates the seafront and stretches away to distant islands. Adrian is out already, taking a brisk walk. I want more brisk sleep. I shouldn't have had the Cointreau, it topped up the wine, and my head is suffering, but I had a good time. Nina had a good time. With a man. Nina had a good time with a man, the first in a small lifetime. *We* had a good time. The *we* sounds good, but I'm not seeing this as a relationship. Not yet.

Last night. Adrian in the bedroom. Should I give him marks, evaluate him like a schoolgirl. That would be bitchy but kind of fun. At least he wasn't as shy as I thought he might be. In fact he made *me* feel shy. He doesn't expect much, and seems grateful for whatever I offer him. Maybe we are both at that time in our lives. Adrian is walking back to the hotel. He spots me at the window and waves a hand, his step quickening.

After breakfast we drive on to Glencoe on an empty road that winds through ever-increasing mountains. Adrian is getting excited. He's like a guide on commission.

Have you spent much time up here, then? I ask.

A fair bit. I've always liked British history and got into battlefields years ago. I'm a battlefield anorak. I've tried to get round them all, you know, from Hastings to Culloden, and everything in between, the big and the small. Even if there's a housing estate on one, or a farmer ploughing a war field, you still get a feel for what has taken place there. Well, I do, anyway. Culloden is my favourite, because it's so eerie, and they've kept it the way it was then.

You really know how to woo a girl.

Sorry, I know it's a bit morbid. We don't have to go to any of them if you don't want to.

He's going red.

I'm teasing you. It's alright. The weather's fine, the scenery's great and I've always wanted to be in Scotland.

Touring battlefields seems right for Adrian. A solid hobby, like clocks, one born of a solitary male lifestyle. A sombre lifestyle. Adrian had been alone on that singles night. Sarah worked on me for months to go, whereas his attendance was an unilateral action. *That one in the corner is giving you the eye, Sarah said, the one on his own. I haven't seen him here before but he's not too bad. Well turned out, anyway. Looks as if he's got a few bob. Get over there, go on, I'm going to the loo.* Sarah even gave me a discreet push in Adrian's direction.

We're hitting Glencoe now, Adrian says.

We're on the main artery to the Highlands, but it seems narrow in the wide valley. The scenery is a stretched-out version of north Wales, essentially the same green, brown and rocky landscape scoured treeless by the wind, shaped by water more than sun.

You couldn't really call Glencoe a battlefield, Adrian says.

No, more a bloodyfield.

That's good.

I boned up on it on the Internet before we left. Very treacherous and gory. Very Celtic, or Gaelic, or whatever Scotland is.

There's not much traffic on the road. A few white vans pass us, the odd truck, a motorbike rider going fast, not much else. As Adrian stops in a lay-by I feel like we're the only tourists here.

This is a good spot. You can see the whole sweep of the place from here, he says. Glencoe means the 'valley of weeping'.

They got that right, didn't they?

Adrian is in his element. He must have been here many times before, but now he has an audience. An accountant, who drives a Mercedes, and has an interest in battles is unfamiliar territory for me. I should be apprehensive, but the man is happy to be with me, and I don't mind that.

There's an atmosphere here, Adrian says, I feel that history is watching over the place, and the past hasn't gone away.

Adrian's right. I'm standing at the side of the road, filling my lungs with fresh air, but this place doesn't feel fresh. The valley is wide, but still closed in, and the stillness is oppressive. Banks of clouds are pushing out the bright sky, rejecting the sunlight. In the distance a small croft catches the last of it. It looks impossibly lonely, a white dot in a vast swathe of green, with the silver thread of a stream running close by. The green is dotted with patches of frost that the sun hasn't budged. Near us, frozen blades of grass resist the breeze like thin white bones and beyond, mountains rise up. Three large peaks dominate the rest, rocky, snow-capped crags that are the guardians of this ominous place. As the light fades their jagged edges blur. By dusk they'll soften into one mass. There's a strong sense of foreboding in this place, it has seen too much, but I'm also moved. Adrian puts an arm around me, tentatively. I lean against him and sense him relax.

Getting dark, he says. Looks like it could snow, too. Magnificent though, isn't it?

I lean against him a bit more firmly.

*

Oi, Read, you 'ad my cider, you thieving bastard. I was keeping tha' for breakfast.

The real world was back. Billy announced it by banging on his door. James sat up with a start, thinking that the shouting was coming from inside his head. The door opened. Before he could deny it Billy saw the empty can. He snatched it up and threw at James, but the missile had no force and James caught it easily. Billy stood in the doorway, shaking, in an old-fashioned white string vest. Almost white. Tattoos decorated his thin arms, one marked his sunken chest like a map, but his mish-mash of bruises and bruised veins outdid them. James did not want to look any further down, he'd seen Billy coming out of the shower once, and once was enough. Billy looked like someone from another time, a black and white creature, walking along Orwell's pier, rickety and underfed. It was 2005, but not in this hostel. Billy lived in a time-warp of lost, never-had, or misused opportunities. He'd started out with a lousy hand, then threw all the cards away.

Thieving bastard, Billy repeated, much more quietly.

It was a matter of need, Bill. I'll get you two cans today.

Two cans? Promise?

I'll bring them back with me.

Billy calmed down. He was sober enough to realise he was up on the deal.

Well, okay, but don' do it again.

Billy stumbled out of the room. James checked the clock. Nine o'clock. Another long day was beginning for him. The clock was one of the few things that had survived from his old world. A fortieth birthday present from Nina. The clock face had a backdrop of Charlie Parker playing sax. He'd listened to a lot of jazz in those days. As a youngster he dreamed of being a musician himself, but had given up on piano, guitar and saxophone, once he realised the work involved. A hat-trick of failure. Now he didn't even have any music to play, or anything to play it on. All the old stuff was in the attic of the Nina's place, unless she'd binned it.

Nina's place. He thought of it like that now. She'd bought him out when they divorced and his share had soon disappeared, racing away on the backs of horses, dogs, all types of sports matches, on cards, and the casino's wheel. Especially that. Something about it mesmerised him. A toy one at the age of ten had started his fixation. He'd play with a few local kids, and always be banker. It must have lain dormant in his mind, to break loose in his forties. The first time he set foot in a casino and saw the real thing it was love at first sight; James felt he was coming home. Roulette was one of the worst ways to bet. It took your money in a series of rapid hits. Gambling was invented to drain saps. Stupid saps, intelligent saps, saps in all shapes and sizes, all looking for Shangri-La, Utopia, Nirvana, the quick fix to another life, another place to live, a way of straightening out that kink in their mind. Saps like him.

It was ten past nine and the social worker was coming at ten. James made an effort to be presentable, braving the dank shower with its antique shower curtain, and shaving carefully with a new razor. He couldn't remember the woman's name, but he knew it was something unusual. He dressed in his least shabby outfit, made himself coffee in the kitchen and searched his wallet for her card. Deborah Skirrid that was it. Like the mountain. It made him smile and he wondered how someone got a name like that.

Billy hated social workers. Pete hadn't been too fond of them either. They had been in the hands of the state for a long time but had not become inured to it. They were tied to it by need, but this did not stop them biting the hand that fed them.

They wanna control, no' fuckin' care, Billy had once shouted.

It was a skewed response, born of shame and selfishness. James understood this, but he had also come to understand people like Billy. People gone wrong, turning to others to sort them out, crying for help but resisting at the same time. Trapped by the duality of their nature. This was their problem, and it created the tension that funded their lives.

Billy stuck his head around the kitchen door.

I'm off out, me ol' son. Have fun with your girlfriend. An' don' forget them cans.

It was early for Billy, and he looked quite fit for this time in the morning. He'd managed to find a clean shirt, though it hadn't seen an iron for a long time. James often thought of him as a wind-up doll, always able to surface brightly, then slow down as the day took its toll, bitterness setting in with the third or fourth drink, until he often became a snarling drunk, someone to be avoided on the street. Someone from *the hostel*. He'd stumble back to crash out, and another day was spent. It amazed James, the amounts he was able to drink, and for how long. Alcoholism must be the slowest form of suicide.

From the kitchen window James saw the woman pull up in her bright red car. He had a good view of the road, which curved around the hostel and loped away to the terraces, ideal for boy racers to strut their stuff. A light frost had followed the rain, just enough for white dust to edge the pavement, and a grey mist hung low over the ridge. James couldn't see the top, but he felt the need to be walking up there, going quickly to keep the cold out, breaking onto the top of the ridge to greet any sun that might be around. Getting a piece of his old life back. He felt the need but he wasn't fit enough any more.

In the car the woman fussed with her hair for a moment. James smiled and doubted that it was for him. She was good-looking, dark hair, china-blue eyes, a combination that would have attracted him once. No, not once. It still did. Not that she'd look at him twice, the state he was in. Even so, he instinctively dabbed at his own hair, before he answered her knock. She brushed past him as he ushered her into the kitchen. He'd already cleared bottles from the table, room enough for her to deposit her briefcase.

So, James, how are you today?

Still here.

You didn't turn up for that GA meeting.

Gamblers Anonymous. Christ, he'd forgotten all about it.

How do you know that? James asked.

Someone mentioned it.

She sat down, took out his file and tapped a pen on it. An attractive, confident woman, not much past thirty, rising up steadily in her job, no doubt, having to deal with a man who was pleased he had managed to shave without nicking himself. James sat opposite her.

I saw Billy going out just now, she said.

Yes. Early, for him.

I was shocked to hear about Pete.

Yes. Terrible.

The standard response. Pete was the last person James wanted to talk about. He felt her eyes appraise him. She knew his history and was thinking that he shouldn't be here, that he was an educated man from the right side of the tracks, the side that provided two parents. A man who'd had every chance.

What are you thinking? she asked. You seem preoccupied.

James put his hands behind his head and stretched. He was already tired, at ten in the morning.

Sorry. I was thinking that today I managed not to cut myself shaving. A minor triumph. Do they call you Debbie – Debs?

They did at school. I hated it. Why did you miss the meeting, James?

It slipped my mind.

Come on, you can do better than that.

GA sounds freaky. I imagine it being like some sort of Revivalist meeting, Puritans about to cast me into the flames.

It's not like that at all, and you know it.

Maybe.

Are you religious? You sound like you think you are damned.

No, not at all. Do you want a coffee? I should have asked earlier.

Deborah looked around at the kitchen, and said yes, to his surprise. He found his one good mug and used that.

They have a good record you know, Deborah said.

Who?

The association.

What, healing minds, you mean, patching up the damaged?

If you like. I'd rather say that they can put people back on track.

Ah, the track. It's just the group idea. I've always had a problem with organised stuff. Boy Scouts, youth clubs, college cliques, school staff-rooms. Especially groups of men. My idea of hell – one of them, anyway.

Deborah swirled her coffee around, with a touch of suspicion. She's wondering if it's safe, James thought. Looking for tell-tale trails of dirt around the mug's rim but

36

he'd taken care with his washing. The blue of her eyes was quite striking. He was reminded of one of Zoe's dolls, Tess, her favourite. She'd been captivated by it, as her father was captivated now. James realised he was probably staring as his keeper opened her file and looked at her notes.

How's your drinking, James?

Going well, thanks. Your support worker has written it down there, probably.

James nodded to the file. He regretted his flippancy but couldn't prevent it. Nerves.

Keep this up and you'll qualify for AA as well as GA, Deborah murmured.

Not really, not if you compare me with the likes of Pete and Billy. It takes a long time to lose yourself to booze. Much longer than gambling. That came on suddenly. Do you think I'm an alcoholic then?

No, but you'll get there soon enough, if you don't change. We'll have to work on this, as well as the gambling.

Ah, the royal use of the word *we*. He hadn't heard it much since school, when it was usually followed by something nasty, but the woman was right. It's not *we*, its me, myself, I, James thought, James Read, in all his forms, has to do something. Last night he was drinking in fantasyland, savouring each drop of Pete's whisky, Billy's cider. He wanted a drink now, in fact, at ten o'clock in the fucking morning. It took his mind off gambling. It made it seem farther away. A new vice to chase out the old. Have a drink, take away the first need, have another because you had the first. Don't have one, be strong, then start thinking about the wheel – *big wheel keeps on turning, proud James keeps on burning.* James felt his face beginning to flush.

Has there been any contact with your family recently, James?

No.

Not even a letter?

Did she know about Clare's letter? It had been re-directed. James didn't care. He didn't want to talk about families. He didn't want to talk about anything, words led nowhere.

His thoughts were drifting. Towards green velvet baize, towards orderly other-worlds where unchanging rituals took place. Elegant hands dealing cards, fine perfumes in a cigar and brandy wonderland. The thrill of chance masked by hushed tones, the chance always there.

This was his dream world, but it had been his real world. Real enough to snatch all his money, steadily, without fuss, exchanging for each lost wad the false promise of another chance.

James?

What?

Try to pay attention.

She was irritated. He was her first port of call, and probably her least productive. Usually, underlings dealt with him, support workers, link workers, he'd seen a number of them. They came with the hostel, all busy with their pens. Now he'd graduated to social worker.

Look, you will go to the next meeting, won't you?

James shrugged.

It *is* voluntary, James, but I'm sure you'd benefit. You've done well to get this far. There is a long waiting list for hostels like this.

If ever a statement defined desperate, this woman had just uttered it.

There's only two of us here, now, James said.

Once we sort out Pete's room someone will be moving in by the weekend. The other room has to be re-decorated.

James remembered why. Two weeks ago young Danny had gone apeshit in there. He'd only been at the hostel for a few days before he trashed his room. James never did find out why, but he remembered the way the kid howled when he was taken away by the police, twisting and turning like a

38

snake on a hot rock. His face full of hate, for himself and anyone his eyes drilled. Smackhead complaints from the underworld.

James had been particularly low that day and Danny's scream summed up everything that had gone on in the last few years. He felt like joining in, leading the others into some sort of chorus of the lost. There was even a moon out that night. Like all of them, Danny looked older than he was, a pinched, deprived street face, prematurely aged. They'd all been afraid of him, and his quick fists.

I'll take you to the meeting if you like, Deborah said.

No, it's alright.

I think I'd better take you.

Afraid the child won't turn up at school?

Deborah smiled.

Her tongue flicked the edge of her lips and James glimpsed white teeth. The front ones had bits of lipstick on them. This woman made him think of toothpaste, clean sheets and comfortable houses. The past. When he'd shaved earlier, he'd forced himself to look closely at himself. The present. Usually he shaved and washed mechanically, seeing what he wanted to see. Sometimes even the man of ten years ago. He'd been good-looking, and had grown up with this knowledge. Only fools weren't aware of their looks, and only imbeciles didn't learn how use them. Nina had helped his character belatedly grow, but his peacock ways never really disappeared, and when he began to show signs of ageing, they reared up again. In shock. As his features started to change, his eyes lost their youthful fire, his hair thinned, and the marks on his face did not go away. A lifelong vanity was assailed, then gradually beaten down. By the time he was forty-five it no longer mattered, because by then he was a hopeless gambler, and on his own.

James thought that stuff like this had petered out, like his life, but fragments of it showed itself now. Ridiculous, pathetic, even funny. This girl probably looked at him the way he'd once looked at bag ladies rummaging in the trash bins of New York. Even so, he scanned her hands. No rings of any kind. James flicked his hand through his hair, and hoped this looked like a casual act. Not desperate.

It's this Friday, at two o'clock, Deborah said.

Right.

I'll pick you up at one-thirty. You will be here, *won't you*, James?

Looks like I'd better be.

The smile again. More teeth.

This time Deborah noticed he was staring. She met his eyes for a moment and looked away. Her hand came to her hair again. She wore it long, quite old-fashioned. Deborah made a few notes. A few paragraphs about him.

Do you want to talk about Pete? she asked. He wasn't part of my caseload, but I know you were quite close.

Who told you that?

You spent a fair bit of time with him.

Oh, jungle telegraph been working, has it? Pete was alright. In his rare moments of lucidity.

Deborah smiled again. This time more pensively.

You talk like someone from another planet compared to most of the people I deal with, she murmured.

Ah, like an educated man, you mean. Someone who shouldn't be here.

Don't be so defensive, James. Do *you* think you should be here?

She turned everything into a question. If it was her way of trying to draw him out it was working. Suddenly, he didn't want her to go. James was sitting with someone who didn't smell bad, and who could talk coherently. He felt his isolation, the fact that he was crushingly alone. For one strong moment he imagined himself breaking his habit, getting out, getting back to normal, whatever that was. Casually asking Deborah out. She was over thirty, and he wasn't *that* old. Then he thought of the image of himself shaving earlier and almost laughed out loud. Fantasies again, James. They got you here in the first place.

It's a roof over my head, James answered. I didn't have one of those for a few months.

No, I know.

And I've sort of got used to the place. It's quiet enough, for a last chance saloon.

Yes, James thought, quiet, apart from that scene with Danny, and Pete topping himself.

I don't know about last chance, Deborah said, but it is *a* chance. Get yourself sorted and we could help you get a housing association flat.

Right.

Well, James, I think we've done enough for today. I'll see you Friday, then.

Deborah got up and put out a hand. James shook it tentatively and said goodbye. He stood on the steps of the hostel and watched her drive off, then smelt his hand for traces of her perfume. It was fresh, summery for November. Alive. That more than anything. From another world. Two kids were passing. One spat on the floor at his feet. James was unaffected. He was hanging onto fresh, summery and alive, and Friday was a kind of date. At least he told himself that. Billy was coming back up the road so James went back inside quickly. He didn't want to break the spell. Not yet.

*

After Glencoe I could have done with things lightening up a little but Adrian is keen to take me on to another battlefield. Culloden. Places of war seem like old friends to him, I'm getting a crash course in Scottish gore. On the drive up from Glencoe he's filled me in on Bonnie Prince Charlie and his grand misadventure. I'm not bored, because Adrian's enthusiasm is infectious. His approach is different, I'll give him that. What you see is what you get with him, a

41

kind of middle-aged innocence and I'm not used to that. I won't buy into this too strongly though. Men are tricky, especially when first met. At Culloden, we park up, pay our entry fee and walk through the shop-cum-museum.

Don't worry, Adrian whispers, this tat doesn't spoil it.

I'm not really listening. I'm struck by the life-size display of Highlander fighting Redcoat, murderous survival etched on each face, claymore and bayonet tip red. Adrian ushers me through and we are standing at the edge of the battlefield.

An expanse of winter heather stretches away from us, undulating waves of washed-out brown and green, pricked with yellow. It's dry, but the Glencoe spell has stayed with us. The sky is a dreary grey, and not many tourists are around at this time of year. We almost have the field to ourselves. The guide in Adrian is muted, he's lost in his thoughts. The killing ground is marked out with the names and positions of the various clans and regiments, faintly moving flagpoles chart battle positions and there's an almost overwhelming presence here. Adrian is clutching my arm tightly, as if we might be charged by a redcoat at any time.

This place is more or less unchanged, Adrian murmurs. Of every field I've ever stood on this is the most evocative.

He sniffs the air, closes his eyes, and sighs.

I know the story so well I can imagine every scene, he says. The Highlanders hadn't eaten for days, some of them were just starving kids. Not just boys either. Teenage girls throwing rocks at soldiers. No, not teenage, that sounds too modern – children. They were children, dying for some fop from France. Most of the Highlanders couldn't even speak English, let alone French. They were following a dream, like the down-trodden always do. Another glorious chapter in British history.

Cold from the ground is creeping into my bones. I imagine the sounds of bloody war myself and wish Adrian hadn't told me about the children. Now I see pinched, slight figures in tartan, empty-bellied, shivering, dirty fingers curling around stones, glaring at advancing redcoats. I shiver as Adrian touches my arm.

I'm not getting on your nerves, am I?

I shake my head and smile at him. He's so anxious to make this work. I doubt that Adrian would be able to change, not now. Something in me likes that, something else is not so sure.

Are you cold? he asks.

A bit. It's a cold place.

Yes, and not just the weather.

Beyond Adrian's earnest face the sky has the same yellow tint as over the sea at Oban, but now streaked with red and orange lines. They look like a roadway in the sky that leads over black mountains.

We'll drive on to Fort William, Adrian says. I've booked us into a nice hotel there. It's got a huge log fire.

He looks up at the sky.

Looks like it will be a fine day for the drive back tomorrow.

Adrian holds my hand firmly as we walk back to the car. I almost expect him to swing it, like a schoolboy. I imagine Zoe's face when I tell her what we've done on our trip and hear her scornful words – *Uh, that's morbid, Mum – get rid of him* – he's *a geek*. Adrian's come as a shock to her. She supported Clare in encouraging me back into circulation, but I don't think Zoe ever thought I'd meet anyone.

Meeting Adrian brings her father into focus again. James is probing somewhere back in my mind, and I'm finding it hard to keep to my resolution. There are so many ways he gets back into my mind. I know that a part of Zoe thinks that somehow I made James gamble, made him lose his job, that I got rid of her adored father. She was just coming into her teens when James finally lost it, the worst

43

possible time for her. The girls knew things were not right but I kept the gambling from them as long as I could, even when he started to raid their savings accounts. I went along with it for a while, and I regret that now, but I hoped the girls might hold him together, that the thought of losing them would bring him back from the brink. It didn't.

There was always restlessness in James, a sense that he could and should be achieving much more, and, underpinning this, the feeling that I wasn't enough for him. I think that at the end he even started to blame me for letting him have a relationship with me. James was capable of that kind of tortuous thinking. He called it lateral. I call it stupid. For Zoe his self-destruction was unforgivable, his abandonment an act of betrayal.

Maybe the gloomy battlefield encourages such thoughts. James seemed a straightforward hedonist in college, but as his layers peeled away I saw other things. Masochism, that more than anything else was what James was founded on. He could never see it, and would never admit it if he could, perhaps that's a good definition of it. It took me years to work this out. There was a stubborn block in him that was his own worst enemy. He had the ability to end things before they really got going and opportunities did come easily to him, at first. James was a good teacher, when he put his mind to it. He could have been a head before forty but always held back, slamming doors in his own face. Then he began to think that teaching was below him, ironic, for initially he thought he was taking the softest option. Teaching proved anything but.

James was delighted with the girls at first, but he began to hold back from them too, especially when they began to have minds of their own. The more they wanted to be part of him, the more he drew away. I blame those freaky parents of his, especially his mother. I didn't see much of them, James made sure of that, but I saw enough to know that each lived in a private world, with not much time for

James. If they'd lived, I don't think either of them would have been there for the girls.

At first I thought James was having an affair. All the signs were there. He became more attentive, taking care with his clothes for the first time in years, buying little things for the girls. Gradually getting shifty, but there was no other woman. Just Lady Chance.

If only he'd agreed to get help when it was all going wrong. God knows where this gambling business came from. He'd never shown the slightest interest in anything like that. It would have been much easier to understand an affair, even James getting hooked up with weird religions and ideologies, but gambling, that will always be a mystery. I think it's a mystery for him too. Perhaps that's why he could never explain it to me.

When he came clean I scoured the Internet for answers. There was lots of stuff there, many theories, plenty of mumbo-jumbo from people on the make, but Gamblers Anonymous seemed worthwhile. I mentioned it to James but he wouldn't hear of it.

Lost in your thoughts?

Mm...?

You're miles away, Nina.

Just chilling out. It's been a long day, and the cold always makes me tired.

A good day?

I squeeze Adrian's leg.

Yes. A good day.

Adrian drives us into a sunset. The mountains look like dark chocolate amidst fading orange.

*

In his room James read Clare's letter again. She was his first-born. Clare hadn't left him, neither had Zoe, a situation had been forced on them. By himself. James was unsure

45

whether to meet with Clare. It was so hard to make decisions these days. Easier to let things slide. Let each day fade into the next, maybe with the vain hope that things would improve.

James picked up a book, from his windowsill library. It was hard to get past the first few pages of any of them. He'd used up a lot of time with his head in books, much of it wasted time, he tended to think in hindsight, passive when he should have been active. Now, when he had all the time in the world, he could not concentrate enough. He'd tried to counteract this by getting hold of old favourites. He'd always looked westwards, people now outmoded writing about times long past, Hemingway, Fitzgerald, Sinclair, the Beat poets and Kerouac's wild road journeys, all old and loved stuff, which had sped off the page in his youth but now bored him within minutes. He could rarely manage more than a page or two. Knowing his background, a helpful support worker had given him a few modern novels, but he hadn't even opened them. The *buy-me* blurbs on the back had been enough.

James was back at his armchair station, where he could track the affairs of the street in a detached way. Watching had taken the place of reading. He often used up time like this. The spitting boys were making their way up the street, a meandering snake of sportswear in unison, each of them with a can of lager in his hand, another badge of solidarity; apprentice Billys every one. It was a cold day but only one wore a top, the others were clad in thin T-shirts, their slight bodies taut, and in denial against the bitter wind. The boys were almost thirty years younger than James, but they didn't have anything to do either.

James saw an old man being blown along the street towards the 'Bush, his arms held out like balancing rods. Beyond him the hillside was almost a featureless slab in the gloom. The village's best times lay in the past, everything about it spoke of former days, old work, old pain, old glories, old hopes faded, and James felt a kinship with it. They were things he could understand. He had lived all of them.

James thought about phoning Clare but what the hell would he say? *Hello love, sorry I haven't been in touch for the last three years. How's your life going then?* There was no phone in the hostel anyway. Danny had smashed the one that used to be on the kitchen wall and they were waiting for a replacement.

James picked up a book of collected poetry from his meagre library. He could still manage a poem, if it wasn't too long. His hands moved instinctively to one of the most thumbed pages, and he read Ferlinghetti's *Sometime During Eternity*. The poem had always moved him, but *Jesus hanging on the tree* had a particular relevance now and the piece had more resonance than ever. He'd read it first at seventeen, Ferlinghetti's hip words buzzing in his head. He'd been full of hip words himself then. It was archaic language now. James thought of the music he used to listen to, new and fresh, and saw his cheap guitar in the corner of his bedroom, the one that was admired, and shown off to friends, then left to gather dust. Those times were just the blink of an eye ago, James smiled at the memory, but it was a smile of resignation that fixed on his lips.

He found himself going back to the past more, because it was a better time for him. James often fell asleep like this, when he could sleep, slipping backwards in time, starting again, or just being there.

He needed to go out, to spend some of his giro on groceries. Mr Singh operated a company store policy, whether he realised it or not. His wife ran a small post office inside the convenience store so that most claimants spent some, if not all, of their money with him, as soon as they had it. His prices were high, but he *was* convenient, and the only option for those without a car. James had taken a bus down to the nearest supermarket once, determined to shop sensibly. He did, then stopped off at a pub, to arrive back drunk, and his frozen food leaking all over his shoes. After this he admitted defeat, and became one of Singh's captives.

Maybe he could creep past the 'Bush without going in. At this time they'd have the racing on. Even now, James hardly knew one end of a horse from the other, but when they were off, his senses alerted, his addiction fired up and the hopeless chances of winning flagged up in his mind.

James had a fortnight's money in his pocket. In the last few months he'd tried to establish a kind of routine, and make sure he ate enough food. He hadn't made a bet for a month, his longest abstinence yet. He'd counted down each day, each small victory that mounted up, though he'd tended too often to celebrate them with a night's drinking. Especially when Pete had been around. James could still see his short-lived friend's face peering round his bedroom door. Ravaged, but always ready to break into a smile, grateful for a few hours of his company. James wished he'd given him more of it now.

Maybe Pete had woken up that morning and realised it was the same one he'd faced for the last twenty years, and did not want to face another. Whatever demons had gnawed at him were stilled now, Pete had drawn a line under them, and his life. A positive act.

James hadn't done positive for a long time. Not many hostel dwellers, or the people he'd met on the streets, did positive. They did not do food much either. It was low on their priorities. Money could not be spared, it was needed for the real necessities of their lives. Drink and drugs, all kinds of drugs, anything they could get.

James had lived on the streets of Cardiff once, in the company of Glasgow Paul, a Scottish street-dweller. It had been the lowest point of his life, so far, and the memory was still raw. He hardly understood a word the man said, so distorted by booze was his Glaswegian accent, but they helped each other out. James offered Glasgow Paul the occasional pie or sandwich, and was given a variety of half-drunk flagons of cider in return. Sometimes Paul disappeared, to return with bottles of Thunderbird, or whatever he could lay his hands on. It helped to keep the cold out. Glasgow Paul had spells when he shouted incoherently at nothing and no one, his voice anguished, his eyes lighting up with old memories, burning in a hairy face ruined by eczema. Then he'd calm down and pat James on the arm affectionately, fat, blackened fingers protruding from fingerless gloves. Paul should never have been on the street, but he was, and so was James. He was homeless, and that was the perfect entry card to Paul's world. *One for all, eh,* he'd bellow in James's ear, admitting James to the inner sanctum of what was left of his mind.

Paul was less generous with his drugs, not that James wanted any, but he did once accept pills that were unknown even to Paul. It had been bitterly cold, wind finding its way through all the layers of rancid clothing, and the wine was gone, so he'd swallowed the handful Paul offered before he could talk himself out of it. They must have been some kind of speed, because the cold went away, and everything spun inside. Within minutes he could hear each beat of his heart pound, feel the blood course through his veins and build up between his eyes. His mind stretched out, all compartments rushed past him as his thoughts went into overdrive. He wanted to grab back the good times, to reach out for Nina and the girls. For a time James stepped outside of himself, far enough outside to wonder what had happened to him. He wanted to know how and why he'd fallen, but this knowledge was blocked. James reached out for answers, but, like Paul, he clawed the air at nothing. He began to understand Paul's incoherent ramblings. Latching onto his secret code, he started to shout himself, putting one of Paul's stinking blankets over his head. Paul joined in. He probably thought they were confirming their union, in a crazy street chorus that bound them together. People passed by even quicker.

Casinos filled James's head. Casino, Italian for confusion, chaos. How right that was. There were thousands of them, passing through his mind like film credits, each one lit up, old friends, that could be relied on. He was floating into one like a baby in its mother's fluid, feeling its heat and smelling all the familiar smells as he drifted towards the giant wheel, taking a ride on the number seven. Whirling around, waiting for the wheel to stop, for someone to pick him. *He* was the jackpot.

Someone was shaking James, and it wasn't an excited punter. A young policeman stood over him, pink-cheeked and boyish in the cold. James remembered thinking how clean he looked. Words were coming from him but it took James some time to understand what he was saying. The cop was threatening him and Glasgow Paul with arrest, but half-heartedly so. He didn't really want to bother, he didn't want to get too close. Even with his brain skidding James could see the boy's nostrils flare with distaste. The young cop just wanted them to be quiet, to go back to being invisible.

Even now James broke into a sweat as he remembered the hell of coming down from that session. Wondering if Nina would have recognised him if she'd passed him by. Wondering what she might have done. All that he'd lost came to him, the girls through all their ages, the wife who had tried to help, whom he hadn't deserved at any time.

The pills had a result. James left Glasgow Paul the next morning and put himself into the hands of the state, his mind wrought with shame and relief. James wondered if Paul would still be in that doorway, in the midst of his citadel of pissy cardboard and reeking blankets, bottles arranged around him like turrets, venting his spleen on the world, and, in the one sound and tiny compartment of his mind, wondering if he could get through another winter.

There was a public phone box outside Singh's which, by some miracle, had not been trashed since James had moved into the hostel. He could phone Clare from there. By the time he'd decided, the rain had stopped and a pale sun followed it. James stepped out into a day that had changed to fine and cold, the sky the lightest of blues, the hillside no longer a slab. It was now defined by its scrubby undulations, its patches of trees, and the stone walls that squared it up. As mist was burnt off, sheep re-appeared, desultory shapes that littered the mountain like grey pieces of cloth.

Mr Singh was in good form. It was giro day. To James, it seemed that practically everyone up here was a claimant, of one sort of another. Singh wore a turban that matched the sky outside. For a moment James had a touch of distaste, for this stranger in a strange land, with his BMW outside and kids down the coast at a private school, then equally quickly felt shamed. Singh was never going to spit past James's head, or steal his milk, or assault him with boot, fist or knife. Or axe, as James had read in the local paper the previous week. Singh was here because no one else was bothered. This was a subversion of old Empire and there was a kind of justice in it.

Ah, Mr Read, good to see you. It's a nice day, isn't it, now that the rain's stopped.

James nodded as he forced his eyes to avoid Singh's drink section. They were well priced, so were the cigarettes. The non-smoking, teetotal, Sikh knew the staple necessities of the area. He beamed at James and stroked his beard, a lustrous black with the beginnings of grey tramlines. James stood in the queue at the post office counter, holding his giro self-consciously. He hated this public show. A few coughing old men were ahead of him, and a young girl trying to keep her toddler calm. The boy twisted and yelled and tried to make his way to the sweet counter next to the till. Singh had everything laid out to tempt – booze, fags, sweets, and at the back, almost as an afterthought, the stuff that should have been important for daily life. The girl had another on the way, James noticed. He stood behind her, and smelt her cheap perfume, mingled with old smoke. She might have been seventeen. Maybe younger. The perfume was quite different from Deborah's, heavy and pungent enough to bring on his sneezing. The girl turned to glare at him, a glare that said *outsider, wanker*. Quite right, James thought, as he kept his face dead-pan. A smile would never do. As the girl stretched to control her son James saw the tattoo above her rear reveal itself, a small blue hand pointed down, and her neck was stitched with love bites, some fresh and red, others older, and turning brown. The necklace of her existence. It should have depressed him but at least she was snatching at a kind of life, the kind this place allowed. No, a smile would never do.

Mrs Singh counted out his money. It always seemed quite a lot, for a few minutes. James took a basket from the front of the shop and quickly walked around filling it with groceries. No alcohol. He didn't take much care with his purchases. It was hard to remember when he'd last enjoyed a meal. Eating had become mechanical, he ate to live, not much more than that.

He approached Singh's counter. It lay beyond the bunkers of drink, arrayed with cigarettes and the myriad scratch cards, all selling a dream for a pound. James tried to adopt a blinker mentality but it was hard. He watched the girl put a bag of sweets into the toddler's eager hand then buy two scratch cards, rubbing at them eagerly before she even left the shop.

You are well, Mr Read?

Alright.

James wished the shopkeeper did not remember his name so readily. He'd tried to keep his head down, to merge into the fringes here, but it was difficult. He *was* an outsider, and that was the end of it. In this part of the valley anyone from more than two miles away qualified.

James looked at Singh's newspapers. All tabloids. Suddenly he wanted to read a halfways-decent one. The interview with Deborah Skirrid had brought this on. A fragment of his old self was appearing.

Today I will be unafraid.

That's eleven pounds eighty, Singh said.

What?

Eleven pounds eighty.

Oh.

Did you want a newspaper? I see you looking.

No. None of them anyway.

I could order you one. The boy will deliver.

James was tempted for a moment, but he knew what papers said. He knew what the world did.

No, it's okay. Thanks.

The girl's scratch cards were on the pavement outside. Her dream had lasted for two minutes. James saw her further down the street, pulling the toddler along. Beyond her was the phone box. It stood out like a beacon, just for him, and James approached it. He read the graffiti scrawled inside. *Carl luvs Cindy, Rob suks, Fuk off, Swansea.* Someone had used the box as a toilet the previous night, and the smell still hung around.

Further on up the road was another beacon. The Hollybush. Its wooden windows had been painted recently, a ridiculously bright yellow, against a backdrop of dark red. The pub was a garish slash amidst the greyness of the village. It defied its surroundings and the yellow said *come on in, you know it makes sense*. It made sense to James.

It was an instant decision. It always was. He didn't have any frozen food in his bags so he'd go in, just for one. He'd sit in the corner and think of what he'd say to Clare. Think how he could take his life forward again. Yes, just one.

The Hollybush was never empty. It was never really

full either. Very few young people went there on weekdays. If they had money they preferred to drift further down the valley, perhaps even as far as Cardiff, where there were more of their age. Most of the drinkers here were older than James, far older, some of them, which was fine by him. He used to like people who had worked all their lives, whose memories were lively, healthy, and full of forward movement. Only the destruction of old workplaces lay like a sad coda at the end of each story. What might be nostalgic nonsense elsewhere was grounded in fact in this village. For working men, at least, things had been better. *Working, man.* Those two words no longer went together that often, James realised, not here. For the young that remained, work had been replaced by scheme after scheme, minimum wage drudgery that led nowhere. He'd seen this from afar, he'd sympathised from afar, made the right noises from afar. That was as close as he got to his roots. Then.

James pushed open the 'Bush door, and was instantly comforted. Nothing like the charge of entering a casino, but enough. Last night's stale smoke and reek of old bitter, the three old boys in the corner, even the blowsy middle-aged woman behind the bar, blended into the welcome. Well, perhaps not the woman. She looked at James's shopping suspiciously as he ordered a pint of Guinness, taking his money and acknowledging his 'hello' with just a short nod of her head. James liked her bluntness.

He looked around and wondered if he should join the old men. They had a box of dominoes in front of them. A game from another age, their age. He was wrong about the racing. Subdued noise came from the television mounted overhead, like another person in the pub talking, but it was a programme about houses, not horses. The television was too high up for anyone to interfere with, people were forced to look up at it, in obeisance. Why not, James thought. It had been god for a generation.

James nodded to the men as he sipped his drink. They

54

nodded back. He took this as his cue to sit down with them. James put his glass on the table a little too heavily and a line of froth spilled from it. One of the old men chuckled.

First of the day, is it, son? Always the best.

Aye.

Aye. Where did that come from? James had pushed in on this world, now he was aping its language. It seemed to come naturally to him, as if his roots were pulling inside. Maybe he was patronising them, but none of them seemed to mind. These men were open and they liked a *youngster in* their midst.

James knew he should be thinking about the conversation with Clare, not sitting with old men playing out their time. Usually he sat alone. He'd almost become used to it. There was no contact with anyone from the old days. He'd made sure of it. Self-destructing was the most personal of affairs, something better done in isolation. Sometimes James wondered what Nina told people, how she explained what had happened to him. If she was wise she'd say nothing. Let him fade from people's minds like he'd faded from her life.

He'd forgotten about Adrian for a while. Now James saw a man walking up the driveway to the old marital home, opening the door with his own key, familiar and comfortable with his new surroundings. He saw him driving Nina to his place in the country in an oversized car. Maybe a Jeep, something with chunky wheels and chrome bull bars, that had more balls than he did, and looked like it should have been roaming Wyoming. James shut this down before he saw anything else.

Do you want a game, son? the oldest man asked.

I'm not sure I can remember how to play it.

It's not rocket science, mun, one of the others added, though the way John here takes his time over a move you'd think it was, sometimes.

That's enough of your cheek. See, kid, I can remember

these two boys when I come back from the war. They was only fifteen then, just started down the Navigation. Jealous as 'ell, they was, 'cos they'd been too young, and had missed the show. Not that the country would 'ave let them go anyway, them being young miners. Not to mention their mothers. I told 'em they were the luckiest kids on earth.

The old man laughed and started to cough.

Don' mind him, old John is getting a bit past it, we reckon, the third man said.

Past it, you cheeky bugger, I 'aven't got to it yet.

James was quite pleased he'd gone from being *son* to *kid*. These were men easy in each other's company. They shared the same experiences and times, and were coming to the end of well mapped out lives of purpose. James decided to play. He was glad to be asked. No one had asked him to do anything in a long time, apart from attend meetings.

These old boys probably knew where he was staying. Maybe they knew more. There would have been lots of talk about Pete, yet James did not feel any hostility. He was just someone playing a game of dominoes with them.

James arranged his pieces and took his cue from the others. He listened to the well-practised routines of the old friends and savoured the drink. John, the oldest, was past eighty, but still sprightly enough. A survivor of war and heavy industry. His eyes retained their bright blue, and he had numerous small scars that matched them. John made a roll-up cigarette from his tobacco pouch and offered the pouch to James.

No thanks, I don't.

Very wise, son. If I'd known I was going to live this long I would have looked after myself a bit better.

The others laughed on cue. The Guinness went down easily and James had another. When he got the third the others accepted his offer of drinks all round. By the fourth he vaguely remembered Billy being in the bar, and that it was dark outside when he stood in the open air urinal at the rear of the 'Bush. Locals called this the Wailing Wall. When James stood there, steadying himself on the clammy stone with a hand, he saw the last outlines of the hillside fading to black. There were no lights up there to challenge the darkness. That was what James liked about it. The absence of man. Something he had meant to do was nagging at the back of his mind, but he was too drunk to bring it forwards.

Billy went back with James, making sure he didn't fall, and carrying the shopping for him. James vaguely remembered Billy's high-pitched waspish voice penetrating his head like a buzz-saw, a happy voice, glad that James had joined in.

The bed enveloped James as Billy dropped him into it, repaying the favour of the other night. He sank down and tried to keep still as the ceiling shifted above him. This was what he hated most about being drunk, ceilings that moved, floors that danced, minor tremors all around. His nagging memory produced the face of Clare for a moment, before everything shut down.

Thursday morning, 10am. Billy was calling him. Billy was in the bedroom calling him, his voice an instrument of torture.

Wakey, wakey, sunshine. There's a piece downstairs wants to see you.

At first James thought it was still last night. That Billy was still getting him home. He rubbed at his eyes until he could see the alarm clock clearly. Billy appeared, rubbing at his ribs beneath his vest. James panicked. Deborah was downstairs waiting for him. He'd got it wrong once again.

Bill, he called out, what day is it? Friday?

I dunno. No, I don' think so. Definitely not Friday. Look you better get yourself sorted. I don' think she'll wait long. Good-looking piece, an' all. Your luck might be in, me ol' son.

Clare. It must be Clare.

57

James sat up, really panicking now. Thank God Billy hadn't shown her up to his room. His head sat up with him. It felt like lead, being slowly smelted. James thought he might throw up, he dared a glance at the small mirror and wished he hadn't.

Bill, tell her I'll be down as soon as I can. A few minutes.

James went to the bathroom, put his head under the tap, then smoothed his hair back over his head. His face was the colour of the off-white wall coating, with as many imperfections, and his eyes looked like they belonged to someone else. They looked like they wanted to belong to someone else. He drank some water and felt a little better. In his bedroom wardrobe he found a creased but clean shirt and put that on. He was still wearing last night's trousers and did not have time to change. He could smell stale beer on them and see Guinness stains amidst the creases.

As he almost fell down the stairs his head started up a drum solo, a bit like Buddy Rich partying with Glasgow Paul. James stumbled into the kitchen, to face a woman he'd never seen before in his life.

Your friend said it was alright to sit here, the woman said, gesturing to the chairs around the kitchen table.

Some of Billy's cans were strewn around, one had spilled out onto the table, leaving a sticky, brown mess. James cursed Billy until he remembered what he'd been doing the night before.

This woman was in her early forties, quite stylish, and she'd hung onto her figure. James was acutely aware of his shabby trousers and beat-up state.

Had a hard day's night? the woman said.

Uh…

Reminds me of Pete, in his early period. Before he really got started.

Pete?

Yes, Pete Davis, the man who died the other week. My

58

husband.

James stared at the woman and wished to fuck that Pete had told him more. All he'd known about was the disaffected sister, and that was only a passing remark. If anyone had seemed a lifelong loner it had been Pete. Jean was that photograph coming to life, and the woman did not look much different. It made Pete's death even more tragic.

What can I do for you? James said.

What can I do for you? What planet are you on, James? You sound like Mr Singh up the road.

James sat down, it was either that or fall down. If ever there was a woman on a mission he was looking at one, with him hung over like hell, and his head thumping out a cruel beat.

You didn't know that Pete was married, did you?

James thought it better to shake his head, though the hangover didn't agree.

I hadn't heard from him for years, Jean said, but he got in touch a while ago, completely out of the blue. He said he was in this place, mentioned you, 'my new mate', he called you.

Yes.

Pete started rambling on about the past, about having had all his chances. I had to put the phone down in the end. He was in a bit of a state. When the police phoned it all came clear…. why he phoned.

Do you want a coffee, or something?

Okay. You look as if you could do with one yourself.

James could, but he also poured himself a large glass of orange juice and drank it as the kettle boiled, glad that his shopping had come back with him intact. He owed Billy one for that.

I should have let him come to see me, she continued. Pete wanted to but I put him off. It would have caused too many complications, and I didn't see the point in it.

I don't know your name, James murmured.

Jean, and you're Jim.

Well, Pete called me that. No one else ever has. Sugar? No thanks.

James put two spoons in his own cup as Billy put his head around the door.

Oi, that's bad for you, Billy said. He winked at Jean. See you again, love. I'm off out – *James*.

There was a minute's silence. The coffee was too hot but James drank it quickly. He glanced nervously at Jean and saw Pete swinging from his tree. If this woman didn't show up at the funeral what the hell was she doing *here*? James wasn't sure if he cared. He *was* sure he wanted to go back to bed.

I hadn't seen Pete for nearly ten years, Jean said. I didn't even recognise his voice at first. After Pete phoned I thought that maybe he'd hit rock bottom, that it couldn't get any worse for him. I even thought he might find a way back. Then he goes and does this. I phoned Dean, but he wasn't interested in coming back for the funeral.

Dean?

Our son. Didn't know about him either, did you? Yes, we had a son, he's twenty-three now. Dean hasn't bothered with his father for a long time. He's working in London now, doing okay. When I told him about Pete he didn't want to come down. What's the point, Mam, he said. Dad's been dead for years for me. I couldn't face going on my own. Stupid bloody fool, she muttered to herself.

Jean's voice remained firm but there was a tremor in it.

Were there many people at the funeral? Jean asked.

Well, you know, not too many.

James saw the empty Crem and reluctant mourners anxious to be gone. He wondered who'd come to his own passing, whether he'd be as far removed as Pete. He thought of Clare again, and his failure to phone her. Jean played with her coffee but didn't drink any.

Did he say anything, before he…?

60

No, Pete seemed fine. Well, not fine, but as he always was. Look, you couldn't have known this was going to happen, none of us did.

Us? How many of you are here then?

Well, there's only Billy and me now, but there are social workers, support people, you know.

There was a lot of guilt in the room. James felt it, old guilt, fresh guilt, guilt about relationships failed, lives stunted, horizons flattened. Jean's mixed with his own.

Your coffee's cold, he muttered. Do you want a fresh one?

No, it's alright.

Jean was dark, almost Latin-looking. Dark brown eyes, naturally black hair, enhanced now to keep out the grey. She was tall too, almost as tall as him. James couldn't see her with Pete, but he'd only known the ruined, lost Pete. This woman must have known someone else.

Why are *you* here? Jean asked. You don't talk like someone living in a hostel.

I made a few wrong moves.

Haven't we all. Will you show me Pete's room?

James hadn't expected this, either.

There's nothing much in it, he answered.

Jean was already on her feet. James led the way upstairs and opened Pete's bedroom door, gingerly, praying there was nothing too strange inside. There wasn't. There was very little in the hostel of Pete at all, what life he'd had lay elsewhere, where the drink was. Jean stood in the middle of the bedroom and looked around. Unlike Billy's bedroom, there was not much evidence of Pete's lifestyle. Just a solitary pint glass on his bedside cabinet, clean and unused. There was a shirt draped over a chair and Jean touched it briefly with her hand. James saw her dark red, varnished nails brush against the shirt, stay there for a moment, then pull away. She stood by the window for a while, but James knew she wasn't looking outside.

I should have gone, Jean said

James saw moisture glisten at the edge of her eyes but she kept it in check. He was so glad he'd attended Pete's funeral. He tried to think of something positive to say, but it was difficult.

Have you come far? was all he could come up with.

Newport. Right, I'll be off then. Thanks for showing me around.

Not much to show.

No, but I wanted to see it. Where Pete ended up... James saw her out. There was a black sports car in the street and Jean got into it. When she drove off James realised they hadn't even shaken hands. She hadn't offered one. This had been a farewell journey for her, perhaps one of exorcism. Jean had mentioned 'complications', which meant she had someone else now. Maybe she'd talked about her new life with Pete, and that had sent him over the edge. Maybe not. Pete might have been glad for Jean, might even have welcomed it. Maybe he'd been let off the hook and sought instant release. So many maybes. That was the trouble with suicide.

The hangover came back. The shock of this woman appearing had pushed it away for a while, now it started up again. It was one of his worst for some time. Pressure was trying to push his eyeballs out of their sockets, he was in a cold sweat, and his guts felt like a cave, with distant echoes of food in it. As he stood on the hostel steps the phone box caught his eye, a silver wink in the morning light. It wanted action but he needed breakfast. As he closed the hostel door James pictured a big fry-up. It was the wrong picture. Buddy Rich played on as he dashed upstairs to the toilet.

*

I didn't expect Zoe to be home. She opens the front door before I can turn the key. I'm confronted by those blazing eyes, so much like her father's. Adrian stands behind me sheepishly. It's quite funny really, it's as if Zoe's the mother and I'm the kid slinking home after a dirty weekend. I daren't smile.

You're back, Zoe says.

Looks like it.

Adrian brings my case in but still stands behind me. I'm really fighting to keep from smiling now as we play the scene out.

I didn't expect you to be here, I say.

I'm going back up to college tomorrow. There are no lectures Monday morning.

I'm pretty sure there are, but Zoe obviously wanted to be here when I got back. To check out if I've had a good time, and see how it went. To know if I'm happy, that above all. Part of her will want that, but a bigger part will be apprehensive. Zoe has come to hate change, for so much has been thrust upon her. *Am* I happy? I'm not sure. I don't think any woman would describe Adrian as a fun guy, but the attention has been agreeable. That has to be a start.

Do you want a coffee, Adrian? I ask.

No, it's alright. I'll pop off. I have work to prepare for tomorrow.

Okay.

Bye, Zoe, Adrian says.

Something comes from her mouth but it's barely intelligible. Then my expert of Scottish battlefields is gone.

That was a bit rude, Zoe.

She shrugs.

Corduroy trousers. Ugh!

Look, I'm tired, love. It was a long drive back. Am I going to be lectured on Adrian?

He's a nerd, mum.

Yes, I think he probably is.

Well then… and he works with Clare. How weird is that?

63

It's not weird at all. Just a coincidence. Look, I know it's a bit of a shock to you, that your mother could possibly meet someone.

Why would you want to meet someone like him? Where *did* you meet him anyway? It was Clare, wasn't it? She set you up.

She did no such thing.

But he's her boss though, right? That's incestuous, if you ask me.

If you must know, I went out with Sandra for a drink. Adrian just happened to be there.

Just happened?

Yes. For God's sake, Zoe, stop playing detective.

She's suspicious, but Zoe could never imagine a singles club. It is too beneath her. She'd never think me that sad. Not that I think I am. Practical is the word I'd like to use. I must keep telling myself this. It *was* unfortunate though, when I found out where Adrian worked. Sandra said that proves it's meant to be, silly cow.

Zoe's standing in front of me, almost a head taller, not quite so pretty as Clare, but perhaps even more attractive. She's the one most like James, she has his high cheekbones and unruly hair, and she'll never have to worry about her figure. She has a swimmer's undulating shoulders and hips, and the waist that most women dream of, at any age. I'm glad that the girls look so good, but looks come at a price. Zoe's angry about Adrian, and more than a bit jealous. I bet he's never had that effect on a girl before. I *am* smiling now. I can't help it.

Mum!

What?

This isn't funny.

Oh, I don't know. Look, it's early days with Adrian. I don't know how it's going to go, not that it's any of your business. Can't you be happy for me? I'm not ancient yet, you know.

64

Not quite.

Oi!

Yes, but what about Dad?

What about him?

I sigh quietly. All I want to do is to sink into a deep bath, think about Scotland, and work out if there is a future with the battlefield man.

I've opened a bottle of wine, Zoe says

Yes, and you've drunk most of it, haven't you?

The shrug again. The slouch of the shoulders as she slopes into the kitchen in front of me. All legs and outward confidence. I know what's inside isn't so sure. I hated the way James made it obvious she was his favourite, that he had a favourite at all. Clare has never said much about this to me, but I know it hurt her.

I put the kettle on and we sit at the wooden table James's parents gave us when we got married. Dark oak and as gloomy as them. I should have got rid of it long ago, but the girls wouldn't hear of it.

Why *were* you smiling, mum?

Oh, I don't know. It was a long drive back. I'm tired.

Zoe slumps at the table with her face in her hands.

I reach out for her hand, expecting it to pull away, but it doesn't.

Look love, I've been divorced for nearly three years now. Dad is not coming back.

I know that.

He hasn't been in touch for years.

Why, though?

I don't know why, darling, but you know how he's living, he's...

Alright! You don't have to go on about it.

For Zoe, Adrian is making the divorce final. Drawing a line under her father. I've got to the age when I'm not sure if anything is ever really over, or forgotten.

What was it like then? Zoe asks, as she picks at her

nails.

What?

Scotland. With him.

Not bad. Adrian's different.

Yeah, he looks it. Dresses like an old man.

Well, he's hardly a young one, but I think it's called comfortable. Who'd you expect me to take up with? A rock star?

You're still good-looking, Zoe says quietly.

I can do without the *still*. You'd soon have something to say if I came home with a toy boy. At my age men don't grow on trees, Zoe. At least he hasn't got much baggage, none at all really, apart from the house he's stuck with. Would you rather someone with young kids around here?

Yuk!

Exactly. Anyway, you don't have to get in a strop about this. As I've said it's early days.

Yeah, but Clare's working with him, though. What happens if you dump him?

Dump him. The language of *my* teens. I'm not at all sure if this *will* last, but I do know I feel more alive, even if Adrian does wear corduroy trousers. Out of them, he wasn't an old man at all.

Now you're looking for trouble, Zoe. Nothing will happen.

By Zoe's standards, this hardly qualifies as an outburst. It will become trickier if Adrian spends much time in the house. Maybe I should have sold the place when we divorced, gone for a fresh start, but the girls had been through enough disruption. I hope, one day, that James will be able to explain to the girls what happened to him, or at least try to. Then make amends. I don't expect anything, with me his words would become locked up with all that goes into James, but the girls deserve an explanation. They need one if there's ever going to be acceptance, let alone closure.

The drive back seemed to take forever. Thank God we were not in my little Fiat. The silences got longer as Adrian drove. Small talk petered out long before we neared home. I could feel him getting tense, as if he was coming back to reality. There's a secret man within, the one he really wants to be. A historian perhaps, but he's allowed himself to be trapped, like so many of us.

My head's hitting the pillow when Zoe starts up with her music. Another one of her new discoveries pumps out noise into my night. It sounds like a young man is being strangled, but I'm too tired to be bothered, or complain. As she remembers I'm in the house, and turns the music down, I'm already falling asleep.

*

James got up shakily from his crouching position. He felt weak but purged. There was just the headache to contend with now. He wondered if he'd just dreamt the visit of Pete's wife, appearing from nowhere like that, into hostel life and out again just as quickly.

He stood in the battered cubicle, trying to keep clear of the shower curtain. It had once been green, now it was mildewed, dank, and streaked with brown stains. Danny had punched holes in the cubicle, and these leaked water onto the bathroom floor. James remembered him running into the kitchen with splinters of plastic in his hands, grinning like a fool. Wild-child Danny, raging against the machine, and himself. Danny didn't do play-acting, he went for it full-on, pure anger his mainline, all other drugs subsidiaries. James had been envious of the boy, in a strange kind of way, envious of the way Danny was able to let it all go. Envy was something James did, he'd always wanted to be someone else, do something else, look beyond what he had. It was just as well that passing exams had come easily to him. Danny was banged up somewhere now, in a secure unit. The recent track record of the hostel was not good. No wonder Deborah Skirrid was working on him.

The hot water soothed his head. James stood under it until his skin started to pucker and last night's beer seeped out of him. It was good he could take his time, there were no heating bills to worry about here, no coins to put in slots, coins that could never be spared, when there was a bet to be made, a drink to be drunk. The state took care of it, like they'd taken care of Pete's funeral.

James dried off and dressed as tidily as he could, for he felt that going to the phone box was like going to an interview. He'd try a short walk first, a scaled down version of what he did in better days. After a hurried, cobbled-together breakfast washed down by strong tea James was out on the street. He smelt keen air, saw the mist lifting and the hillside starting to appear, wet, brown and steaming as it firmed up in the November sun. His early life had been mapped out by a similar environment, but in a less desolate part of the valley. James had come back, whether master of his own fate or not, and he doubted if many did. Getting out was usually a one-way ticket.

It was cold, but the wind had eased. James walked past the usual suspects outside Singh's. They were getting used to him now, and sometimes couldn't be bothered to insult him. They still spat though, small, gobby projectiles launched from under Burberry caps passed close by him. They were meant to threaten not to hit, he'd learned that now. He was an unknown quantity, and street boys knew how to be careful.

Alright boys.

Wanker.

Cheers.

The usual exchange. A ritual being played out, as perhaps it had been for thousands of years in Wales. Insular locals trying to resist interlopers, and always failing. The irony of the valley's situation struck James as he began to

68

leave the terraces behind. There was nothing left here of value, apart from the people, and no one wanted them any more.

James was gasping after less than a mile, and, two-thirds up the hillside, he stopped to rest. The last terrace curved up towards him, like a wavering line of stone trying to get away from the rest. Concrete tiles did not catch the sun like the old slate ones but the roofs of scattered cars did. As he got his breath they flickered below him like the shields of Solomon.

James sat on a rocky outcrop and looked at the valley twisting its way down to the coast and the Somerset levels beyond, the lead slug of the channel lying between each piece of land. He was worn out, but still felt at home. He sucked in the air and thought about the spirit that had always been in this land. As his head cleared, James found he was able to put a line of coherent thought together. Like a line of cards. Or dice. Immediately, the wheel turned in his head, colours dripping off every part of it. It needed no further encouragement. James sighed, and tilted his head, like a predator sniffing prey. It took him a moment but he was able to cut off these images before they really got going. It was getting a little easier each time, a small result, the type he might report to Deborah Skirrid.

James closed his eyes as the sun warmed his face. He brought Clare into focus. Clare, the practical one, the one he'd taken for granted when Zoe was born. Zoe the gorgeous, shining one. Having a favourite was lousy parenting, and he tried to avoid it, but it came so easily to him. He'd never minded not having a son but as he looked back now James wondered if he hadn't treated Zoe like one. She'd always been up for anything, his partner in crime. He'd divided the girls up, Clare with Nina, Zoe with him, but Clare was the one looking for him now. The practical one.

James couldn't manage the top of the ridge but the

walk was a start. One small step for Read. He descended the hillside behind the Hollybush, trying to ignore its honeytrap sign. One of the older terrace dwellers had set free his pigeons. There were several lofts perched precariously at the top of terrace gardens, brightly painted shacks, ramshackle, but vibrant and still alive, much more than remnants of a lost past.

The birds cavorted above him, a dozen or so of them turned as one, like a giant swallow energetically writhing in its freedom, then screamed down the hillside in an arrow. They had it made. A wild display of stamina then back to a roof over their heads, where food, warmth and sex was on tap.

James was getting close to the phone box now and still had no idea what he'd say, but at least the boys were gone. When they drifted away it struck him how still the village became. So unlike those old images of movement, milling people amidst smoking endeavour. The valley had been cleansed by having its life removed and James doubted that this was a fair exchange.

The box smelt a little sweeter than last time. He picked up the phone and wiped it with a sleeve. It needed wiping. James dialled the number Clare had given him. Jim Reeves was singing in his head – *put your sweet lips, a little closer to the phone*. It was a long six rings, then Clare answered.

Clare?

Who's this?

Dad.

…God, I didn't recognise your voice.

I've had a cold.

I can't believe I didn't know it was you straight away.

He heard the shake in her voice. His was doing the same.

Don't worry. Uh, I got your letter.

I sent it ages ago.

I know. It's been round the block a few times.

There was a few seconds of silence.

How are you, then? he managed to ask.

James just about stopped himself calling Clare 'love'. Not an appropriate word after so long.

Yeah, great. I passed all my final exams.

Yes. I read that in the letter. Excellent.

I thought you weren't going to bother, Clare said, when I didn't get a reply.

No no, it just took a while to reach me.

Where the hell are you?

At the top of a valley.

What are you doing up there?

Not much.

What type of place is it?

I've got a… a flat, part of a terraced house.

James was in a cold sweat. He felt it prick at his skin.

Eh, how's your mother?

She's okay. Fine. She's on the way to Scotland

Scotland?

Yes. With Adrian. I told you about him in the letter.

I see…. for her fiftieth birthday.

More silence.

Can't you even stay in touch, Dad? It does my bloody head in. You're not divorced from me, or Zoe.

I know. It's just…it's…

His tongue stuck to the roof of his mouth. He had no spit. And the street boys were back. As they passed the box, one of them made rapid hand gestures at him, and whacked the door of the box. The others laughed and wheeled away. They shambled up the street to stop outside Singh's. Like the pigeons, they seemed one entity. This was his world now. On the end of his line his first-born was living in another one. Thank God.

Dad? You still there?

Yes. Just finding some more money.

He put another pound into the slot. James wondered

how much his daughters really knew about the gambling, how much Nina had told them. Clare was doing her A Levels when the marriage fell apart, more a final rend, as Nina finally lost patience and admitted defeat. She'd only held on that long for the girls' sake. It was only weeks away from Clare's exams but she still managed to do well.

Dad, you're gone again.

Sorry. So, the job's okay?

Yes. I think I'll stick with Johnsons for a while, they seem like a good outfit.

Anyone special around?

No, not special. Not since Russ.

Zoe?

Oh, she's always got someone on the go, boys worship her.

He wanted to ask about Adrian but it wouldn't do him any good. James watched the boys spray each other with coke from their cans. Shaking them up and using them like fire extinguishers. Marking out their territories. This was a place of territories. Old drinkers, spitting boys, pigeons, hostel dossers, all living in their own micro-worlds.

James had forgotten Nina's birthday. He told himself that she deserved some happiness, an antidote to her last years with him.

Look, Dad, can I come up?

What… here?

Of course there. Where do you think I mean?

Well…

Please, Dad. This has gone on long enough.

I could come down…

Never mind about coming down. I'll come up to you. You can see my new car.

Alright.

The word came out in a panicky croak but it was all that was needed. They arranged to meet the next Sunday. That would give him a few days to collect himself. He gave

72

Clare directions. They'd meet outside the 'Bush. He'd have to prepare her for the hostel in stages.

At one, then, Clare said

Yes, I'll be outside the pub.

James found it hard to get his breath. He imagined Clare appearing with Nina and Zoe, his past presented in one package. Sweat poured from him once more as the hangover tried to make a comeback. He lurched out of the phone box like the drunk he so often was, his thoughts racing with his breath as family pictures passed through in his head. Each one accused. John, the domino man, passed him.

You alright, lad?

Yeah, no problem.

Coming up for a pint?

No, not now, thanks. Maybe tonight.

His legs almost followed John, they knew what James needed. He noted the top of the ridge above the village, an exposed spine of shale and scrub, and determining to reach it before he met with Clare.

In the hostel, Billy was singing *Volare* in the kitchen, already on his second can. Billy's eyes were shut, his red face screwed up, his mountain range of broken teeth revealed as he gave the song full throttle. He was oblivious to James's presence; Billy was in a micro-world to end all micro-worlds.

The GA meeting was on Friday afternoon. For James, Friday was not a good day. As another weekend loomed, his situation grew a little more real, time became even harder to kill, and his addiction took advantage. It gnawed at him, wanting to be set free and demanding space to roam, but James had to keep it caged.

Billy had made himself scarce. He was already on *his* weekend, but people had been in the hostel, doing up Pete's room, and putting in a new phone. James dreaded the thought of two new inmates. It would be wise to keep on Billy's good side, or it could easily be three against one.

The smell of fresh paint affected his chest. It had been better for a while, but now it geared up for a Welsh winter, which would be more rain than ice. He could hear it wheeze as he breathed in, a small, almost musical whistle, like a pea trapped in his ribs, a lesser intimation of the old miners that were scattered throughout the village.

James thought that perhaps he could work out. He smiled at the thought of joining the muscle-bound body builders of the village. There were more than a few of them around, older versions of the phone box boys. It seemed to him that they pumped up their bodies to deny the reality of their existence, controlling the one thing they could control, but, if their bodies were temples, it was only of self-worship. They'd piss themselves at the sight of him in their gym. *Mr Puniverse*. James gave himself a few puffs of Ventolin. It wouldn't do to be breathless in front of Deborah.

She was on time, and James was ready. He opened the door just as she knocked.

Oh, James, you startled me.

Can't think when I last did that to anyone.

He'd scrubbed up as well as he could, and had tried to control his hair but he'd never been able to iron, and his shoes should have been retired long ago.

Ready then?

As much as I'll ever be.

Try to be positive. This is for you, remember.

James sat in the front seat of her car, one of the few times in the last year he'd been in one. The police car in Cardiff was the first. He'd been trying to stagger back to his squat after a session of fruitless betting had been chased up by compensatory boozing and had been arrested for being drunk, but not particularly disorderly. They'd let him sleep it off in a cell and he was released without charge. For eight

74

hours he'd lain on a grubby bunk-bed, not sure whether the clanking of heavy cell doors and the station's midnight chorus of anger, complaint and despair was inside his head or real.

The meeting's at a community centre a few miles down the valley, Deborah said.

Will there be lots of other stuff going on?

Probably. Don't worry. It's in one of the back rooms. Quite private.

Oh.

Nothing was that private in the valley, but James doubted if anyone would be interested in a bunch of hopeless losers. A few of the phone box boys smirked at him as he got into Deborah's car, but nothing was shouted out. They were at the centre in a matter of minutes.

I'll introduce you to Dave Connolly, Deborah said. No one is really in charge, but Dave is the co-ordinator.

Another social worker?

No, but he does do a bit of support work for us. Dave's a fellow traveller. Everyone at the meeting is in the same boat as you.

All rowing their way to hell, James thought. He was nervous, his hands clammy, his chest tight. He thought of his old college performances. Words rolling off his tongue like bright marbles, some sincere, most for effect. Used for women mainly, to snare and secure. There'd been many before Nina, a few after. At first she didn't even stand out from the crowd. He was spoilt for choice. James Read, ladies' man, lads' man, everyone's man. Not really belonging to anything, but always popular. Having the best of both worlds. That had been back in the seventies, still close enough to the golden sixties to bask in their glory, but a time of change. He'd revelled in the crumbling of the Heath government, and thought of himself as a class warrior then, determined to stay *us* and not become *them*.

By the time college was over James had a presentiment

of things to come. Life was greyer, everything from politics to music, the country flat, bloated, and at a dead end. Fertile grounds for zealotry and a zealot duly came. It was easy then to convince himself that caution was the answer.

Caution bled into conformity. College had provided him with Nina and a profession. He'd teach English, and she French, not too exciting, but safe. Safe is what he told himself was needed at that time. A future was mapped out. They'd have kids, and be happy. What everyone did, or tried to do. Social and political concerns could be given lip service, but not much else. Marriage would be enough of a test, James told himself, a move forwards, but always something chipped away at him inside, a voice of doubt. It got louder as life got more difficult. Eventually it began to shout, and have its way.

Are you going to get out of the car, James?

What? Oh, yes.

I'll introduce you to Dave then I'll be off.

You're not staying?

No need. You'll be fine. Dave will give you a lift back.

Deborah led the way through the main entrance. James heard bustle around him but kept his head down. He felt like he was in another dimension, looking in on this world but not really a part of it.

Deborah was introducing him to someone.

Hello mate.

A large hand was offered. James looked up at a tall man, powerfully built, with close-cropped reddish hair. His eyes were sharp, piercing even. James was reminded of Van Gogh's self-portraits. Enlarged and brought to life.

How do. I'm Dave, Dave Connolly. Nice to have you here, James. Do they call you Jim?

Not really.

Okay. James it is, then.

Dave wore a brushed cotton shirt and looked for all the world like a lumberjack who'd lost his forest.

76

The handshake was reassuring. Firm but not bone-crushing.

Right, I'll be off then, Deborah said.

James scanned the congregation. There were a dozen or so men in the room, most of them sitting in pairs at tables. This looked like a chess club without the boards. James gave a small prayer at the absence of women. Their presence would have been too high a hurdle too soon.

You're living up at the hostel, then, Dave said. Cheerful spot, innit?

Immensely.

Come on, I'll introduce you to the boys.

Dave conducted the tour. There was no one young here, no one that old. James wondered if gambling addiction was an affliction of middle age, or that it did not go very well with longevity. One man stood out, small, slight, and dressed as a teddy boy.

Do you like Elvis, butt? the man asked, as they shook hands.

Uh, yes, I suppose so.

The King, eh?

I'll get you a coffee, Dave said. You want one, Tony?

Please.

Milk and sugar, Jim, sorry, James?

Yes. Two sugars.

Three for me, Tony said. I'll never be sweet enough...*Love me tender, love me true*.... Come and sit by here.

Tony tapped the chair next to him. He seemed harmless enough, and cut quite a dash. His string tie was immaculately fixed, it described a perfect bow against his crisp white shirt, and his black leather waistcoat went well with his skinny frame and drainpipe trousers. Thinning hair had been coloured and gelled back, maybe with Brylcreem, and fashioned into a ridiculous pig-tail at the back. Only the carpet creepers were missing. Tony wore trainers which rather spoilt the effect. Despite what he was feeling inside, James could still smile. He guessed Tony was about sixty, but wasn't sure, for his face was pink and unlined. Only his watery-blue eyes were old, and they did not fix on anything for long.

Weird, the first time, isn't it? Tony said.

Yes...

We're all in this together, mate, that's the way to think. Tony lowered his voice. Look at Dave, big, powerful, bloke, 'in he, but he lost the lot, just like the rest of us. 'Ad his own building firm, big 'ouse, nice wife. It all went tits up, with the gambling, like. Getting on his feet again now, wife's gone though, she's in Australia, an' his kids. You married?

No.

Dave came back with the coffee.

Ok, James? Tony not annoying you, is he?

Not at all.

Dave moved to the other side of the room. Nothing much seemed to be happening. There was a low murmur of conversation, but James did not feel threatened. No one was bothering him. He focused on what Deborah had said about boats. No one here was better than him, certainly no one worse.

When did you start, then, James?

Start what?

Tony played with the string of his tie and looked directly at him. It was the longest his eyes had stayed still.

The gambling? What else?

James's natural reaction would be to clam up, but he knew that wouldn't do. Clare would appear in a few days, he needed to front up, try to be positive, like Deborah said. This might be his last chance. *Try* was a word that had become so difficult. He'd used it on himself many times before, only to have it disappear on the spin of a wheel or drown at the bottom of a glass. Then it became *try again.*

Look, Tony said, you don' 'ave to say nothin', but this is a good place to talk. When I come here first I hated every bloody thing. Blamed everyone and 'is brother for what 'ad 'appened to me. We all bin through it – still goin' through it. All the fuckin' time. They say gambling is like booze, once it gets into your blood it'll always be there. You 'ave to learn to control it, see. Everyone 'ere 'as lost out big time. *You* 'ave. But there is a way back, boy, an' tha's why we're 'ere.

About five years ago, James said quickly.

Uh?

You asked me just now when I started.

Oh aye. Five years, eh? Christ, you're just a beginner. Got a preference, horses, dogs, cards?

Yes. All them.

Tony laughed.

You got it bad, alright.

If I had to pick one thing it would be roulette.

Posh fucker, eh? No offence, mate, jus' joking. Bit above most of 'em in 'ere, though, casinos would be. Don' mind me asking, but you're a professional man, ain't you. Or were?

Am I? Was I? Why do you say that?

No offence again, but you stick out like a dick on parade. You dress like us, sure, an' you got the right look in your eyes alright…..

… Thanks.

Tony winked.

… but you *ain't* like us. I could tell tha' straight off. Maybe you fallen further than anyone 'ere, 'part from Dave. You probably 'ad further to fall.

What do you mean, 'the look in the eyes'?

Well, sort of hungry like, but a hunger that can' be satisfied. Your eyes are still looking for it. It'll stay with you for ever now, stalk you like a ghost. A part of you will always want it. You gotta put up with it first, then you learn

79

to ignore the fucker. You 'ave to.

Have you?

Getting there. 'Aven't 'ad a bet for six months now.

Tony leant closer. He smelt of old tobacco.

An' I'll tell you another thing, son. Them that do get the big win, it don' change nothing. They still wanna go on. Lose it as quick as they gets it, most of 'em.

James was surprised at how easily Tony had assessed his background. At least he hadn't called him an *educated man*. He knew now that intelligence was not a buffer against anything. Some of the most inadequate people he'd ever known were intelligent, but theirs was a paper intelligence, useful for fixing paper problems. Literature was full of them, they were the glue that stuck together thousands of books, multitudes of the fallen, the lost, and the crazy, people of low moral fibre skulking through its pages for the last hundred years. People like him.

Low moral fibre. James was surprised that such a phrase could still enter his mind. His grandfather used to utter it like it was a message from God. To that old man it was, symbolising a code of behaviour he'd followed all his life, welcoming its constraints, only to die embittered at the state of the nation. That had been a period of family deaths. His heart-attacked father went soon after. James was already married to Nina when his mother followed on a few years later. For her, diagnosis to death had been very rapid. She had lung cancer, yet had never smoked. Neither had his father, or drunk, apart from a small glass of sherry at Christmas. They should have lived much longer. James was aware that genes for a long life might be lacking in the Reads, but there had been times in the last five years that the thought of his own death had been quite sweet. Pete's suicide had crushed such fraudulent notions. James had coped well with the passing of each parent, maybe too well. By then he'd created a world for himself, a bomb-proof nuclear family of three females who adored him. He

80

thought he had.

Life with his parents had been strange. James had gradually realised that as he grew up. By looking around him, at the families of the few friends he'd had, he saw what the Reads lacked. Three people had been locked into three private worlds, but James's was not of his own choosing. He could not remember ever doing much with his father, just three things, three pinpricks in a childhood that seemed to last for ever. Three events that still stood out sharply in his mind, such was their rarity. A visit to the cinema, a trip on a steamer and being violently sick on the choppy waters of the channel, and going to a zoo. That was with both parents, a strange, one-off occasion. He'd been eleven years old then, old enough to sympathise with the caged animals, to share their distress, and want to go home. He remembered polar bears restlessly pounding their compound, continuously shaking yellow heads back and forth, looking for the life that had been taken from them with eyes that were still wild.

Even at that age James knew such singular interaction with his parents was not normal, but did not realise to what extent until much older. The old man had been locked into books and ideas that never went anywhere. He was a local government officer who thought he deserved better, but did nothing about it. And his mother, even now, James still wasn't sure what had made her tick. Certainly not her husband, or her son. She'd taken laissez-faire philosophy to extremes, and he'd made his own choices from the age of fourteen. *As long as you're happy, dear,* rang in his head even now. The testament of his youth. He'd inherited a double dose of selfishness, then added his own. The Reads had been three dysfunctional people, but one was a child.

When the gambling started and James began to lose heavily, so the drinking followed. The bottle forced him to look deeper within, spurred on by the raw edge of a bet. Parts of him he had kept hidden or was unaware of were

81

exposed, forced out of their secret cell into the open. A latent resentment towards his parents flared up but it was far too late. At first, the thought of the Big Win became compensation for his past, then, as it grew, it began to feed on itself, a rough beast that he couldn't control. Money, that stuff he told himself he'd never been interested in or motivated by, now became a cure-all. He ripped through the family funds amazingly quickly before Nina knew what was happening, high on guilt, but unable to stop himself. Whatever money he had left after the divorce went just as fast.

Tony was right. The GA might be his last chance.

Lost in 'em, 'an you?

What?

Your thoughts. Lost in 'em. I was the same, first time I come. A meeting like this, sort of triggers it off, like. You're off on one. Thinking 'bout all the stuff that got you 'ere. Tha's good. You gotta start thinking 'bout it, before you can starting talking 'bout it. Then maybe you can start doing something 'bout it.

James smiled as hopefully as he could.

What you do then? Tony asked.

Well, I haven't done anything for some time.

Look a bit like a brief, you do. Lots of *them* gamble.

James looked around him. He was in a nondescript back room, sitting on a cheap plastic chair at a cheap plastic table. Heat pumped through the room to steam up the windows, they streamed with condensation, and if the valley was outside he couldn't see it.

What do *you* do, Tony?

Good God, kid, I 'aven't worked in twenty years. Used to be a binman on the council. The job was the first thing to go, then the missus got rid when all the money kept disappearing down the bookies. You're a loser, she told me, an' tha's all you'll ever be. I didn't know wha' she was on about at first, I was so wrapped up in the betting... I do now. 'Course, once I was turned loose the drink got going. I'd always liked a pint on a Friday night, but every night was Friday then. Drink-gamble, gamble-drink, like two fuckin' big fists battering me. When I lost 'alf my giro on the horses, getting pissed on the rest took it all away. For a while. But you know all this, don' you, James?

James nodded.

Tony slurped at his coffee, holding the mug in two hands.

I got a kid somewhere, too, he continued. Shelley. We only had one. Pity that. You should never have just the one. Strange girl – like her mother. Never saw that much of her, even when we was all together. Couldn' tell you where she is now. Who knows, I might be a grandad. Sad, innit?

Twelve ruined lives were in this room. James was amongst a collection of weakness and wrong moves; he was a part of it.

You gotta get over it, son. Move on.

Son? How old do you think I am?

Tony's blue eyes appraised him.

Oh, 'bout forty, maybe a bit more. Am I right?

Just about.

James retained enough vanity to support the lie. His confidence was lifted a little, and he began to talk to Tony about casinos, describing Roulette wheels like they were old lovers, opening up, and captivating his audience. Each man feeding off the other's addiction. Dave rejoined them.

How are things going? Dave asked.

Fine, mate, fine, Tony said, 'aving a right old chat, me and James 'ere.

Good. Can I have a word, James?

James nodded and got up from his chair, following Dave's beckoning hand. They stood against the wall at the far side of the room, and Tony wandered over to another table.

How'd you find Tony? Dave asked.

Ok.

He's probably the most talkative here. I thought it would be be best to start you off with him. We go for a 'buddy' approach here.

Buddy approach?

Yeah, a member who'll keep an eye on someone, 'specially new boys. Bit like a sponsor, I suppose.

Is it always *boys*?

Well, it is here. There are women members of GA's further down the valley. They get hooked on scratch cards these days, more than bingo and fruit machines. Chasing dreams. Just like us.

You want me to have a sponsor?

Think about it, at least. You've made the first step by coming to the meeting. Everyone here will tell you that's the hardest one.

The meeting was packing up. James couldn't believe a few hours had gone by so quickly. It was not what he'd come to expect from time.

Come on, Dave said, I'll run you up.

You know where the hostel is?

Course I do. I was the first one in there when they opened it.

Dave drove an oversized Jeep, like the one James had imagined Adrian driving. It was like a civilian armoured car.

Ridiculous vehicle isn't it, Dave said, right bloody gas-guzzler, but when I got back on my feet again I wanted people to know.

When they stopped outside the hostel the spitting boys around the phone box took note. They liked it. They liked Dave. He was the type of man they could respect and there were no hand signs or jeers.

Dave roared off with a wave and two blasts on the horn before James was inside the hostel and the boys across the street reverted to type.

Oi, doss-house man, one shouted over, been out with your boyfriend?

Got any skunk? another added.

James wasn't sure what skunk was but he shook his head anyway, and went inside.

James was stuck on a giant playing card. James instead of Jack. He was dealt. Giant hands moved over a giant table as the card tumbled down. He looked up into the cavernous nostrils of giants, saw the tawny seas of whisky in their glasses, sailed through low clouds of cigar smoke, and was blinded by the glint of gold rings. Then he was back in the pack, being crushed, the light shut out, hard to breathe, before being freed again, flying through the clouds and landing on the green plain below. He was in the winning hand, part of a royal flush, snapped down on the table triumphantly, face up and out of breath, cigar ash falling on him in a grey waterfall. The queen of diamonds winked at him.

James sat up in the bed, twisting a sheet in his hands. He was soaked through with sweat but felt instantly cold. He got up shakily and turned the wall heater on, praying that it would work. It did, and he sat near it, letting it warm his back as he collected his senses.

He felt need. The need to make a bet. It was like a stab, a quick insertion, as his addiction punished him. James shivered and hugged his ribs. He'd seen this in Pete and Billy, he'd seen it in Danny as he smashed his fists against the kitchen wall, until they were bloody, and so was the wall. He'd seen it in many others in the last three years. A need that was blind to reason or control. Glasgow Paul had taken it to the ultimate level. This won't be as bad as heroin or cocaine, he told himself, not as bad as booze. Brave words, but as James sat shaking, with a blinding headache, he wasn't sure if he could live up to them.

It was Sunday. Clare's day. James looked out of his

bedroom window at dawn breaking. It was almost a reluctant start to the day, as grey light began to seep in at the edges of the sky. He could still see a few stars, cold white flicks slowly fading in a lightening sky. James was meeting Clare at one. Now he wished he'd suggested an earlier time. There'd be less chance of him worrying himself into a nervous wreck. Less chance of having a drink. He must present himself sober, that most of all.

He went down to the kitchen to make coffee, and eat stale cornflakes that turned to soggy cardboard in the milk. It was eleven o'clock before he could get going, it took him that long to get the nightmare out of his system. James heard Billy clumping around. He'd had a quieter Saturday than usual. Maybe Billy was finally slowing down. Not by design, just that time was creeping up on him. Billy had told James his liver was *like an old flannel* a few days ago, not without pride. The doctor told him he had perhaps another six months, if he kept drinking.

Billy was singing something. He was always singing something, today it was his favourite, *Whisky In The Jar*. For once Billy sang clearly, and well, without the usual drunken slurring and splutters. He had the trademark club tenor's warble in his voice, like he was gargling marbles, but James was still impressed. Real emotion dripped from the words as Billy *wept for his Daddy-o*. Billy's past was in the song. Every life that fetched up at the hostel had so much to tell, most of it locked up with shame, anger and regret. A new inmate was coming soon. He might be another Danny, he might be worse.

James told himself that the GA meeting *had* been beneficial. Tony had been a willing audience and it had been a long time since he talked like that to anyone. He'd made a start. Today he hoped to make another.

James stared in the bathroom mirror at his foam-covered face. As he shaved, with extreme care, bits of it were revealed. Little windows of skin, each one telling a story. He'd had several drunken falls in the last few years. In his teaching years he'd been used to flattery about his *boyish features* from colleagues, even if it was tongue-in-cheek. He'd seen one of the heads he'd once worked for a few months ago, in the town at the gateway to the valley. His first reaction was to cross the road but it wasn't necessary. The man didn't recognise him. He glanced at James then looked away quickly.

James wanted to use the scraps of confidence that were building inside him. He was already eating better, now he had to learn to sleep better, lessen the blue-mountain ranges beneath his eyes, and change his clothes more often. He'd managed it for Deborah, and the GA gathering, now he'd manage it for Clare.

Last night James had spent an age trying to iron stuff for this Sunday meeting. The hostel had a communal iron and board in the kitchen, it had been there for a few years but was new and unused. His technique was non-existent. He'd attack a shirt from every angle, and be thwarted at each turn as creases came back to haunt him. James's ironing provided a pre-pub floorshow for Billy. Billy sat at the kitchen table laughing. Eventually James called a truce with his clothes and told himself they looked ironed, in an individual sort of way.

Yesterday morning, buoyed up by the GA meeting, James had enrolled at the library further down the valley. Social services had given him a form to prove who he was, and where he lived. Things like driving licences, passports, had been lost in a succession of bed-sits, and he'd long since been stripped of bank accounts and credit cards.

James came back with a few books, and had looked through them last night, as the drunks in the street outside went through their Saturday ritual. The late night chorus of men's voices that led from pub to dwelling place, interspaced by the occasional woman's laugh, shout or squealed anger. James had grown used to it, he liked the way each group faded away into the night, to be replaced by another, and another, until finally the night fell silent, and everyone was home. It told him that he was in his room, relatively sober.

A plane often went over about this time, maybe a late flight to the sun, or the end of a holiday. His ears would track its progress over the valley, straining for the last drone. Cars grew fewer and fewer, until by the early hours they were rare and isolated, so that he could hear the individual swish of their tyres on the wet road. This was his routine. The routine of the solitary he'd become.

The library books were on gambling. How to cure it. Control would be a better word than cure. James wanted to find out about compulsion. How he could lose the plot so quickly, lose everything, for something so senseless. There were plenty of people who wanted to tell him. He was amazed at how much stuff was available. He was living in a time of theories, and people wanted to sell them.

James killed time in the kitchen. Like a kid on a first date he checked his clothing time and again. His hair could do with cutting, it hung over his ears in black and grey wings, but it was too late now. He'd have to do. As James walked out into the keen air he thought of the last time he'd seen Clare. So much of the last three years was a fuzz, snatched imagery, scarcely remembered episodes, all set in the territories of his vice, but he remembered that meeting all to well. Meeting her that time had been a turning point for him, he realised now, or at least the start of one. Standing close to the ornate double doors of the Hollybush, James thought back a few years ago, to the memory which stood out as sharply as the hillside opposite him. Like its contours were cut into the landscape, so it was cut into his mind.

Halfway through her degree Clare had found him in a squat in Cardiff. He'd been in that place just before his time with Glasgow Paul, and what had happened there had driven him out onto the street. James had shared a crumbling terrace with a few crack addicts, and a man who should have been in care somewhere. A schizophrenic who had somehow freed himself from the system. A large man about James's age, who wore battle fatigues which made him look like a soldier in search of a war. Each man had his own space in the squat, usually not much more than a pile of fetid rags, broken furniture and a sleeping bag. No one bothered much with anyone else; they were all locked into their own hell. That suited James, for his addiction was in full flow, and his descent in overdrive. The schizophrenic seemed to take a shine to James, which was probably worse than having him for an enemy. He'd hang around and try to talk to James, mouthing bits of gibberish.

It was a Friday and he'd just lost most of his DSS emergency money, on a horse called *Morning Glory*. James remembered the name. He'd been doing horses then because there was no way he could get into a casino. There was enough money left for two cans of White Lightning. He smuggled them into the squat, and drank them quickly. Empty stomach, cold and wasted, into nine percent rocket fuel equals instant pisshead. He passed out in the corner of the downstairs room he liked to call his. It was the one no one else wanted.

James came to with the schizo-soldier kneeling beside him, pulling at his clothing and making strange noises. The man's hands were tattooed. *Hate* was on one finger, *Love* on another. *Help me with the voices*, the man was shouting, *get them to leave me alone.* James managed to struggle up, shaking himself into consciousness as he pushed the man away. They wrestled for a few moments then James broke free, finding a strength he never knew he had. The man crashed against a wall and didn't get up. He lay there moaning and pressing his hands to his head. One of the boys upstairs was playing something on his ghetto blaster which sounded like James felt. Someone rapped, snarled words, pounding bass, and a guitar that sounded like metal being shredded. He had to get out, get away.

James stumbled out into the street, and just about fell into the arms of Clare. They were both startled. She didn't know him at first. When she did tears came to her eyes.

Dad. What's going on?

James looked at her blankly. He almost turned and ran away. His life had just about been tolerable as long as it was secret. Stripped bare, it was not worth living. Clare looked stunning and so out of place in his new world. James stared at her make-up being ruined by the tears tracking down it.

Clare! What are you doing here? *How* are you here?

Dad, look at you. God, you look like a tramp.

Her tears threatened a revolt now. James just stood there. Caught like a rabbit in headlights. Clare collected herself before he did.

Come on, let's get off the street, she said, taking him firmly by the arm.

Clare led the way to a cafe, where the owner looked at James suspiciously. James felt like shouting out that this was his daughter, bursting with pride and shame in equal doses. Clare bought two large mugs of coffee but James doubted he could drink any. His stomach felt like an empty vault in which White Lightning sloshed around. Clare dabbed at her eyes with a tissue.

My make-up's ruined.

How did you find me?

Never mind about that. I wouldn't have to if you kept in touch. For Godsake, Dad, Zoe would freak out if she saw you like this.

How is she?

Settling down a bit now. It's taken her a while.

And your mother?

Alright.

Clare's hand reached across the table for his. He fought down the instinct to draw away, when really he wanted to snatch her up and deny everything.

What the hell was that place? Clare asked, and what was going on?

Uh, just a temporary bed-sit. I'm in line for a council place. Nothing was going on, don't worry.

You shot out that door like a bat out of hell.

James shrugged.

Clare wore a dark blue coat with a silver brooch on the lapel. He recognised it. One of her eighteenth birthday presents. They'd brought it back from Milan, where he'd gone with Nina for a short break. Their last. He'd already started his secret life by then, but it was nothing to worry about, he told himself. Just a temporary blip. So what if he missed a supply day? They had no money problems. Gambling was just a diversion, a touch of excitement in his early middle-age. A d*ivertissement,* as Nina might say. He'd always be able to handle it.

Why did you disappear like this, Dad? It's not fair.

I know. I'm going through a bad patch. It's…

Bad patch! You're practically living rough.

Not practically, James thought. He didn't know what to say. Nothing could speak more plainly than his appearance, and he hoped to God he didn't smell too bad. He saw his reflection in the cafe window, and he saw Clare's. Beauty and the Beast.

Zoe still thinks it's Mum's fault, Clare said. Things have been difficult between them. It's the only way she can explain what's happened, especially as you vanished off the face of the earth not long after the divorce.

Look, she mustn't think that. None of you have contributed to this. It's all my own work.

You should tell her that yourself. *I* know it, but Zoe doesn't want to think of her father being that useless. It *is* bloody hard to understand. What went wrong, Dad?

The trillion-million-dollar question that he'd been asked so many times before. He'd never been able to answer it. Not for Clare. Not for Nina. Not for himself. James tried to drink some coffee but it had gone cold.

It *would* help if you got in touch, talked to Zoe.

Yes.

You haven't answered my question.

He looked at his hands, as if they had the answer, but they only wrung themselves together.

I don't think I can, love, not yet. It was just something….something that took over me. I tried to tell you this before the divorce. Addictions are never sought.

Bullshit, Dad. That's a nice neat phrase but it doesn't mean anything. Where's this going to end? With you freezing to death on the street?

I'll get on my feet again. I promise…

Don't make promises so easily! You've done that too many times before.

They were silent for a while. Clare looked so stylish, like the Milanese women of that last trip. Nina had been excited and zesty that weekend, but he'd been on automatic pilot, thinking ahead to the next bet.

James was getting over the shock of seeing Clare and being called *Dad* again. It sounded strange, an inclusive word, from warmer times.

So, how *did you* find me? he asked.

One of Mum's friends saw you in this area, so I asked around. It wasn't hard. You stick out like a sore thumb

Your mother doesn't know where I am?

No.

James sighed. He should have got further away. Kept his shame a bit more private. He was involving the family even now. In a moment of clarity, fighting against everything buzzing in his head, and still smelling the schizoid's foul breath, it dawned on James that he would always involve them. Just by being alive.

He glanced out of the window. His fellow squat dweller was passing, probably looking for him. Watching his strange, loping gait James tried to shrink. He kept his head down, almost level with the coffee mug.

Are you hiding, Clare asked. From *him*?

Clare flicked her head towards the man, but he didn't look into the cafe.

It makes for an easier life.

Yeah, yours looks very easy.

Her eyes were starting up again. James willed his not to follow suit, and fought to keep a tremor from his voice. He reached a hand across to hers and touched it hesitantly. Clare grabbed his and held on tightly.

Don't get upset, love, James said.

Clare started to shake, attracting the attention of a woman at the table next to them.

Why not? You are.

He rubbed at his own eyes quickly.

What did Jerry Lee Lewis once say? It's only sweat.

You and your old fogies.

Look, James said. Tell me about *your* life.

Clare calmed down and ordered more coffee. This time James could drink some of it. Clare filled him in on the details and when she pressed him James made promises he knew he'd never keep as soon as they left his lips. Promises like he'd try to get help, get a better place to live, get in touch with Zoe. Even as they talked James was thinking of going to the DSS tomorrow, to try to get more money. To beg. A few weeks ago one of the young staff there recognised his name, then, eventually, his face. The boy was one of his old Comp students. He called James *sir*, putting as much insult into the word as he could but James had been too desperate to feel much humiliation. Like any addict he was focused on his next fix, and the means of getting it. Nothing else mattered.

An hour passed. Words came to a halt and Clare left with his promises in her ears. It was a reluctant parting, he had to push her away gently when every fibre of his being

93

wanted to hold onto her. Clare tried to push money into his hand but he resisted. That would have been too much to bear.

James watched her mingle with the shoppers in the street and savoured the last touch of her hand on his. Then he hurried back to the squat to fill a bag with a few things before schizoid man returned. It was too dangerous to stay there now. Ghetto blaster boy came down to see him off. He was in his early twenties, over six feet tall and under nine stone in weight. Brown eyes sunk so far back in his head they looked like two smudges of pain amongst his face stubble and eyebrow piercings.

Got any loose change, man? the boy asked.

James fumbled in a pocket and came up with fifty pence. It was all he had.

Cheers. Nice one. You off? See you then.

This was squat life. Ships passing quickly in the night, barely seeing each other, never touching. To get away was a good idea but James was collared as soon as he went through the front door. Schizoid man was standing on the steps.

Wassamarra, pal? don't you like me? Too good for the likes of me, are you? What you doing here, anyway, you poncy bastard? You're not one of us.

I'm not one of anything, James muttered.

The man's tattooed fingers bunched up into fists. James was about to be hit by *Love and Hate* but he rushed past him, using his sad bag of belongings as a shield. Schizoid man was left shouting on the steps, but he didn't follow.

The force is with *me,* not you, you wanker, the man shouted. I'll see you again – arsehole.

James turned to see the man addressing the heavens, like the crazed king of a mad kingdom. He gave silent thanks that he was not pursued. The shouts echoed down the seedy terraced street that had been his home for a few months. Some houses were boarded up, some had small

94

landfill sites in their front yards, some rusting metal sculptures that once might have been cars. One held the upturned body of a bicycle, part hidden by weeds, its one wheel turning gently in the wind. It was only a few minutes from the centre of the city, but very much its tawdry underbelly. Houses that had gone wrong, like the people who lived in them.

That night James was on the street, getting acquainted with the great outdoors. He found another insane kingdom. The realm of Glasgow Paul, lord of piss-stained cardboard and matted blankets. Another lunatic.

James watched Clare drive slowly up the street, looking for the Hollybush. Recent instinct almost made him step back into the shadows, to blend into the red brick of the pub with his brown anorak, but he stepped out onto the pavement as confidently as he could, and beckoned to her.

Clare parked in the small area at the back of the pub. Her car stood out amongst the others, which were motors as geriatric as their owners. Clare wore the same silver brooch, but this time on a dark red coat. It caught the weak sunlight and made it stronger, setting off the red background, and her black hair. His daughter was even more striking than last time. Finishing her exams, getting a good position, had put a touch of maturity to her young face. Maybe she's always had it, James thought, from her mother. It's Zoe who was more like him, his quixotic young diamond. He brushed his lips against Clare's cheeks and she hugged him briefly, before he could step back out of range.

Well, you look better than last time, anyway, she murmured.

Thanks.

This your local, then?

Not really. I come here, now and then. Some of the old boys here know me. I thought we might have some dinner.

In this way James hoped to keep Clare away from the

hostel. The 'Bush did a good trade in Sunday dinners but he wondered now if this was a good idea. There'd be a few diners choking on their beef when they saw Clare. It would be more than a snippet of gossip for the domino boys, something to be pushed around with their pieces. Clare raised another problem.

Have you forgotten, Dad?

What?

I went veggie years ago. I don't think there'd be much for me here, especially in November. It's hardly salad weather, and I don't really fancy a microwaved vegetarian *option*.

He must have looked crestfallen enough to make her laugh.

Don't worry, I had a late breakfast. Let's just have a drink. I want to talk with you more than eat, unless you are hungry, that is.

No, I'm fine. I had a late breakfast too.

They went in, to the back lounge, almost an old-fashioned snug, with worn, leather-look armchairs and a stained glass window. A drinkers' church.

This is quaint, Clare said. I didn't think pubs like this existed anymore.

There's still a few around, if you know where to look. There's no incentive to change it, and I don't think they do themes this far up the valley.

They were alone in the lounge. Food was being served in another part of the pub. James heard the low murmur of voices, a Sunday murmur, the drunken choir that passed his hostel window every Saturday night was taking time out, re-grouping for next week. He smelt the Sunday dinner smell that had marked out every weekend of his childhood, a time when the boredom of the Read family peaked. It was almost like the Sundays of old in this village, perhaps not by choice, but James liked it. A day of rest had always seemed like a good idea to him.

What do you want to drink? Clare said.

I'll get them.

The barmaid's eyes widened when he ordered a white wine for Clare and a Diet Coke for himself. They looked over his shoulder and begged him to tell her who Clare was, but the woman managed not to ask. As James turned to go back to the table he understood her interest. Clare was out of place in here, he felt like he'd won a prize and was exhibiting her.

Two meetings in two years, Clare said, we mustn't overdo it. Nothing much has happened, has it, Dad? You soon scarpered from that awful squat and there's been no contact with Zoe or me until you phoned the other day. Nothing. That *bad patch* still going on, is it?

James drank his Coke too quickly, spilling some of it onto his shirt. He felt Clare's slender fingers pressing down on his hand.

Don't be so nervous.

I've wanted to get in touch, James blurted out. Things *have* improved, but it's taken time to get this far. I'm getting…well I'm getting help now.

Help?

Well, at least I've got a decent place to stay.

He closed his eyes and thought of Danny running amok, Billy falling through doors. Pete swinging from his tree. He felt the pressure of Clare's hand increase.

I have support from people now.

What people? You mean social workers?

Yes, that type of thing. Uh, I went to a meeting, too.

Meeting?

For people like me. Addicted gamblers.

You mean like Alcoholics Anonymous?

James nodded.

That's good, Dad.

He nodded again. A few people looked into the lounge. One of them was John, the dominoes man, with a younger couple. He saw them and came straight over.

I thought it was you, John said. Who's this young beauty, then?

Eh, Clare – my daughter.

John stepped back

Good God.

John stretched out a firm hand.

Nice to meet you, love. Your Dad is a bit of a dark horse. Getting to be a good dominoes player, though.

John gestured to the couple to join them. James winced, his spirits sinking.

Well, since we're doing daughters, you can meet mine, John said. This is Ann, and her husband Mike. They're treating me to Sunday dinner.

James got up and shook hands with a woman of his era, and her man, who eyed him somewhat disdainfully. John's shrewd old eyes appraised Clare.

Come on, Mike said, they'll have stopped serving soon.

You're not having dinner? John asked.

James shook his head.

Bye then, John said. See you again, love.

I haven't been 'loved' for ages, Clare murmured.

It's still old school up here, James said.

I don't mind. He's a sweet old man. You've made friends, then.

I wouldn't say that, but the older ones seem to tolerate me.

Time passed. Clare filled him in on recent events in her life, and Zoe's college activities.

She's doing a media studies course. Bit of a Mickey Mouse subject, but you know Zoe. We'll probably see her reading the news in a few years, or performing on TV.

Performing?

She's learning bass guitar. She plagued Mum until she bought her one last year. She's in some sort of band now.

Really?

Clare rummaged in her handbag.

Here's a photo of them – *The Balancing Stallions.*

The what?

I know.

James looked at a photograph of his daughter and three boys. All hairy, and very sixties.

It's called retro rock, Dad. Trying to capture the sounds of the past.

Why?

I don't know. Maybe because there's nothing new left to do.

Oh.

When you left Zoe went through a lot of old photos of you and Mum. There was one from college, you playing a guitar. I think it's what gave her the idea. She's quite good at it now. Sings a bit, too.

That's great. Perhaps she'll stick at it. I didn't. And you, is the job alright? It is it what you want to do?

Well, someone in the family has to be sensible. I know what people think of jobs in finance but I don't want to end up…

…Anything like your father.

I wasn't going to say that, but I want my own place by the time I'm twenty-five.

That's only two years.

Yip.

There was a lull in the talk. No one else came into the lounge, which helped. Is he alright then, this Adrian? James asked.

Seems to be.

Is it serious?

Oh, I don't know, Dad. It's early days. Zoe hasn't taken it too well, but you'd expect that. You know how possessive she is.

Yes. Do you think she'd talk to me now?

Only one way to find out. I told you that last time.

James needed a drink even more than he needed to eat. He'd come as far as he could dry.

What's your flat like, then? Clare asked.

Oh, it's alright.

She wanted to see it. James was alarmed, and got up suddenly.

I'll get us another drink. Another glass of wine?

No, I'm driving. Get me a soft drink. Look, let me pay, Dad.

No, I'm fine.

He was at the bar before she could say anything more, ordering a large whisky for himself. Using his dinner money. Blanking out the questing stare of the barmaid.

Did you need that? Clare asked

Oh yes.

Well at least you're honest.

Oh, I'm that, alright, James thought. About drinking and gambling I'm very honest, and loyal. Unswerving devotion to duty. The drink calmed him and the warm glow that seeped up from within was welcome. James sighed audibly.

I'll have to be getting back soon, Clare said, I've got some work I want to write up on the computer.

On a Sunday?

I want to make a good impression early on. It's a good job, Dad.

Okay. Look, I do want to phone Zoe, it's just that I don't want to upset her.

Don't be such a wuss. That's all been done, you know that.

James finished the whisky and wanted to drink more. To celebrate this small step forward.

I know I've asked you this before, Clare said, but can you tell me now, before I go? Why the hell did you started gambling?

It was the trillion-million-dollar question last time and

was now. James drank the rest of the whisky.

Try.

James wondered how many times he had asked himself
this. He was asking himself now. Checking out library
books, trawling through all the psycho-babble theories,
social, religious, moral, even sexual, and back again.
Depending on his mood, every one of them seemed to fit
him, and none of them did. John came through the lounge
on his way to the toilets. He smiled at them but did not talk.
He'd been fed and watered, a rosy-cheeked old man at
peace with the world.

Dad?

I *am* trying.

It's not just your problem. You do see that?

James smiled.

I feel as if *I'm* the child. Of course I see it. I've lived it
every day… what I've done to you, and Zoe.

And Mum.

James fingered his empty glass. Suddenly, he wanted
out. He wanted to bet. The stalker loomed large in his mind,
and for one mad moment he thought of trying to get down
to Cardiff. Even asking Clare to drop him off. He'd learnt
recently that Cardiff was trying to attract a new super-
casino. Initially, the addict in him thought of this like a bear
thinks of honey, but James knew it was a crazy idea, one
which said a lot about the world he'd left behind. He
banished the stalker, and just about held it together.

James reached out for Clare's hand a bit too quickly,
and knocked over one of the glasses. When it smashed on
the floor it seemed like the loudest sound in the world. The
barmaid glared at him, hands on hips, as James waved a
hand in apology, his face reddening.

I'd give anything to change it back, James said. Clare,
you do know that?

Yes. I'm not so sure about Zoe, though.

I'm going to the loo.

James needed the air. The barmaid was brushing up the evidence when he came back.

You haven't answered *my* question, James said. About phoning Zoe.

You won't know until you try, I told you in that Cardiff café. You still haven't tried, Dad.

Have you got a mobile number for her? I wouldn't want to upset your mother if I phoned the house.

I don't think you would. Mum would like to know that you're okay. You still care for her, don't you?

Of course I do.

Well then, why do you think she doesn't care for you?

Clare wrote Zoe's number on a piece of paper for him and James put it away safely. He lost things easily these days.

It was mid afternoon when they left the Hollybush. The elderly diners were leaving with them. He watched one or two get into cars, and the rest walk up the street. Each old person carried a bundle of stories inside, stories that had straddled quickly changing times, and all would be snuffed out within a few years. For James, this was one of the saddest things about death, the way it extinguished vital personal histories at a stroke, leaving behind the inconstant memories of others

James stood by Clare's car, almost willing her to get into it.

You don't want me to see your flat, do you? Clare said.

Well, it's not really a flat. It's a shared place.

Shared?

Yes. For people like me.

You mean a kind of hostel?

Yes.

Why are you trying to hide that? Dad, your life of the last few years hasn't been much of a secret.

Yes, but I haven't been there long. I want to fix up my room a bit. How about next time?

Will there be a next time?

Yes.

I'll hold you to that.

Clare hugged him. She got into her car and wound down the window.

Phone Zoe, Clare said.

Then she was gone, her car disappearing down the village road to join the main valley artery. It would be clogged with Sunday traffic as people pursued the new religion of shopping but Clare was on her way back to a worthwhile life and James thanked God it was so.

He walked back to the hostel, stopping at Singh's to get a pasty and two cans of Guinness. His Sunday dinner, at last. Buoyed up with meeting Clare, James felt a wave of affection for the turbaned Sikh. The man was always open.

It was getting dark, but the phone box had its usual array of inhabitants. James wondered at *their* internal stories. They would be short, but not too sweet. There was no spitting today, no abuse. One of them even said 'alright'. James almost stopped in his tracks. He wasn't sure if this meant anything but he felt good, a small sense of belonging. He wanted to keep it for as long as possible. It had become very rare.

*

Since Zoe went up to Warwick I've been alone in the Read house. I like it, I think. At least for the time being. Clare comes over a few times a week but she's forging her own life. Adrian would be here every day, if I let him, but that would be moving things on too quickly for me.

Now that I have the time, and opportunity, I plan to tackle the back room that was James's book emporium. For someone who loved reading James showed little interest in taking many books with him when he left. Perhaps a dozen in a hastily filled holdall. I wonder which ones, which books he'd thought indispensable. There must have been a few of his American road novels. He always made out he was born too late. James would have liked to ride around the States in the 50's, on a Harley Davidson, probably, looking to get shot by some redneck farmer. I think dreaming was the cornerstone of his psyche, it made him restless and I think he always wanted to be someone else. Maybe to the point where reality was pushed out. Gambling might have been his cry for help. I hate this cliché, for it excuses so much. James had a self-destruct button that I was not aware he was pushing until it was too late.

I was tempted to get rid of all the stuff in the back room when the marriage ended but the girls wouldn't hear of it. Especially Zoe. She'd often mope around in there, thumbing through James's stuff, her way of trying to hold onto him, I suppose. Not that she's ever read anything much, neither girl has. They follow newer, more practical ways. I can't handle many of James's books myself. Too heavy, too miserable, too male. Perhaps I can box up the books, and store them in the attic. Better still, I can sell them. Zoe would accept this now.

Adrian followed me in here the other day. He's a book man himself, and was interested, and he's also getting bolder. Adrian looked through the books and nodded approval. He's discreet, but he's too eager to involve himself in every aspect of my life. I was irritated. I don't want to share my past with him, I want it to stay past.

Every shelf of books in the back room encapsulates an era, even books from James's childhood are here. He was a born hoarder. I sit down and open a few. Stirring boys' own stories. Cowboys and coral islands. James's fantasy past which might have bled into his present. I think of his strange, silent parents who never came into my life and how glad I was that James was so unlike them. I was wrong. They shaped James more than I ever could. He became a married loner, the worst kind of all.

James was complicated, with too many conflicting forces inside. The more I knew him, the more I realised this. His parents were gone before I could get to know them, and I'm sure the reasons lay with them. The one lasting memory I have of his mother is her silently knitting in the corner of her living room, more interested in the pattern than anything else, her life marked out by the clicking of her needles.

I scan through *Zen And The Art of Motorcycle Maintenance*, one of his favourites, and wonder if he thinks of me much. I doubt it. Certainly not as much as I think of him. I hate myself for doing it sometimes, it makes me feel weak, silly, even vain. I feel that he doesn't deserve these thoughts, not now, but can't cut them off.

My parents more than made up for his, especially when Zoe first practised rebellion. This ran parallel with James's rapid descent, and our divorce. What an incandescent time that was. My mother is a safe haven for Zoe, and she still runs to her, from time to time. Mum is able to balance sympathy with realistic appraisal, as clear-sighted at seventy-five as she ever was. Dad died two years ago. I managed to contact James, it was the last time we spoke, but he didn't show up, which was another hammer blow for the girls. At least I think he didn't, but when Dad was going into the ground, and emotion was at its rawest, I thought I saw him lurking at the edge of the ceremony, but it was a big turn-out and I couldn't be sure.

I think Zoe is starting to think she'll never see James again and I'm praying she's not right. It's hard to believe, but everything he's done in the last few years is hard to believe. It came out of the blue and when James's addiction forced itself out into the open I almost drove myself crazy searching for reasons, answers. He didn't provide either and I've come to terms with this, for myself, but it would be so much better if he could communicate with the girls, tell Zoe the stuff she still wants to hear from him.

The phone rings. It's Adrian. His day is not very busy and he wants to take me to lunch. I decline, and hear the disappointment in his voice, but, sitting in the back room, breathing in the dust of James's books, I don't feel in the mood. I tell him I'll see him later in the week.

I notice one of my books, *Germinal*, amongst his American collection, its 70s cover still bright and lively. As I pick it up I wonder how many others of mine are in here. Photographs drop from a book, photographs of us. One is a shot that is a little out of focus, but it looks as if James is holding court in the student bar. In the other we're out in the country somewhere.

I start grouping the books into loose categories. They chart James's development. How he read his way through English and American literature, then French, German and Russian, then books from anywhere, each adding to the store of knowledge that ultimately proved useless. It didn't help him in his day-to-day life, but James was great for general knowledge quizzes.

I'm getting annoyed. Old resentments return, and it's time to stop what I'm doing. I liberate *Germinal*. It's in the original French and I think I'll read it again. I take the photographs too. I remember the country scene now, James all teeth and tan in a white T-shirt. It was the long summer of '76. The landscape behind us is parched and brown, African savannah more than English field. I remember that camera too, a good Nikon from my parents, with a self-timer on it. I'd run back to James and the camera moved a little on its stonewall as it clicked. I can still smell the still heat of that day, a long, lazy end-of-term day, in the summer that seemed to last forever. James loved it. I used to think him part lizard, but maybe it was more snake.

I'll keep his childhood stuff, and box up the other books, but I won't sell them. I'll phone a local charity shop later in the week and they can come and collect. I'm probably throwing away money, there's plenty of old hardbacks here, some leather-bound, but I'll also get rid of a lot of bad memories. As I look out onto a garden now frost-bound I see James reading them, swinging gently in that ridiculous hammock he had. Looking for all the world like some idle Edwardian bachelor, with time and money on his hands, rather than a husband and father of two kids.

James took so little with him. Just a hastily packed suitcase of clothes, the handful of books, and a few other bits and pieces. *I don't want anything else*, he said. At the time I thought that the final insult. Now I think it was blind panic, James running away from the headlights.

*

James obeyed his Charlie Parker alarm clock. It was part of his new regime. A nine o'clock start to each day, hardly the crack of dawn, but near enough for him. The clock had a punishing alarm, a sax-like wail, guaranteed to cut through the muzziest head. It was cutting through his now. James had read a Laurie Lee book when he was twelve, which spoke of the tyranny of alarm clocks. It had sunk into his young head and stayed there ever since, but all through his life they had been necessary. Until his fall. Recent years had been clock-free, time had been just night and day, all people had ever needed once. Now it was being counted out again and James was resigned to his raucous wake-up call. It might signify his return to the real world.

Old routines came back to him. The quick shower, the spat with the girls, the rushed breakfast, or no breakfast at all, then out to another school, hoping he wouldn't have to peddle Shakespeare to kids who at best weren't interested, at worst, hostile. Teaching badly because *he* was no longer interested. James punched the button on the alarm and managed to turn it off at the third attempt. He had to fight very hard not to sink under the sheets again.

James got up and stood with his hands near his rough

windowsill, looking out at the hillside as he rubbed sleep from his eyes. This had become a morning ritual, it was as if he had to check that the world was still out there, and he was still part of it. The hillside was well wintered now, a sodden brown edged with washed-out green, dotted with the usual moving grey specks. Water and sheep. What Wales did best, he thought. More sheep than people now.

For James, patriotism had always been a slippery beast, if not a force for evil, but returning to the valley had brought on thoughts about his country; he had the time. In the past he'd been a fence sitter, diffidence his middle name, but, sitting with the old men in the pub the other day, he'd realised there was still a sense of belonging in him. This came as a surprise. The scrubby, scarred and re-moulded landscape around the village symbolised Wales as a providing nation, serving outsiders, in the main. It had fuelled the growth of the English Empire that had been called the British Empire. Add drink, religion and sport to enforced drudgery and you had the melting pot from which the main artery of his countrymen was tapped. Thicken with a twist of a last vital ingredient, in-fighting, and a full and potent mix was achieved.

James doubted that anything here had ever been truly agreed, or stuck to, for long. A characteristic that had been seized on by interlopers across several millennia, Roman, Saxon, Norman and what Norman became. There were people long before the Celts, lost in time, but no doubt displaced or assimilated just the same.

James had given himself his own course on Welsh history once, when it was apparent his school would never provide one. So many chances had been lost, his people always having to adapt to the new ways of powerful neighbours, whilst coping with their own deficiencies; a struggle that had usually defeated them. *My people*, James thought. The phrase sounded strange.

James wasn't sure if Wales now was a nation in

anything but name. Too small an indigenous population had been asked to absorb so much new blood, the country had fractured into many societies, little Englands east and west, to challenge and prick the main body in the most deadly way. By ignoring it. Maybe the last chance for true unification had left the field at Worcester, with Glyndwr.

Nina had tried to get him to join her in learning Welsh once. They clashed over this and the girls' schools. Nina wanted Welsh-language ones, but James distrusted them. He had enough old socialism in him for that. So they settled on the compromise of a different school for each. Clare learnt Welsh, and her mother learnt with her, Zoe and he maintained their monoglot existence, Zoe relieved and resentful in equal doses. Perhaps this was the start of the family misfiring. James wasn't sure if he was thinking of new beginnings, but that old, slippery beast wouldn't lie down, go away, or rest easy in his mind.

At least it *was* in his mind. The longer he resisted his addiction the more he was able to think again. James wondered how long he'd be in the hostel and if there really was a way forward. He tried to think of possibilities. Teaching was out. He'd never be able to hack that again, even if anyone would have him. Detached as he was, James was still aware of the many changes taking place, each one chasing the tail of the other. He was part of the old guard now, and had been left well and truly behind.

The library books lay alongside the clock. James took one up, sat against the heater and thumbed through it. There were many avenues to explore, but he put the book down and remembered his resolution. Wake, shower, shave, eat breakfast. What normal people did.

He went downstairs to get a drink. Billy was slumped in a chair, head on the kitchen table. He hadn't made the bedroom last night. A half-drunk can had fallen from his hand and frothy white spots trailed like spores from Billy to fridge. James slipped on White Lightning and careered across the room into the cooker but the noise was not enough to wake Billy. The drunk snorted a few times then fell back into deep sleep. James was relieved. He had thought Billy might be dead. To lose two flatmates would be more than carelessness.

Come on, Bill, let's get you up to bed. That new chap is coming today.

Billy was a dead weight. James pulled him up the stairs as Billy kept up a conversation with himself, spraying James with reminders of his cider. Billy was a master of *drunken*, that secret, alcoholic mix of sighs, splutters, curses and pleas. James lay him face down on the bed, the best way for a drunk, less chance of them choking to death. Billy settled into the mattress like a basking seal.

James carried out his resolution, then picked up one of the library books. He was still looking for answers, solid reasons for his actions. Clear-sighted, objective reasoning had never been a strong point. Self-deluding bullshit came easier. He'd failed to give Nina anything like an adequate explanation for his actions, let alone the girls, for he'd never been able to give himself one. How do you tell teenage daughters that gambling had become more important than they were? He was so used to asking himself these questions they lay like stone tablets in his mind. Unanswered.

Someone knocked on the front door. James looked down from his window to see Deborah, with a stranger in tow. He went down to open the door. Standing next to Deborah, dwarfing her, was a man in a duffel coat. He carried a small, scuffed, suitcase, and wore black leather gloves on very large hands.

Hello, James, Deborah said. This is Colin.

Colin was tall, square-shouldered and about James's age, but his face was much more ragged. Rich seams of wear had cut into it, sparse hair was cropped close to his skull, and his grey eyes were very distant. James noticed that he had small yellow teeth that were much too perfect for his face, but most of all, Colin had a face tattoo that slanted sideways from his cheek to his neck. It was a dragon, with red body and blue wings. A white scar bled into the dragon's tail as it stretched beyond Colin's ear, as if the beast had been attacked. There was something familiar about the man, James couldn't put his finger on it, but, even at the height of his gambling, he doubted he would have forgotten someone with a dragon on his face.

Colin will be staying here for a while, Deborah said.

She smiled at James reassuringly.

I'll show you the bedroom, Colin, she said.

James said a belated 'hello' but Colin did not respond. Deborah led the new man upstairs.

James sat in the kitchen, waiting for them to come back down.

Anyone want a coffee, he said, as brightly as he could, when Deborah re-appeared.

No thanks, I'll have to be off, Deborah said. I've left Colin to sort out his room. Can you show him the kitchen and bathroom, when he surfaces? Oh, how did the meeting go?

Okay, thanks. I saw my daughter Clare, too, on Sunday.

Really? That's great James. I'll see you soon. Can you give Colin this?

Deborah handed him a front door key.

He's got the one for his bedroom door. Don't look so worried. He's not as fierce as he looks.

Are you sure?

Colin won't be anything like Danny, or even Billy. He's pretty quiet, you'll hardly know he's here. He's had a tough time of it but he's coming on well now.

Coming on well from what?

You know I can't tell you that.

James saw her out. A few days ago he was getting himself in a state at the thought of meeting Deborah, now

111

he didn't want her to go. At least she left her fragrance behind her. It cut through the smell of stale cider, and left its impression on him.

As he shut the bedroom door behind him Colin rested his back against it. He checked out his drab surroundings and smiled glumly. SOS-same old shit. What he expected. What he was used to. Not that it mattered. None of the outside stuff did any more. He was living on the inside now, in the land of a thousand voices, and they needed space, time, above all quiet. He listened for noise in the hostel but all was still. A good start.

Colin did not move for a few minutes, until he heard the social woman drive off. He liked the feel of the wood against his back, it was always good to have something solid behind him. Then he began to take out what possessions he had from his bags, putting most of them in the plastic-wood chest of drawers that came with the room. There was a duster and a can of furniture polish at the bottom of one bag. Colin began to clean the room, humming tunelessly to himself. When he'd finished he looked out of his small window onto the village and there was another glum smile.

Colin took particular care to clean the top of the chest of drawers. Here he placed a series of photographs. Each one was a reminder, a chart of his military history, what had made him the man he was. He was young, almost fresh, in the first shots, then bored in German barracks, drunk in Gibraltar. Pride of place was a yellowed newspaper cutting placed into a cheap frame. His platoon walking into a Falklands sunset. He was the back marker, carrying the heavy radio set, British flag fluttering on the top of it. *Our Boys,* the caption said. Colin saluted the frame. It still made him shiver.

James knew he looked considerably better than a few

months ago, but he wished he could buy some new clothes. He was on the edge of a fantasy. Asking Deborah out, imagining her saying yes. Ridiculous thoughts. Sex was a hazy memory. Libido was the first thing to go for addicts. It got crushed out, sacrificed in the chase but as his last bet got more distant James felt it coming back. Not with a rush, more a slow awakening of its old self. He'd been celibate for almost four years, unwillingly at first, then it became a state he was comfortable with, another distraction taken away as he concentrated on his gambling. He was not comfortable with it now.

James made more coffee, and took it back to his room. Decaffeinated. It didn't taste very good but he was trying to get used to it. He'd been overdosing on caffeine, and it jerked his thoughts around, made them march too quickly.

As James thought about sex, life and the road ahead, it came to him. Colin. He *had* seen him before. James spilt some of the coffee down his trousers as he remembered where. The coffee narrowly missed his crotch and he jumped up, cracking his knee on the radiator. He was the schizoid from the squat. Of course he was. The dragon was new, and he'd been cleaned up, but it was the eyes James remembered. The way they looked when Colin had closed in on him that time. Distant, yet full of life and pain. They'd been like that in the squat and they'd been like it a few minutes ago, as if they were focusing on him from some far-off place.

James didn't want to believe it and argued with himself for a while, but he was certain. It *was* him. Great. Absolutely fucking great. He wondered that they could house someone like Colin here then he filled in the answers. Deborah said Colin been through a lot. That meant he'd been institutionalised somewhere. Sectioned, probably, then stabilised, until the state felt able to put a stamp on him that said *safe*. Safe enough to live with people in a hostel anyway.

James was sure Colin hadn't recognised him. Perhaps he never would. Colin could have been listening to any voice inside his head at the time. Agreeing with it, fighting it. James's face would be one of hundreds from his shaky past, most of them blurred and distorted by his illness. It had been in full flight in that squat. Everyone there had been soaring on something. Anything to take away the pain. H, crack, any kind of dope, uppers, downers, booze. Running from bastard parents, bastard partners, bastard life. James was the only one who had no such excuses.

Dave Connolly talked about challenges ahead; Colin might prove to be one. James picked up one of the gambling books again, positioned the chair near the radiator, and rested his feet on it, letting its warmth track up through his socks to his throbbing knee.

Today I will be unafraid.

*

I'm taking Zoe to Warwick. She's conned me into it, and has sulked her way through breakfast, but there's been no explosion. She'd like me to say that I'm going nowhere with Adrian, that he's already yesterday, but at least I know she'd be the same with anyone I met.

I'm still tired after Scotland. Driving more than a hundred miles into the Midlands was the last thing I wanted but I couldn't face another row. Zoe shows no interest in learning to drive, but she doesn't do public transport much either.

Meeting Adrian has shown me that she still hasn't come to terms with the divorce, she's hanging onto the past because James plays no part in her present. Zoe was too young to grasp what was going on when James cracked up.

Maybe James thinks it's better this way, that by removing himself he removes the problem. It could be that his selfishness is going from strength to strength. Perhaps I should never have had children with James. It's easy to be wise now, but it took me years to know that he'd never be able to offer the commitment I wanted. By then it was too late. He convinced himself that he could. He convinced me. Maybe I knew, deep down, he could never change, but love is not so easily broken. At least not for me.

James had a firmer grasp on reality. He tried hard to hide it, but I realise now his take on the world was quite pragmatic. *Nothing has really changed.* I remember him telling me this when we left college. It was in early July, a magical day, when we'd walked for a last time through lush Warwickshire fields. James standing on a five-bar gate, hair wild as always, tipsy on wine, his crumpled notification of a scrambled second class degree hanging out from a pocket. *Nothing has changed, we'll soon be absorbed into the system,* he shouted.

I'm sure James is the reason Zoe chose Warwick. She's trying to retrace her father's footsteps, but it's a mighty different place now, in a mighty different world.

You don't have to come in, Mum, Zoe says, as I park near her hall. I haven't got much to carry. Tell Clare to phone me.

Okay. When are you next coming down?

I dunno. I'll have to give you space now – for your new romance.

Oh shut up.

A gangly youth appears, to carry Zoe's bag. He's wearing a multi-coloured fleece, has lots of dark hair, and is very good-looking, in a pre-Raphaelite kind of way. This must be her new boyfriend and fellow band member, but there's no way she's going to tell me. I receive cursory thanks, cursory wave, and am dismissed. I would have loved a cup of coffee but know it's better to make tracks.

On the way back I decide to stop off at Stratford, to see if the teashops are as good as I remember. They are. I find one with small, leaded windows, and sit with the blue-rinse brigade, eating a cream cake and drinking good coffee, served by a Greek. My antidote to Zoe, and Monday. I rarely do supply on Monday, it makes the week go much better. Less money but more time, and time equals freedom. A whiff of it, anyway.

In the café I let time drift for a while watching the ducks bob along the silver Avon. Thinking of the first time I ever came here, the fifth form trip to see Lear. Some of the boys were ejected for rowdyism and the school banned trips for a while. That seems yesterday, and a million years ago. By the time I drive on I've washed my sulking daughter out of my hair. I'm taking the scenic route, listening to Radio Four and watching the sky brighten over huge fields.

Wa's he like then, this Colin guy, Jimbo? Nor a freak, is 'e?

Billy was standing in the doorway, a can of lager welded to his hand.

I only saw him for a few minutes. He didn't say anything.

Aw no, a silent bugger. They're the worst.

James shrugged.

'Ere, Jimbo, look what it says on this can. The taste of Britain. Tha's good, innit. I'm all for a bit of tha'. Wanna swig?

No, you're alright.

E's in there, is 'e? Billy asked, pointing to Pete's old bedroom.

Huh huh.

I'll give 'im a knock. Say 'ello, like.

James caught Billy's arm

No, leave it for a bit, Bill. Let him settle in.

Oh, ok. I'm gonna get a bus down to the White 'art. Nice li'l pub, tha' is. No food, no bandit, no bloody kids. Wanna come?

For a moment James was tempted to put some distance between himself and Colin but he declined.

No, I might go up the 'Bush later.

See you then.

James heard a few noises in Colin's room. The man was talking to himself, it sounded like a low chanting. James turned to go silently away but something stopped him. He stood on the landing, hesitating for a moment, then knocked on Colin's door. Nothing like taking the bull by the horns, he thought, ignoring the advice he'd just given to Billy. The noises stopped and the door opened.

What?

Colin's powerful figure filled his bedroom doorframe. It looked like he'd been working out all his life.

It's James. We met downstairs just now.

Why are you telling me that? You think I can't remember things that happened a few minutes ago.

No, of course not.

Colin came up close. He smelt of onions. His tattoo came with him. James was very near the snarling dragon and its trail of red fire that bled into the scar.

Like it? Colin said.

What?

My face painting. You're staring at it.

Uh....

I wanted something to mark me out, see.

Right. It's very striking.

I like a quiet life, Colin whispered.

So do I.

So there's not a lot of noise here?

No.

Colin looked him up and down.

Boozer?

Sometimes.

If only sometimes why are you here?

I made a few bad moves, James said.

Haven't we all, mate. Haven't we fucking all.

Colin seemed to relax a little. Large fists changed back

117

into hands again. They were gloveless now, and James saw *Love and Hate*, his old adversaries. Colin pushed his bedroom door open.

Poxy room, this is, he said.

It's a roof over our heads.

Aye. You been living rough, then?

Now and then.

What's the other guy like? The runt.

Billy. He's okay. He's out a lot.

Aye, and I know where. Drunks make me nervous. They make a lot of noise. Break things. You're not like that, are you?

No. And Billy's okay.

Right. Colin thrust out a hand.

James took it, expecting his fingers to be crushed, but Colin's handshake was surprisingly soft. It felt like a bag of water, no firmer than the vicar's in the crematorium.

I like a quiet life, see, Colin repeated.

He went back into the bedroom, shut the door and started talking to himself again. James knew Colin would be sailing on a raft of medication and hoped to God the man kept taking it. He'd have to warn Billy about noise, though getting that one to be quiet might be like trying to hold back a wave.

James went back to his own room. He thought about a walk. He needed to get fitter and if physical tiredness did not turn off thoughts it at least kept his body occupied. He was lucky there was no betting shop in the village. The nearest one was further down the valley.

The monkey on his shoulder had got excited in the library though, when it saw the computers there, lined up and ready, all willing to place a bet for him. Their colourful screens reminded James of that first time he set foot in a betting shop. The overhead TVs lit up, waiting just for him, like the fairground lights that had entranced him as a child.

It was Grand National day, an event that had always

passed him by. James had taken an interest in most things as a young man, but never gambling, and certainly not horseracing. He'd been reading the Saturday paper after another pointless row with Nina. They'd got to that stage. Routine bickering, unable to still their tongues, until they'd rubbed each other's nerves raw. Breakfast toast tinged with disappointment and recrimination, and the girls stepping carefully through the war zone.

Heart of Gold. That was the name of the horse. It caught his eye as he looked for the football. James remembered it was the name of a song that went with happier times, it struck some kind of chord and he looked at the list of runners and wondered about the machinations of betting.

James finished his breakfast and tried to put this out of his mind, but it stayed put. An idea began to form. A bet would be a new experience, something he'd never done before.

While Nina shopped with the girls James yielded to the idea. He sought out a bookmaker's, one on the edge of the estate on the other side of town. He parked the car around a corner and tentatively entered into its acrid air, his eyes immediately smarting from the low cloud of smoke. James picked up the air of expectancy as he adjusted to the haze. Hope, dreams and poverty mixed here, poorly dressed people clutched slips of paper and urged on their horses, eyes glued to the screens. Some noiselessly moved their lips, others exhorted loudly. One man's enthusiasm was abruptly cut off as his horse fell. A few looked at James suspiciously; he was an intruder

He had no idea how to make a bet. After a few minutes he asked someone but was waved silent as another race started. The bank of televisions on the wall formed a banner of light, which beamed down on their expectant congregation. There was something akin to religious fervour here. Every punter wanted to believe.

A younger man approached him. James quickly learnt a few essentials. With his new friend at his shoulder he placed a twenty pound bet each way on his chosen dream. All the money he had on him. He felt like he'd stepped back in time. This place could have been a Victorian gin-house, filled with Dickensian characters snatching at furtive pleasures. He liked it. There was no responsibility here, and he liked that, too.

It was just minutes to the race but James had to step outside for a few lungfuls of fresh air. It was a sunny day, and he was struck by the difference in atmosphere. He had a moment of self-doubt, and felt the healthy air willing him to stay out, but re-entered, to shout with the others at the screen. This was the nearest to male bonding he'd ever achieved. *Heart of Gold* came in second. He was a modest winner.

See, the young man said, if you'd bet on the nose you'd 'ave won fuck all. I always bet each way, me.

Then he screwed up his slip and threw it down in disgust. James queued for his winnings like a guilty schoolboy. An exhilarated, released schoolboy. Aged forty-two. He felt lighter in body and mind than he had for an age. It was ridiculous, and made no sense, but he was on a high. The hook was sinking into his gut. Soon it would begin to pull.

James no longer had access to credit card, or bank account. Otherwise, he doubted that he could have resisted the lure of on-line betting. They did Roulette online now, he'd seen an advert in a newspaper. There was a tug on his heart as he thought of the Wheel, rotating prettily on the world wide web, like the alluring planet of another universe. James shrugged this off. He had things to do. He was going to write to each daughter. A Monday job if ever there was one.

He'd bought a writing pad and a few pens. Together with the library books, and his thin stand of books, they lent an air of his old life to the room. When he married Nina, James commandeered the small back room of the family house for a study. He'd laden it with books. He'd kept them all, from the age of ten. He had read some several times. There'd always been time for reading, no matter how many girls there'd been, how many dreams to pursue. No matter what state his young body was in when it fell into bed, he always turned to a book, if he was alone. It had been his precursor to sleep since early childhood. James had provided himself with his own bed-time stories, a ritual set in stone until his fall.

Many dangers had lurked on those pages. Weakness could be encouraged, vanity preened, elitism nurtured, laziness taught to masquerade as something else. Particularly the latter. James had always intended to write himself. He had it all worked out before he left college. Beautiful wife, beautiful offspring, comfortable job – writer. His fantasies were kept in neat compartments then, and early life had led him to believe success would inevitably come.

James hadn't managed a chapter of anything. There'd been a lot of false dawns, sketched ideas, opening paragraphs. *They* came easily, then nothing. He'd been like Sartre's clerk, endlessly re-writing his opening sketch of the beautiful woman riding her horse in the Bois de Boulogne, re-writing it until it became a lifetime's work that lead nowhere. A slow burn of insanity. James had more or less given up by the time he was forty. It came as a shock to realise that he didn't really have much to say.

That first bet led to the buying of a first lottery card. An innocent bit of fun, he told himself, but he hid it when he got home. Hid the fact that he, cool James Read, could possibly do such a thing. Buying a pound's worth of dream at ridiculous odds – more chance of being struck by a lightning bolt than winning. He memorised the numbers and when they were broadcast on the TV could hardly contain his excitement when two of them were in the first three. Nothing else came up and embarrassment flooded through him. Nina had asked if he was alright, but she had been pre-occupied with Clare that Saturday, out on her first date.

James sat at his table. He'd got it a few weeks ago, at a re-cycled furniture place, cheap for people on benefits. It cost ten pounds and they delivered it free. The table tended to shake somewhat, but he'd propped up one leg with beer mats to steady it. Now he hoped to make it his work station. Brave thoughts on a Monday morning for a compulsive, penniless gambler, living in a hostel at the end of a blind valley, but James was determined to hang onto them. He might even write a book on it; he *had* things to say now.

Writing to Clare was not too bad. Ice had been broken yesterday. He thanked her for her visit, and said he'd phone her again soon. James was careful not to use the word *promise*.

Writing to his youngest daughter was another matter. James got no further than *Dear Zoe,* before he put down his pen, and started to gaze out of the window. There'd been enough frost in the night to top the landscaped tip opposite the hostel with a white nipple. Landscaped was the wrong word. Roughly shaped and left to chance was more accurate.

The pigeons were out again. Two lots today, competitive formations that tested each other like warring fighter planes. One arrowed past his window, close enough for James to see the birds' eyes standing out like orange buttons. The twisting, undulating wings seemed to sum up his new mood. He took up his pen again. *Dear Zoe...*

It took him an hour but James managed to scrabble together a letter. He read it through many times, changing it until it satisfied him. Then he wrote out the final version, finding the use of a pen strange, and almost forgotten. His handwriting was shaky, he was shamed by his unsteady scrawl on poor paper, but it was the best he could do. James knew Zoe better than to try to offer her explanations with words on a page, but he did offer an apology, and, as an afterthought, wrote down the address of the hostel.

Zoe was at Warwick, Clare had told him. It had been all seventies concrete and privilege in his time. New build trying to compete with old red brick. It was probably twice the size now, sprawling over yet more green fields.

Zoe's birth had not been easy for Nina, James doubted if birth ever was. The way his life had gone, blood, pain and tearful screaming seemed a suitable way to enter the world. It had taken Clare a while to adjust to the new addition, but the girls had got on well. There had been no problems within the family, until he started them.

James wrote *I can't understand it myself* at the end of the letter. This was true but the phrase sounded obvious, and empty. He could hear Zoe's snort of disdain. If she did not reply, James was not sure what he'd do. He didn't have a plan 'B'.

James suggested a meeting with Zoe, when she was next down from college, leaving the place up to her. He went out to get stamps from Singh's and posted the letters. It was now past midday and he felt he deserved a drink at the 'Bush to mark the occasion.

The dominoes players weren't in the pub but Billy was. He caught James before he could back out of the bar.

Jimbo! Fancy meeting you in this fine establishment. Le's have a drink. I got money.

What happened to the bus?

I couldn't be arsed in the end.

Within minutes James was enjoying himself, his pint cool and familiar in his hand.

Is 'e a big bloke, like? Billy asked.

Big enough.

Billy looked at his pint thoughtfully.

Thinking of Danny? James said.

Aren't you?

123

Danny was young, this man isn't. I don't think he'll be any trouble.

James was trying to convince himself as much as Billy.

Maybe. I wish Pete was still around. He was good at cooling people down. Le's 'ave another drink – for old Pete.

Billy went up to the bar but James paid. Pete was *old Pete* now, he noticed. Billy hadn't liked Pete that much, but death was great at bringing on respect. In another few weeks he'd be *good old Pete,* incorporated into Billy's personal folklore. The arrival of Colin made the loss of Pete rawer for both of them, but the visit of his wife, though a shock, had been the catalyst James needed to phone Clare. He'd managed to keep up the momentum by writing the letters. At the next GA meeting he'd have something positive to report.

James imagined Zoe getting her letter. When she saw his writing on the envelope she'd treat it like an unexploded bomb, at first. Conflicting emotions would surface. Disdain, contempt. Love. She would put it aside for a while, even think about binning it, then she'd read it over and over. At least the girl he'd left would have. A lot might have happened in three years. There was a moment of acute sadness and guilt, and the sounds of the pub were stilled. He was outside it all, and for once, his addiction did not come to his aid. He had such a large bridge to rebuild. James closed his eyes, and tried to call up a suitable commandment.

Just for today I will try to strengthen my mind.

Here you are, Jimbo. Get that down you.

Billy was buzzing, he thought James might become his new drinking buddy.

'Ow 'bout coming down the valley? Billy said, go on a bit of a pub-crawl?

No thanks, Bill. I've got things to do.

Things to do, be fucked. Like what?

I've got to go down the DSS.

Oh, right. What time you coming back?

I'm not sure. You know how they are.

Too fuckin' right, I do. Well, I'll probably stay here, then. Pop in on your way back.

Okay.

This was an excuse Billy could understand and there was little chance of him remembering this conversation anyway.

James left Billy to it. As he stepped out of the pub the pigeons were returning to their lofts. They sped down from the hillside, crossing the century of pit spoil that had been grassed over and left, like evidence from a crime. He felt his legs willing him up the slopes, then he thought of placing a bet. He was surprised it had stayed away this long. It was a quick sear of his senses, a remembered snatch of hope and desire sated for one glorious moment. It almost brought a sigh to his lips. This was the seductive part of his addiction. For the true gambler money was just a tool, the collateral needed to feel like this. Once, at his most desperate, James had tried dummy gambling. Writing down bets on bits of paper, trying to manufacture the same feeling if he won, but it was hopeless, ridiculous. Like trying to drink from an empty glass.

A headache was starting up. Daytime drinking usually brought one on. Small fingers of pain started to press against the back of his head, then it became a hand that began to move around, until it settled behind his eyes. James forced himself not to walk past the hostel to the inviting air of the hills. If Colin was to be a problem, better to face up to him now.

Colin was in the kitchen. James could hear him moving about and muttering to himself. Habit encouraged him to creep past up the stairs but he obeyed the commandment and pushed open the kitchen door. Colin was pouring himself a cup of tea from an old-fashioned teapot. He had an army-type camouflage jacket on which did nothing for James's confidence.

Hello, mate, Colin said. Want a cuppa? It's loose tea. Much more civilised

The man was quite different, lighter in tone. James made a mental note to pick up a book on schizophrenia from the library, then made another one which said don't bother. A little knowledge might be dangerous.

Okay, James answered. Thanks.

Colin poured out another cup. The teapot had a Union Jack on its lid and *Colin* had been taped across it. Colin gestured to a chair and James sat down at the table. He felt the eyes of the dragon on him as Colin sipped his tea and started humming to himself. Slurped more than sipped. His tattooed fingers settled around the mug. It was caressed with *Love and Hate* as the pigeons flew past the window.

Flying rats, Colin murmured. What the point of keeping them?

Each to their own, James said.

Colin rubbed his dragon.

I like that, he said.

Colin's eyes appraised James, then they seemed to look right through him, and settle back with disinterest on his mug of tea.

Yeah. You're a boozer. Been down the pub already, haven't you? Well, I don't mind that. As long as you're quiet.

James knew he should be telling the man to mind his own business but didn't think it was wise.

I don't drink, Colin said. Not even in the army, and God knows I had cause to then. You're not like the runt though. He's a real pisshead.

Yes, Billy likes a drink, but –

Quiet?

James nodded reluctantly. He wondered why Colin seemed obsessed by noise. Something in his army past,

126

perhaps.

Good. I'm off, then. Might go for a walk. I never went out much at all after I was discharged. I went from being fit to being fit for fuck all. Lay around a lot, just staring at the ceiling – half man half mattress, that was me. Saw muscle starting to turn to flab and that got me out of it. I'm back to my old self now.

Colin tapped his muscled arms, attempted a wink and left James in the kitchen. The headache moved up a gear but James resolved to stick it out without tablets; he'd taken far too many of them. He went back to his room and tried to look for answers again in one of the library books.

James woke with a start, the book falling from his lap. The headache woke with him. Wind tugged at the window, rattling its rotting frame. The weather had changed. Rain was bringing mist with it as visibility faded. For a moment James thought it was the wind shaking the front door, then realised it was Billy outside. James heard him going through his usual fumbled key routine, no doubt getting soaked to the skin. James went down to open the door. He was too late. Colin was doing the honours. Billy tried to step past him but stumbled and fell onto Colin, who straightened him up with one hand.

Alright, mate, Colin said, quite softly. I'm Colin, the new guy.

Billy's wild eyes tried to focus.

Jimbo?

No, Colin. You're a noisy little bugger, aren't you?

Billy chuckled.

I've 'ad a drink, like.

You don't say? That's nice. A good thing to do on a wet Monday. Do you want a hand up the stairs?

No, i's okay.

Billy saw James at the top of the stairs. He tried to scramble up them to this familiar figure, like a child seeking the safety of a parent. He almost made it, but fell before he could reach the top. Billy sat on the stairs in a heap and looked down at Colin.

It's okay, Colin murmured, don't worry about it. I don't mind a bit of noise. Never minded a bit of noise, me.

James got Billy inside his room quickly.

Eh, Billy said, 'e's not so bad. Quite a friendly bloke, in 'e?

Sleep it off, Bill, and for Godsake get something to eat.

Drink is my food, Jimbo. You knows tha'. My food, my life, my woman, my everything... Billy broke into a few staggered lines of a song.

Colin was still standing in the front doorway when James stepped back out onto the landing.

I don't mind a bit of noise, he repeated.

Colin winked again, but the eyes of the dragon stayed open.

*

I've just come back from one of my least favourite Comps. Over-zealous New Labour head, interfering governors, jaded staff room fed up to its back teeth, and kids worrying about their futures at the age of fourteen. Not an uncommon scenario these days, but not good for a cold and wet Tuesday, especially as they've meddled with the clocks again and it's dark before five.

I hear someone pulling into the drive. It's Clare. She let herself in and finds me in the kitchen, unpacking the shopping I got on the way home.

Got enough for two? I've brought some wine.

Might have. I don't know about drinking on a Tuesday, though.

Did you take Zoe up to Warwick?

Yip. Yesterday morning.

You fell for that one, didn't you? 'Bout time that girl

learned to drive.

Don't knock it. She'd want a car, then.

I was reading an article in a magazine dinner-time. It said that kids expect everything as a right now.

This is the voice of experience talking, is it? Kids were not like that in your day, eh? All of a few years ago.

Well, you know what I mean.

I did, actually, and Zoe *was* like that. Even with just four years between the girls I can see the difference. Parenthood seems to be divided up into micro-generations now, things change very quickly, and not always for the better, it seems to me. Education mirrors this, change upon unnecessary change. Thank God I'm not nailed to the classroom. Maybe it's an age thing. My age.

Mum?

Um?

You're miles away.

Am I? Make us some coffee. Do you want tuna, I've got a few steaks I was going to grill. You still eat fish, don't you? There's some salad too.

Great.

Clare has come over to find out how Scotland went, but she seems in no hurry to ask me. She's quite subdued, in fact. I worry about how hard she works, but know I can never stop her. She'll go far, and will earn it. I bring Scotland up myself in the end.

Go on then, ask me what it was like?

What?

You know what. Scotland. With Adrian. Adrian the geek, the nerd, as Zoe so kindly calls him.

Yeah, she would. He said you both had a great time.

Oh, talked about it in work, has he?

Only to me, and only to say that.

Well, great is pushing it a bit, but it was quite good. He'll take a bit of knowing, your Adrian.

He's not *my* Adrian. It is a bloody coincidence I work

with him, though.

Zoe thinks you set it up.

Is she playing up about him?

A bit. She thinks we're ganging up on her, but she'll be alright. A few years ago it would have been much worse.

I know.

Open your bottle then. It's been a hard day.

Ditto.

Do you want to stay over?

No thanks. I've got stuff to work on later.

You're not overdoing it, are you?

No more than anyone else. It's the way it is these days, Mum.

Don't I know it.

We are quiet for a while, sipping good Rioja which Clare has spent too much on.

I've seen Dad, Clare says quietly.

At first, I'm not sure I've heard her right.

What's that?

Dad. I've seen him. Sunday.

I spill a few drops of the wine onto my skirt. Dark red spots on grey.

Damn, I'll have to get that off straight away. Where's the salt?

You did hear me, Mum?

Yes.

I try to pitch my voice as calmly as possible but it comes out more like a mouse squeak.

How?

I wrote to him, some time ago. It took a while for the letter to find him. I'd almost given up on him, but he eventually made contact. We met last Sunday.

You've kept this quiet.

It was what he wanted. He made me promise.

Yes, I bet he did.

I'm sorry, Mum. I knew you'd be upset. I'm not sure I

130

should have told you now.

Oh, thanks very much.

I dab at my skirt with a damp cloth then top up my glass, and drink half of it.

Where is he?

Holed up at the top of the valley.

God, Clare, you make him sound like Lord Lucan.

He's living in a hostel. He told me it was a flat but I know it's a hostel.

It's a shock to me to know how much I want to know. What he looks like. What he's doing. How he's doing. A hostel doesn't sound very good but it's better than a squat, or the street. When I found out he'd been seen living rough in Cardiff I felt the ground opening up in front of me. I didn't want to believe it at first, I felt shame, then anger, and, when I'd calmed down, pity. It was what you read about, saw in films. It didn't happen to people like us. Thank God Zoe never found out. Clare is waiting for me to say something.

Well, is he alright?

Better than I thought he'd be. He looks older. Going a bit grey. He says he's stopped gambling and he's going to Gambling Anonymous. That's a big step for him, I think.

Yes, it would be. James must be desperate; he never could stand organisations. If this was true, there might be some hope for him. He might have turned a corner. *If it's true*. Our last few years together were taut with his lies, and half-truths.

How did he get in this hostel?

Social services.

So, James has placed himself into the hands of the state. I'm relieved, but also vaguely annoyed. He always did have a dual effect on me. It's always necessary for someone to look after him. I don't think he'll ever go back to teaching, even if teaching would have him. He thought I locked him into it, that committing to me led to unfulfilled

131

dreams for him. What *they* were I'm not sure. James had vague ideas about freedom and living an unconventional life, but he was always much stronger on thought than action. He did mutter about *being born in the wrong time* now and then, but I doubt that another time would have put up with him, unless he was born rich.

When the girls came, and time to himself was more precious, James came out with *the need to write*, another slogan that did not go anywhere. Uttered with increasing bitterness. I could feel him moving away from me on the back of regret, but could not prevent it.

Maybe gambling was a way out from all the things he couldn't control. *Maybe*. Any evaluation of James is full of maybes. Every time I thought I knew him another man would show himself.

Am I being too negative? Divorce is good for that. It would be easy to let such thinking crowd out all the good stuff. His charm and generosity, and the wit that was the last to go. James was miserly with himself but never with us, and even if his kindness had a certain ebb and flow, it was always there. I think the immensity of family life overwhelmed him. What he became part of, and tried to buy into, was essentially alien to him, so unlike anything his own life had prepared him for.

I went over it so many times when James first showed signs of cracking up. Almost drove myself mad trying to work it out and having to try to come up with reasons for the girls. Trying to explain things I didn't understand myself. Resenting the fact that James needed so much attention, and that any problems I might have had didn't exist. He expected me to be strong, so in his eyes I conveniently was.

Adrian comes to mind, a much more uncomplicated man. At least this is how it seems, but I doubt if there is any such thing.

The buzz of Scotland is fading fast. I feel some of the

excitement of a new relationship but know it will be hard to go through all the finding out again, even more so the sharing. I've got used to my own space. It was bought with a lot of pain and I'm not sure I want it taken away from me again. Perhaps some of James's selfishness has rubbed off on me.

I put the tuna under the grill whilst Clare prepares the salad, something her sister would never even think of doing. I'm a little angry with her for being so secretive, but she's got that from James. He might be absent but he still has a hold over the girls, even if they don't realise it. This would be fine, if it was positive, if he could re-enter their lives without ripping them apart again.

Do you think we should tell Zoe? Clare asks.

I don't think so. Not yet, anyway. Look, what did James say? Did he talk about where he's going? The future?

Not really, but I think he might be able to sort himself out.

What was this hostel like?

I didn't go there. We met in a pub.

Bloody typical.

No, it wasn't like that. He hardly drank. Dad was really trying. That must mean something.

I'd like to agree. We might all be around for a long time, even James, if he cleans up. Something might be salvaged, but it's not easy. I have so much evidence for the prosecution stored up in my mind.

Are you going to see him again? I ask.

I think so, and I told him to contact Zoe. It was obvious the thought of that frightened him but if he does it'll be another step forward.

Hmm….

We eat the meal, and I drink more than is wise. Adrian phones. He wants to come over, but I put him off.

He's really keen, Mum. He was floating around the office Monday, cloud nine or what? And he's loaded, you *do* know that?

Clare!

Oh, sorry. I forgot about your *principles*. Right, I'm off then. I'll give you a ring on the weekend. Zoe's not coming back for a while, is she?

I hope not. She's got to settle up there.

I see Clare out, into a filthy night and shut myself back in the house, before the rain comes in with me. I do not feel so secure in my solitary state tonight. News of James has affected me, even excited me, if I'm honest. Pathetic, after three years of divorce, and a few more years of hell before that, but there has never really been closure. If James had left me for another woman that would have been final, anger and hurt would have shut the door and bolted it firmly. But gambling was such a crazy, inexplicable reason.

There's work to do for tomorrow's school but I doze instead, in front of a useless TV programme, fodder for the brain-dead, the life-crushed, the people who can't be bothered to turn it off. The latter is me. My mobile wakes me up. Adrian is texting me goodnight.

*

James had not seen much of Colin. Their newcomer went out and brought back bags of shopping that first night and had labelled his stuff in the kitchen. COLIN had been neatly taped onto cornflakes cartons, soup and bean cans, a mug, and his beloved teapot. On a jar of coffee he'd added an exclamation mark after his name. He'd created his own space in a corner of the kitchen but did not spend much time there, which suited James and Billy.

James heard Colin going out and coming in a few times, but all he saw was the man's back as he hurried past the kitchen and up the stairs. Billy was as noisy as ever, and nothing had happened. Maybe he'd over-imagined the threat. It could be the experts were right after all.

Another man was coming soon. Billy already knew his name.

Aye, Martin, 'e was down the other place with me for a bit, 'til 'e went inside, like. Young bloke. 'Bout thirty, 'e is.

Drinker?

Oh aye, amongst other things. Mart likes a drop. Parents threw him out years ago. Used to be a good-looking boy, but 'e's had a few hidings over the years. Bit of a tea-leaf as well, see.

James sighed. They'd have a schizophrenic *and* a thief in their midst.

Dave Connolly had asked James to give a talk at the next GA meeting. The first call he'd received on the new wall phone. At first he tried to get out of it.

You've done the hardest part, Dave said, by just turning up. Get through this and you'll have something to work on. A solid start.

It's all a bit public.

Of course, that's the idea, but you'll be amongst your own. You're not going on the bloody telly.

Three days later James took a bus down to the community centre. The day was suitably grey, the sky leaden, the light less than half strength. Rain tried to establish momentum as it trickled down the windows of the bus as James sat hunched up in the back seat. He'd been up most of the night, preparing his GA talk. Trying to prepare it. He'd never been shy but this terrified him, his chest was getting tight and he was sweating. A cold sweat that had been with him all day. It made his skin prickly and told him that this would be a giant step forwards, or a disaster. James closed his eyes.

Just for today I will be unafraid.

The bus dropped him outside the centre and James pushed through the usual assortment of people with time on

135

their hands. He made his way to the back room, where Dave Connolly was waiting for him, with Tony and the others. There was a full house of expectant faces. James sat down, shuffled the few notes he'd made and waited for Dave to introduce him.

Tony flitted from table to table, acting as his agent. He had his best Elvis gear on, set off by a striking red waistcoat with gold buttons, 'for the occasion', he whispered to James, flicking back his pony-tail theatrically. Each time James heard 'you can do it, my son', and 'they're gonna love ya,' his spirits sank a little lower. Dave pressed down on his shoulder with a large hand. He had a mug of coffee in the other.

Bet you're shitting yourself, Dave whispered.

Quite.

We all are, the first time, but it's an important step, James.

I know, but that doesn't help much. Do you think I should start with something like 'I'm an addicted gambler'?

Like the boozers, you mean? If you want. Yeah, sounds good.

It didn't sound so good to James, it sounded bloody obvious. He felt his shirt stick to his back, and knew his face was shining.

Dave introduced him and talk amongst the tables subsided. James got up from his chair, hardly aware of his legs, and stood in front of his audience. It was more a kind of floating up. After his opening line, which broke through his reluctant lips in a sudden out-take of air, he wasn't really aware of what he was saying. He heard a few murmured responses from his audience, but the rest was a blur. He got to the end of it on a wing and a prayer and was surprised by the strong ripple of applause and a heartier clapping from Tony.

You done okay, Dave said.

He done more than okay, Tony added, bloody great, I'd

say. How do you feel, butt?

Dazed.

That's about right, Dave said. You've let a lot of stuff go today, James.

Right.

James wasn't sure what he'd 'let go' because he wasn't sure what he'd said, whether he'd kept to his loose plan or not. He realised that was the first time he'd ever shared himself so publicly, despite twenty years in the classroom. It went against the grain. His grain. The instinctive secrecy he'd always had to fight against. There was always something he'd kept back from Nina, a secret compartment that was his. Even when the girls came it could not be prised open. Maybe it had been prised open today.

James was surprised Nina ever stayed with him. More so when she agreed to marry. He remembered that time well. His proposal was the culmination of months of frustration, the first time that he'd really began to look back on his strange upbringing, and resent it. There was a tension in him that he looked to ease. Marriage seemed the best move but it was all about him. He had vague notions of providing for Nina, being a good husband, but he never moved very far away from having himself at the centre of his universe, and he said little about his upbringing to her at the time. That was a mistake; the marriage had begun with one.

James was sitting at a table with Tony and Dave when Deborah Skirrid came in. He was so fazed by the talk that he did not notice her until she sat down.

Hi, James. How did it go then?

Oh, hi. You knew about it?

Yes, Dave here mentioned it. I thought I'd drop by.

It went bloody great, Tony interrupted, bloody great, it did. It was different class, listening to James.

That's good, Deborah said.

Dave and Tony left them. Tony wanted to stay but

Dave shepherded him away, as he winked at Deborah and flicked back the remains of his hair.

Did you hear any of it? James asked.

Some of it. I was standing by the door.

Thank God I didn't know that.

It *was* good, James. You went from being anally retentive to open in a few minutes.

And that's good?

I think so.

A few more gamblers came up to James and congratulated him.

How's Colin settling in? Deborah asked.

Well, it's early days, isn't it?

You don't sound too confident.

He's not someone I'd choose for a housemate, but beggars can't be choosers, can they?

James wanted to tell her about the squat incident but thought better of it. He was coming down from the talk now, focusing on Deborah. What she was wearing, how she smelled. Her perfume drifted over to him, fighting against the smoke of the congregation. He stifled a cough, fiddled with his shirt and wondered how he looked.

Colin's on medication, I suppose, he said.

That's his business, James. He's had a rough time over the years, but he's okay now though.

Okay, James thought. Maybe *better*. But not *cured*. Colin could never be that.

I'm completely knackered, he said.

Public performances do that to you. Come on, I'll give you a lift back.

Thanks.

Colin was walking away from the hostel as they pulled up outside. It was the first time James had seen him out. He was reminded of that time in Cardiff. The same loping walk, and long-legged strides. Colin moved along with his head down, as if intently studying the pavement, his battle outfit blending in well with the mossy stone wall alongside him. Deborah hadn't noticed him and James didn't mention it. Billy would also be out, so James asked Deborah in.

Well… I've got lots on today.

You've got time for a coffee, haven't you? Call it a celebration.

Okay then, just ten minutes.

The kitchen was in quite a good state, and the floor did not look as if people had been sleeping on it. Colin had improved it. Things were mysteriously cleaned when no one else was around. James put the kettle on.

Just popping to the loo, he said.

Upstairs, he dashed some water into his face and tried to tidy his hair. It was as unruly as ever, and laced with grey, but at least it was still with him. Most of it, nature had spared him baldness, so far.

James knew he was being stupid but couldn't help himself. Instinct made him view Deborah as part of his awakening, and instinct was still the strongest part of him. She was too young, and probably well sorted with a live-in partner anyway, but he was on a roll. Feeling an echo of the rush he had when betting, being dangerously carried along to unknown destinations. This time Deborah was the wager.

James went back down to the kitchen and made the coffee. The kitchen was lit with cruel strip-lighting but Deborah still looked good.

Strong with no sugar? he said.

You remember.

He made his own sweet and milky and prayed that Billy didn't fall through the door.

There was more than a moment's silence.

It's my birthday in a few weeks, James said.

Really? How old?

Forty-eight, he said, quietly.

Not quite a baby boomer, then?

Not quite. The 70s was my time. Big hair, flares,

platform shoes, bloated rock music, dying politics. Then punk – the antidote. All pretty naff, really. The films were good, though, probably the last golden age for Hollywood. You probably weren't born then.

James, are you fishing for a lady's age?

He felt himself colouring. Deborah smiled.

Don't worry. Just teasing. I'm thirty-three, actually.

His mind started to play the game. Using the card it had been dealt. Thirty-three, she might be almost thirty-four. Fifteen years, that wasn't so bad. He'd have to keep telling himself this, until he believed it.

Thirty-three. He had two kids by then.

Well, you've made contact with them again. That's a start.

Yes.

Deborah glanced at her watch, for the second time.

Uh, I was thinking, James said. I haven't celebrated a birthday in years, there's been no reason to, but... would you like to come out? On my birthday, I mean. For a meal or something? I'll save up.

It just came out and he hoped to God it didn't sound like desperation. He wished he hadn't said he'd save up, it sounded so hopeless, but at least she didn't laugh out loud.

You don't even know if I'm single. And you're a client.

Not really. Not like Billy or Colin. I was more of a referral.

I'm not sure my boss would see it like that.

Well, are you? James asked.

Am I what?

Single. Sorry, I'm being rude, now.

Deborah smiled and finished her coffee.

Yes, as it happens. Between traumas, you might say.

I'm just thinking that a little intelligent company would be a change... for me, that is. Sorry, I shouldn't have said anything...

James, don't be so bloody nervous.

Sorry.

And don't keep saying sorry.

Sor… eh, right.

I'll get back to you on it, Deborah said. I'll have to go now, I'm running late.

So you're not saying no.

I'll get back to you.

As he waved her off James told himself that she was just being kind He caught sight of himself in the mirror and thought she was being very kind. Even so, a fragment of the old vanity reared up in him, he saw himself with some of the wear taken away, scrubbed up, in decent clothes. He did have a good overcoat, courtesy of a charity shop. James fought to keep in check the excitement he felt. She hadn't said no.

*

I've gone to Adrian's place for the first time. When we turned into his drive I felt a bit like the poor girl in the Hollywood film, the one who falls for some billionaire's son. Turning a corner and gasping at the splendour of the family pile. Wondering if it can ever work. Well, perhaps not quite, but the house is very large, far too large for him. It was his parents' house, Adrian tells me, a five-bedroomed Victorian country house in a few acres of land. I wonder if Adrian had planned to fill the bedrooms with kids. If so, he's left it too late. With me, anyway. *Woodlands* is displayed on a free standing wooden plaque. I hide a smile behind a hand.

Just about all the original features are here, Adrian says, as he shows me around. I've kept everything in good order. This place costs a bit to maintain, but, well, I haven't had that much to spend my money on.

I wonder how Adrian has remained single. How anyone hasn't nailed him long ago. He shows me into a study.

Bookcases obscure every wall, and they are full. Battles, wars and soldiers leap at me from everywhere. I almost expect to see a rocking horse and a few catapults on the floor.

My inner sanctum, Adrian says quietly.

I sense the loneliness that comes with these words. Perhaps emptiness is a better word. The place is full of a few generations' baggage, but it feels sterile. I can't imagine any warm life ever being present here. The books speak of the past. I look up at a portrait of two stern, middle-aged people.

Mater and pater. Look a bit fierce, don't they? They had it done on their twentieth wedding anniversary.

They must have got married quite late, for they both look in their fifties. I feel a certain responsibility already settling on my shoulders. If I don't want this I'll need to get out quickly, Adrian will be hurt badly otherwise. No, this is wishful thinking, it's already too late. Everyone takes a chance, when they meet someone. Not that Adrian is everyone. He's a one-off, a throw-back to another time, another way of life. A gentleman, that's the word I'm searching for. An antique word. I hope he doesn't think the fact I went to Scotland with him seals our future.

Woodlands is a place where children would have to know their place. I imagine the solitary life Adrian must have led as a child. I know the solitary one he's led as an adult. Clare has told me that her older colleagues cannot remember him with anyone. At least he's not damaged goods, Mum, she tells me. I'm not so sure. The house does not inspire, and the grounds about it are not much better. Just an expanse of paddock-like grass, fringed by shrubs.

A man comes to cut it in the summer, Adrian says. I don't do much with it, as you can see. Well, what do you think?

It's not exactly a humble abode. There must be so many memories here for you.

142

Not as many as you might think. My parents packed me off to boarding school, as soon as they could. It was my mother's idea, funnily enough. When my father became ill, I promised him that I'd never sell *Woodlands*. Mother wanted to when he died, but she became ill herself soon after. I was stuck with my promise. Stuck with *Woodlands*. I'm not sure I'd still be here otherwise. Property developers phone me from time to time, stick leaflets through the letterbox, asking me if I want to sell. It's in a prime spot, and, if someone could get planning permission, there's room for a small estate here.

How old were you when your parents died?

They were both gone by the time I was twenty-seven. I was a latecomer for them, you see. I was starting to do well by then, working my way up, like your Clare. Everything was in place to go forwards. I did. I have. Work-wise, that is

Talking of work, I haven't thanked you for giving Clare the job.

Nothing to thank me for. She was an ideal candidate. I found it hard to believe you were her mother. Such a coincidence.

Yes, isn't it.

I wish it wasn't. Clare working for Adrian just complicates matters. Her meeting with James has also stirred things up inside. Part of me has begun to think things are simpler when you're alone. That's the safe route, but safe isn't all it's cracked up to be.

Adrian's promise to his father is typical of the man. He's trapped himself in this gloomy mausoleum. Childhood is always a moral void; his must also have been a cold one. He has this in common with James, but not much else, I think.

It's a nice view, isn't it, Adrian says.

Yes.

It is the best thing about the place. Soft, lush country

leading down to the coast. The land around *Woodlands* has long since been shaped by man, it has been tamed and lent an air of privilege.

I'll get us a drink, Adrian says. Red wine? White?

Red please.

*

James moved Deborah's card around in his hand as he drank coffee in the kitchen. It had her office and mobile number on it. It was Tuesday and he would be forty-eight on Friday. The last three birthdays had crept by him furtively, one had been forgotten altogether, though there was still a residue of shock at passing forty. Now he was bearing down on fifty. Age had rushed up on him, all the *time flies* clichés of his elders taking on weight, until they became his own. He wanted to mark this birthday with something other than depression, drink and a wild bet. The addict inside told him that a small, sensible bet might be allowed but there was no such thing, not for him. James dismissed it.

Just for today I will strengthen my mind.

James didn't really expect to hear from Deborah and no news might be telling him something. Colin had brought a semblance of order to the kitchen but it still retained an air of dereliction. James was in the midst of second-hand furniture, recycled goods, a ruined table with dirt-crammed cracks, and an inappropriate carpet that always showed evidence of drinking. Lager spills could be dated by their colour. Fresh and light brown for the recent, a darker stain for the older ones. Like certain pubs he'd been in the carpet also had a tendency to stick to feet. James sunk further into his thoughts and didn't realise Colin was standing in the doorway.

Nice and quiet, isn't it, Colin said.

James dropped the card.

Oh, didn't startle you, did I?

No.

Good. Wouldn't want to do that.

Colin had his usual gear on, high laced-up boots, matching combat shirt and trousers, cropped hair on bullet head. He looked like a man in search of a war. James wondered if his background really had been military, or if Colin might just be obeying one of his voices with his outfit.

Do you want a drink? James asked.

Okay, if you mean tea or coffee. I'm teetotal, remember.

Christ, that must be a first, for this place.

So, ask me then?

Ask you what?

I don't drink, gamble, thieve, am not a junkie, so why the fuck am I here?

Uh....

I've had a few problems upstairs, see.

Colin pointed to his head, then let his hand linger on the dragon for a moment.

Oh, I see.

Don't be stupid – James. Of course you don't see. No one does. I don't myself. There was so much going in here – the finger taps his head again – so many voices, that sometimes I thought there was nothing of *me* left. Do this, no, don't do that, do this... got so bad I took a few wrong turns. Ended up on the street. I could have done with a friend then, but you only meet shit there.

I can imagine.

Too right. Always keep a roof over your head, that's the most important thing. Even if it's only a squat.

James felt Colin's eyes probing him.

I'm okay now though, with the medication and stuff. I'm fine now.

Good.

145

James made the coffee.

No sugar for me, Colin said, I've got all the energy I need.

Colin drank his coffee as if it was soup.

Don't mind me slurping, do you? Old habits die hard. The missus hated it.

You've been married?

Oh aye. In my army days.

So, he *had* been a soldier. This made him more dangerous, in James's eyes.

Been over for years that has, Colin said. Donkeys' years. I got invalided out after the Falklands. She couldn't handle it. *I* couldn't handle it. Mandy was just another voice in my head, getting at me. I'd changed, she said. 'Course I'd fucking changed. Who wouldn't?

Any kids?

Nah. She probably has though, by now.

I couldn't get my head around that fire, Colin said.

He stared at his coffee mug, swirling the liquid around.

Fire?

Every squaddie knows that the army will fuck it up if at all possible, 'specially if the fucking navy's involved, but stuck in that bloody barge all that time, that took the biscuit. Even half-blind Argies couldn't miss it. They didn't. A lot of my mates went down.

Are you talking about Bluff Cove?

'Course I fucking am. Turned to beef burger, they did. I've had a thing about fires ever since. Don't want to be near the bastards. Had a problem with a pub fire, once. You know, one of those country places, a grate full of burning logs. I started staring at it, then it all kicked off. The voices went crazy. Busted the landlord's jaw. That was the first time I got arrested.

That must have been years before the squat, James thought. That meant Colin had been treated before, and pushed back out before. Unlike him, Colin had reasons for going wrong, tangible reasons, being bombed, burned and shot at reasons. James wanted to go, his eyes flicked to the wall phone in the hallway.

You expecting a call?

No, not really.

Haven't you got one of those mobile things?

No.

I have.

Colin took a phone from a pocket and held it out.

Here it is. I've hardly used it. People like us don't have many people to phone, do we? I don't have any, come to think of it. Useful though. For emergencies.

Emergencies?

Well, you never know what might crop up, James.

No, I suppose not.

People like us. A few weeks ago this inclusive phrase wouldn't have worried James. Now it did. He wanted to move out of the hostel. Move on. James tried to think what he might move on to. Then he thought of Colin stuck in the hold of the *Sir Galahad*, choking on the acrid air as his comrades began to burn around him, desperately trying to get out as the seeds of his illness were sown.

Do you want to use it? Colin asked.

What?

The mobile. It must be a woman you're waiting to hear from. I know the signs.

It's not important.

But it will be if she phones, won't it?

James tried to grin but it probably came out more like a grimace.

You're a college guy, aren't you? Colin asked.

Please, please don't come out with *educated man*, James thought. He felt trapped. He wanted to think of his ground-shifting speech at the GA meeting, he wanted to think of his daughters, the future. He didn't want to be stuck here with Colin. The past. He didn't want to be *people like*

147

us. Not any more.

You are, aren't you?

I'm just someone living in this hostel, like you.

Don't be fucking ashamed of it, mate. I've spent the last twenty years trying to educate myself. I've lost count of the libraries I've been chucked out of, 'specially when I was living rough. Colin closed his eyes and started to recite.

Hate and love, if you ask me to explain
The contradiction,
I can't, but I can feel it, and the pain
is crucifixion.

Colin held out his tattooed hands, as if to illustrate the verse.

What's that?

Catullus. Roman guy. A few thousand years ago, but still right, eh? I keep a lot of stuff like that in my mind. Little snippets of things. It helped with the voices, when they were rampant. Christ, once I got into learning I was like a kid in a sweet shop, flitting through all those shelves. Then someone showed me how to use a computer and I became a total geek then. The boys in the Guards would piss themselves laughing if they knew. Not in front of me, though.

James doubted that anyone would laugh at Colin. He'd obviously been keeping himself fit. He was muscular, but not muscle-bound and his frame had the type of latent power that the village hard men could only dream of. His hands were very large and the tattoos made them seem like weapons. James could clearly see them reaching for him in that squat.

Is that why you had the tattoos done on your fingers, James asked, because of the poem?

Nah. They were done years ago, when I first joined the army. I saw someone like it in an old film once. Looked kind of cool, I thought. I added this later.

Colin touched the dragon on his face, his fingers

probing its flaming maw, as if feeding it.

Thought I'd celebrate when I got out of hospital. New start, new identity. Cost me ninety quid.

Colin slurped the rest of his coffee, whilst James waited for an opportunity to go.

James, you know anything about King Arthur, all that stuff?

James looked at Colin blankly.

The Knights of the Round Table?

Oh, right. Not too much. I read a book by someone called White once.

Yeah, I know it, *The Once and Future King*. After Bluff Cove I really got into that stuff. It was the names of those boats. Sir Galahad, Sir Tristram, all the boys used to wonder what the fuck that was about. Then again, a lot of them thought The Falklands was somewhere off Scotland. Squaddies, eh? No good for thinking, good for killing, being killed. Expendable. Doing the dirty work for slimy bastards behind desks, like they always have. Yeah, I learnt all about that chivalry stuff. It was another world, and I needed one. It helped to keep my thoughts on something. Helped for a while, anyway, until old Arthur became another voice. He started to tell me things, like the rest of them.

James did not know where this was going. He didn't expect to be talking about Celtic mythology with Colin. He didn't expect to be talking to him at all. This might be a good sign, but his sense of unease did not leave him. James heard Billy coming in. Stick your head round the door, Bill, James thought. *Please.*

Billy must have heard Colin, because he didn't appear. James heard him hauling himself up the stairs, chuckling in *drunken*.

Pisshead little runt, Colin muttered. What good is someone like that?

Colin moved his hands around, *Love and Hate* were

pressed together. James knew the film that had influenced Colin. Ironically, it was one of his own favourites. Bob Mitchum playing a psychopathic killer and phoney clergyman, directed by Laughton. Perfect art.

I'll just see if Bill gets to his room okay, James said. I'll catch you later.

James started to get up, but couldn't. Colin was holding his arm. He felt the strength in the grip.

I want to tell you more about Arthur.

Okay, but later.

You're interested, though?

Eh, yes.

I'll tell you what Arthur told me to do, if you like.

Right.

The grip released and Colin smiled, but it was not a smile that instilled confidence. James went upstairs, past Billy's open door. Billy was sprawled on his bed, arms behind him, as if he was diving down somewhere. He muttered into the pillow as James shut his door quietly. James would have to tell him to get into the habit of locking it from now on.

James felt a new dimension had been added to his hostel life. Colin was another test, another reason to get away. James heard him also come up stairs, then stop on the landing. Colin stood there for a while, then went into his own room.

James sat on his sentinel window armchair, picking idly at its exposed padding. Orange bands cut into the evening sky and said fine, cold weather was coming. He hoped to get out in it, to inject some activity into a life that had stalled. As he watched the patterns in the sky, James doodled on his notebook, wondering what else to say to Zoe. The girls were quite different. Grovelling, begging for forgiveness, would be more in order than explanation for his youngest. She needed open displays of emotion, feelings up front, things that had never come easy for James. He felt

150

it was important to start another letter, whether she replied to the first or not.

James wasted an hour without writing anything, then, on a whim, he put on a coat and went down onto the street. As light faded he walked over the discarded scratch cards, sweet wrappings, crisp packets and crushed drink cans outside Singh's, past the brightly lit Hollybush, and the huddled group of boys near the phone box. They scarcely noticed him now.

An old woman was using the phone box. This surprised him. Daytime, it was usually empty. At night kids used it for sex and shelter. Everyone had mobiles these days, apart from the old lady, it seemed, and him. James walked on for a while, letting the cold wind scour him free of Colin and the kitchen atmosphere. Pavements were drying and the smell of musty wet stone in this moist community was all around him.

James looked back down the street, to see the old woman hobbling away, prodding the pavement with a stick, her head encased in a woolly hat. He went back quickly, to claim the box before the boys. He put a pound in the slot and dialled Deborah's number, before he could change his mind. She answered on the fifth ring.

Hi. It's James.

Who?

James. James Read.

Oh, hi.

Silence. His mouth was dry, and his tongue locked.

James?

Yes, sorry. I was wondering, you know, what we said, about my birthday?

What you said, you mean.

Well, what do you think?

Another silence.

I did say I'd get back to you. It's really sweet of you, James, but I don't think it's a good idea.

No, I suppose not.

It might put me in an awkward position.

It was just a drink.

No, it wasn't, you liar. You're so headshot you're fantasising over an attractive thirty-three-year-old. You're almost forty-eight, for Christsake. Who the fuck do you think you are? You have no home, no car, and no money.

Look, let's take a rain check on this Deborah said. I don't think you'll be in the hostel for very long. You could be back teaching again within a year.

Yes. Sure.

Okay then. Thanks for calling. It is nice of you.

Right. Thanks.

He put the phone down. There was something final in the click it made. Dismissal. James felt in his pockets, for his wallet. In it was all the money he'd saved in the last month. It was just about enough for drinks and a meal – with her. The front windows of the Hollybush were a soft, welcoming yellow in the increasing gloom. Windows of invitation. He saw the barmaid drawing the curtains, locking the light in, and him out. James sighed, cursed himself for a fool, and walked up to the pub.

A few old soaks were in the bar, no one in the lounge. James went in there, he'd make it no one plus one…

Billy was tugging at him. James could just about make him out. His face came in and out of focus amidst a sea of colour and noise. Music played somewhere. James wondered why Billy was in his dream and looked around for the casino.

Jimbo, mun. Wake up. Fuck me, you tied one on tonight, 'an you. Betty behind the bar says you been at it since five o fuckin' clock. If I knew you 'ad so much money, I would have borrowed some off you.

Wha…?

I better get you 'ome, boy.

152

James knew this wasn't right. *He* got Billy home. He was being pulled up. Others were helping Billy. Faces leered at him, coming close, fading away. His legs were moving but his brain was not engaging with them. The floor rushed towards him and he wanted to join with it but Billy held him up. In the corner of his eye a television screen revolved. It turned tricks, changed angles, spun around, James thought he heard people laughing, maybe clapping, but couldn't be sure. He couldn't be sure of anything, then they were through the front doors and the cold air hit him. The crisp November night collided against his burning face and he was instantly clammy, and ill. His stomach geared up to complain as Billy hunched under his left arm and tried to shoulder him along. A black sky was above him, a clear black sky shot through with stars. He saw the brass eye of the moon go past and wanted to catch it, but it was moving too fast. They fell over after a few yards.

Christ, you're bloody 'eavy.

James's stomach lurched. He turned away from Billy and threw up into the gutter.

Aw, fuck me, Jimbo. Charming, tha' is.

This sobered James up a little, just enough to take stock of his situation, to know what the next morning would be like, and shudder with despair. Loose change was falling out of his pockets. Billy pursued it.

You go' money to throw away, you 'ave. Le's see w'as 'ere. 'Bout three quid. Oh, an' a note. A bleedin' twenty! You're bloody rollin' in it. They said you was chasing pints down with double whiskies like there was no tomorrow. You'd 'ad a skinful by seven o'clock. Christ, it's only nine now.

The rest was less than a blur. James had hazy images of the hostel stairs coming to meet him, each one a challenge that his feet dragged on. Someone standing on the landing. Words being said. His head reverberating with Billy's babble. Then he was sinking down into something soft.

153

Something soft and wonderful. He never wanted to come back up.

*

So, what was it like, then?

Clare pours me a large glass of wine.

Oh, not that much, love.

Why not? Where's Adie, anyway?

Don't call him that.

Come on, let's have the goss. In work they say his pile is worth a million, at least.

Woodlands. Yes, it probably is, if anyone would want to buy it. It's all dark wood and gloomy rooms. It is in a nice spot, though.

You can sell it as soon as you reel him in.

Oh, don't be silly, Clare. Give me the wine.

You're touchy, Clare says.

I am, because I don't want to talk about Adrian. There are enough questions of my own I want to answer without the girls prying.

You haven't said much about Scotland, Clare says.

It was alright. Lovely scenery. Look, it's early days with Adrian. I'm not sure if it's going anywhere yet.

I bet Zoe is still in shock…

…That her mother could meet anyone, you mean. Yes, I think she thought I'd stay single for ever now. Me being the advanced age of fifty.

I think Dad would be surprised too.

It's none of his business.

I take more than a sip of the wine.

Mum?

What?

Why do *you* think Dad started gambling?

We've talked about this before. More than once. I didn't have an answer then and don't now. I don't think

154

we'll ever really know because I don't think your father will ever know.

Before he left, Dad said it was nothing to do with us.

No, it wasn't. Your father was always looking for something he couldn't have. That's what made him restless. He was like it in college. I thought it would fade away when you and Zoe came along, but I think he always thought he deserved better.

Better than us, you mean?

No. Don't ever think that, and don't ever say anything like it to Zoe.

What do you mean then, *better*?

It's hard to explain. I think James wanted to have lots of different lives and lead them all at the same time.

That's just childish.

Of course it is, but some men are like that. Most of them learn to temper it, come to terms with the life they have. *Get real*, as Zoe would say.

But not Dad.

No, not James.

Dad was a dreamer, wasn't he?

Oh yes.

I was looking at some old photos the other day. You and him in college. He was gorgeous.

Well, that's something you and Zoe can be thankful for. You've both got his looks.

And yours, Mum.

Thanks, love. Look, you never knew your grandparents on his side, I didn't see much of them myself, but enough to know that they were odd. Distant, locked into themselves, somehow. It's hard to explain, but I don't think they were ever there for James, not in the way he needed. In fact, I think his childhood was as cold as it gets. It's difficult for a kid, then. I know you'll think this is stupid, but, deep down, I think your father is very shy.

Shy? Dad?

155

I said deep down. I doubt if he knows it himself.

That doesn't make sense, Mum. He was always the life and soul of the party.

I know, but sometimes that's just a front. James kept a lot hidden, from all of us. When his parents died he wasn't exactly grief-stricken but it did affect him. It started off a train of thought. He started to go on about what he hadn't had in the past, what might have been. Stuff like that. He began to distance himself.

From all of us.

I don't think he ever meant to, not from you and Zoe. He got caught up in something that took over him.

Gambling. It's so stupid. You make it sound like it wasn't his fault.

It's complicated, but that's the only way I can explain it. Now that he's made contact, maybe he'll be able to talk to you about it.

I hope so.

Are you going to tell Zoe?

What do you think?

I'd leave it for now. Let's see what happens. I don't want her to have any more disappointments, if we can avoid it.

She phoned me from college the other day. She's going out with someone in her band – public schoolboy.

Yes, I think I saw him. When I dropped her off. He was rather nice.

I drink the Rioja and smile to myself. I don't tell Clare that Zoe's young man reminded me of James. Same hair, same air of arrogant nonchalance. I imagine that youngster filling the doorway, trying to shake James's hand, and James not even bothering to hide his hostile despair at the thought of his little girl being taken away from him. James got his moving away in first.

As the wine starts to take effect I close my eyes and savour the current peace of the Nina Read household, an aftermath of calm that is not to be sniffed at. Whatever the girls might get up to will be within the realms of normality. The road James took was twisted. He plunged over the edge of safety, and almost took me with him. In a way I'm impressed he's kept away for so long. When he hit rock bottom I expected him to try to thrust himself back into our lives. I'm trying to picture him now, but from what Clare has told me, it's difficult. The old James crowds out the new.

Do you want any more wine, mum?

Yes, I think I will.

I'm getting quietly tipsy. Watching my eldest daughter with love. Taking pride in her good looks, her effortless figure, and the guileless smile. Beyond her Zoe peers at me from her wall photograph. Another beauty. Shallow thoughts perhaps, but of the utmost importance to any woman.

Mum?

Mmm..?

Watch your wine. You're nodding off.

Oh. It's been a long day. I don't think teachers have much of a weekend feeling anymore. There's always more to do.

Not so much for you, though.

There's enough. Supply teachers still have to do marking, you know. You're not saying your old mum is getting lazy?

As if. You've worked hard all your life. You should enjoy your weekends now.

Clare's right. After the furore of the divorce, quiet weekends were welcome, but once Zoe discovered boys and was out of the house most of the time, they began to drag. I had to rebuild, body and soul, and it's taken me this long to get as far as Adrian.

Shall I open another bottle? Clare asks.

Certainly not.

157

Come on, it's Friday night. A bottle is nothing.

Not for you, maybe. *I'm* not one of the girls. I've seen how you all drink. It seems like anyone under thirty has hollow legs these days.

We're only catching up with men.

They are nothing to aim at.

We both laugh. I think Clare would call this a *girly night in*, something we haven't had for a while. I wish Zoe was here, cutting in with her barbs, pouting as she plays with her fingers, but always coming round in the end. It seems like yesterday that they were babies, and I, we, were facing the long haul of parenthood. It did not prove to be long at all.

Talking about Friday night, I say, why are *you* here?

Clare shrugs.

Thought I'd keep you company, for once.

Men a bit thin on the ground? Surely not for you?

I want to focus on the job at the moment, make an impact. You know, new broom and all that. I have to impress Mr A.

Hey, that's even worse than Adie. Have I made it awkward for you?

Not at all. It's not that type of place. Sure about the wine?

Yes, but you open it if you want,

Nah, it's alright.

Clare rummages in her bag. You still like old films, don't you?

When I get round to seeing one.

Try this then. I got it from a specialist place on the Net. It's even older than you.

Gee, thanks.

Clare hands me a bag. I open it and look at the DVD. *Letter From An Unknown Woman* – Joan Fontaine and Louis Jordan. It *is* old. I wonder if Clare has picked it at random or does she remember something from her early childhood, for this was one of our films, James and I. We had films as well as songs. He was the buff, and I the willing participant. As they grew up the girls would pretend to throw up when we watched black and white films. James collected art house films from around the world, the bleaker the better. When the gambling took hold his tastes disintegrated. I'd find him slumped in front of the TV watching rubbish. Like I do now.

Memories of watching *Unknown Woman* are vivid, on that Ferguson video player that seemed to last forever. James fussing over pregnant me, plying me with incongruous food. Caring. The wine's getting to me and I dab at an eye, very discreetly.

What made you get this particular film? I ask.

Don't you like it?

Yes.

Thought you would, and it was on half-price special offer. These old films are bloody dear, you know.

We put the film on. I relent about the wine and we drink our way through another bottle. There's more than a hint of James in the Jordan character, and I dab at my eyes a bit more. I remember the first time we saw it, snuggled under blankets on a bitter November night, squinting at James's small black and white portable. I can still smell his college cell, he'd put nothing on its walls, none of the usual student's stuff was present.

Clare stays the night, she has no choice and I'm glad of that. I'll be able to blame her for my hangover in the morning.

*

James's eyes would not open. It seemed like he'd been trying a small lifetime. He felt like a dead man with pennies on his eyelids. Then his brain let him open one eye. It was a mistake. Light blinded it, and it quickly closed. James tried

159

again, a few more times until both eyes opened. They blinked in unison as winter sun came looking for them through the window. He was Ray Milland trying to get through his Lost Weekend, but there were no giant spiders on the walls, no pink elephants. What James did have was very real. His head was being used as a gong, his guts were like creased cardboard, and his tongue was a dried-up slug trying to crawl in the dust of his mouth. He was freezing, his body felt like it had been left out on the arctic ice to die. It trembled as he made an attempt to get up. He made a few more. On the fourth he managed to roll out of bed.

James shivered in T-shirt and boxers in front of his mirror. He didn't look too closely at his image. At this point he should be throwing up but nothing was happening in that department. Perhaps he already had. He sniffed around his bedroom suspiciously but there was no evidence. Memory was slow to come back to him. In a series of jump-cuts he recalled being in the phone box, leaving it bitterly disappointed, like a kid on his first knock-back. He remembered chasing down the first three pints with large Grouses in the 'Bush, then nothing.

There was a knock on the door. More like a clap of thunder. It activated the gong in his head and he shook like Quasimodo under the bells. Billy appeared in the room.

Alright, Jimbo?

Seeing the shuddering figure of James trying to clasp itself with both arms Billy burst out laughing. For James's head the sound was rapid machine-gun fire, each bullet hitting him with deadly accuracy. He sat on the edge on the bed, and suffered.

You're in a right state, arn' you? Impressed me last night, you done, me ol' son. Didn' know you could drink like that.

James pressed his head gently with his hands, as if looking for wounds.

Don' worry, Billy said. It's still there.

Bill, don't shout.

I'm not. Look, I put what was left of your dosh on the table.

Thanks. You got me home?

Aye. Just about. You're no lightweight. That Colin was on the landing when I was getting you up the stairs, standing there with 'is 'ands on 'is hips, like Lord bleedin' Muck. Didn' 'elp at all.

Was I very noisy?

Nah. You was too rat-arsed for that. I was though, I'd 'ad a fair drop myself, see. The drunk leading the blind drunk – eh, tha's good, innit?

I've got to get in the shower, Bill.

Aye, I think you better, my son. Billy winked at James. Coming out again tonight?

James's stomach lurched, but it was running on empty.

The look on your face. Nice colour. Sort of a dirty grey, like, with little red eyes.

Billy turned to go.

Bill, thanks again.

No problem. You done it for me, 'avn 'u.

James got to the shower. He wanted to stay there for ever. It was the most wonderful place in the world. He loved its dank curtain, stained floor, tiles and scummy, broken soap holder. He wanted it to steam clean his body, then start on his mind. Teasing out all the devils that lived there, a procession that might take some time.

Hot water trained on a hung-over head was good and James felt his head clearing. By the time he stepped out of the shower he looked like something about to be grabbed from its cage by a French chef, but he felt better. He was ready for coffee, and lots of water. Then he remembered it was his birthday.

Colin appeared in the kitchen as James busied himself at the stove. He moved very quietly for a big man. James had no idea he was in the room, until he heard the fridge door opening.

It's no good for you, Colin said.

Oh, I didn't hear you.

People rarely do. Suffering, eh?

Not so bad, now. Do you want some coffee?

Alright.

Look, I'm sorry if there was more noise than usual last night.

Colin didn't answer. He sat at the table and closed his large hands around the mug James gave him.

I just see it as drunken knights making merry.

What?

Celebrating after coming back from one of their quests.

Oh, that type of knight.

James sighed inside. He needed to get away from this place as soon a possible. The fact Colin had given himself some sort of learning curve made it worse. He thought they had something in common.

James closed his eyes and tried to order the headache to stay away. Last night was a blip, this is what he must tell himself. Yesterday was starting to return. He thought of Deborah, and that phone leaden in his hand as she turned him down. He sensed himself reddening at the thought of it and hoped to God that she didn't hear about his Hollybush night.

Love and Hate prodded James's shoulder.

I could let you have a few books, if you like.

Books?

Yeah. The Celtic stuff, Arthur. You said you'd read that White guy?

James wished he hadn't.

Yes, okay. Thanks.

I'll drop them in later. See you then.

Colin took his coffee with him. The man seemed to be coming out of his shell but James didn't want him to. He wanted him to stay in the land of his voices, to get lost there. Please don't like me, James thought, and for Godsake please don't remember where you've seen me before.

James rubbed a hand over his stubble. He thought it was steady enough to risk a shave now. The phone rang in the hallway. He wasn't disposed to answer it but Colin did. James heard him come down the stairs. He was getting to recognise his tread now, when he heard him at all. It was solid, and each step he made sounded like a decision. Colin came back into the kitchen.

It's for you, he said.

Me? Oh, okay.

Maybe it was Clare again. James liked the thought, when a few weeks ago he would have panicked.

It was a shock when Deborah spoke. He winced. Maybe she'd already heard about his pub escapade.

James?

Uh, hullo.

Does that offer still stand?

What?

I was thinking that perhaps it would be okay. Just a drink. I was a bit rude to you on the phone.

Uh, yes. I mean no. Of course you weren't rude.

And yes?

Pardon?

Do you still want that birthday drink?

Oh yes, absolutely.

Yes, he wanted one like he wanted a hole in the head.

Okay, Deborah said. I'll pick you up if you like. Not at the hostel, though. How about outside the Hollybush?

Tonight?

It *is* your birthday, isn't it?

Yes.

Well then?

Yes, fine. Thanks. About eight?

I'll see you there, then. Happy birthday.

163

James blurted out his assent without thinking. If elation could mix with despair and combust he would have gone up in smoke. It was hard to believe the phone call had just happened, hard to believe she'd changed her mind. This was the elation. Life was so strange. Every twist and turn of it hung on fateful moments like this. He'd spent more than half his money, he looked like shit, felt like shit, and would be struggling to surface from the hangover for most of the day. Its second wave was already starting to wash up against him. This was the despair.

Colin was watching him from the kitchen doorway.

Lady friend? Colin asked.

Uh, no, just someone I know.

I'd like to have a lady friend. Haven't for a long time. That bloody war put paid to that side of things as well.

James wanted to get away from him as quickly as he could, without making it look too obvious. He could not get the image of those *Love and Hate* hands reaching for him out of his mind. He wasn't sure at the time if Colin's threat had been physical, sexual or both. He wasn't sure now.

Don't forget this, Colin said.

He held out an envelope.

Came for you earlier. I just remembered it.

Thanks.

You're a popular man, James.

Hardly. I'll see you later, Colin.

It was a birthday card from Clare. She'd added Zoe's name to it. This set the seal on Deborah's phone call and elation started to edge ahead. It was only later, when he was shaving, that James realised Colin must have taken the card up to his bedroom.

*

Adrian is ringing the front door bell.

Did you know he was coming over? Clare asks.

No, we haven't arranged anything.

He's getting bold. Watch out, Mum, he'll be claiming squatters' rights soon.

My head is thumping. Too much red wine last night. We're having breakfast, but it's almost noon and neither of us is dressed.

Feels like the bell's inside my head, I mutter.

You only had a few glasses of wine. Mum, most of the girls I know drink more than that as a starter before they go out.

Well, I'm not one of them.

Adrian rings again.

Don't look at me, Clare says. At least you've got a nice dressing gown on. This is one of Zoe's and it's pants. He won't go away, mum. Our cars are on the drive.

I go to the front window and give Adrian an uncertain wave. He beams back at me. I'm more than a little irritated. This man is trying to rush things and already I'm feeling smothered. It's my fault. I've encouraged him, but, for Adrian, just allowing him to be present is an encouragement.

I'm going up to the bathroom, Mum, Clare shouts. Leave you to it.

Since Clare told me about James I'm not so clear-sighted about the future. I've learned that the past can't be locked away so easily. I thought that three years James-free would be more than long enough. God, I know women who take less than three months, but in one meeting with her father Clare has brought James back into focus and as soon as James becomes present tense again he's in my mind.

As I open the door flowers are thrust into my face. Beautiful flowers.

Got them from a little shop near Woodlands, Adrian says. Oh, are you just getting up? Sorry, but I was passing and I thought I'd drop in.

Do you always drive around with flowers?

No, that is, I thought…

Only teasing. Come on in. Clare's here. She stayed last night.

I take Adrian into the kitchen. It still smells of last night's wine.

It's a nice, brisk day, Adrian says. I fancied going for a run along the coast. Perhaps get a bit of a walk in. 'Course, I should have phoned. Stupid of me.

Fresh air sounds good, but my tongue takes over.

There's a pity. I've arranged to go shopping with Clare, that's why she stopped over.

I hope I'm not colouring up. I don't lie very often and I'm praying Clare doesn't come down for a while.

Oh, I see. Not to worry.

I'll find a vase to do justice to these. Do you want a coffee, Adrian?

Yes, thanks.

He makes a poor job of hiding his disappointment. I feel a bit of a rat. Adrian is watching me closely. He's sitting at the kitchen table like a greyhound about to leave the traps. I think he might propose to me soon if I keep this going. He won't be able to help himself. He's a lonely man on a mission, and I'm it. I pull the dressing gown around me more firmly, and smile as confidently as I can.

I thought I went into this with Adrian with my eyes open, but now I'm not sure what I want. Yes. I *am* sure. There's a moment of blinding clarity as I make the coffee. It makes the headache jump. I think of Woodlands, security, giving up work, I think of a rich man with a minimum of baggage who's stuck on me. I think that maybe I won't get another chance.

Shall we do something tonight? Adrian asks. Are you free?

Eh, yes, alright.

A meal? I know a good place near the house. They're usually booked up well in advance but they know me.

Alright.

He finishes his coffee.

You stay here, Nina. I'll let myself out. It's cold outside. Shall we say eight?

Yes.

I offer a cheek but he wants lips.

He holds me by the shoulders and looks at me carefully.

Everything is okay, isn't it?

Yes. Drank a bit too much wine last night, that's all.

Ah, I thought that might be it. Happy shopping, then.

He didn't stay long, Clare shouts down.

No, you can stop hiding now.

Adrian's right about the cold. I watch from the front window as he drives away, the car's exhaust letting out a thin trail of white smoke into the still frosty air, like the Vatican making a decision. I have also made a decision.

*

James's life was changing. For five years he'd fed his addiction, allowing it to grow until responsibility was a bad dream. He was lost long before it peaked. By the time it did, James was aware of his need, but not much else. He lived to mainline on the sweet rush of a rare win. Even now, James closed his eyes in memory of that feeling. He paid homage to it, the joy that fired up his spirit in tragically short bursts; the win that made sense of it all.

As his last bet became farther away, and his head continued to clear, James wondered if he'd always been setting himself up for his fall. The literature of his youth had been littered with disaffected losers, sensitive loners, anyone that couldn't or wouldn't fit in. He'd always had a sneaky regard for people who could take on life with nothing much more than a personal code. He still didn't know if what had happened to him was conscious design,

167

accident or fateful destiny. Perhaps it was a combination of all three. Colin might say it was a quest, something calling James from the black parts of his soul.

James arranged his capital on his bedroom table, the muddied twenty that Billy had rescued, and some loose change. To boost his confidence a little, he placed Clare's card besides this modest hoard, then rummaged through the old wardrobe that came with the room. It was taller than him, its thin, walnut veneer patterned with concentric whirls that looked like dark brown islands. It reminded him of the gloomy furniture of his childhood. Inside was his one good Oxfam overcoat, an old anorak and a few shirts and trousers on plastic hangers. He took out the best shirt, and the most decent pair of trousers he could muster.

The twenty caught his eye again. Elgar winked at him, and for a moment James thought of a bet. He couldn't believe it, but his habit was a patient stalker. It told him he could triple the twenty if he backed a sure-fire favourite, the horse that couldn't lose. The horse that didn't exist. He thought of rotating numbers, the wheel stopping for him. It was a long moment, long enough for James's mind to step into a casino, feel his feet sink into the deep red pile of the carpet, and sigh as warm air rushed to meet him, his meagre note burning a hole in his pocket. His addiction was as sympathetic as it was stealthy. Now it crooned to him softly. Willing him up and off in search of the game. James remembered Tony's words. This was the time cold turkey got colder.

James walked around the bedroom, clenching his hands into tight fists. He went to the window, put his hands on the sill, and breathed in deeply. The view was unchanging, and he was getting used to it. A welcome familiarity that was the only constant in his life. Everything was where it should be. He liked the way the poorly landscaped tips declared their independence by refusing to merge into the hillside. He liked the fact that isolated, wind-bent trees could hold their place in the rocky shale of the upper slopes. He liked the way each part of this scene bled into the next. James liked the closeness of it all – that more than anything. This was just a small parcel of land going on in an old world. He calmed down and the twenty became just a crumpled piece of paper again. Elgar faded away.

James tracked a man walking on the hillside, his black and white collie running on ahead, looking back, then running on again. Its energy sparked the scene and made James want to join with it. It was an instant decision, his antidote to turkey. Before he could change his mind, he put on his anorak and wrapped up as warmly as he could.

James walked quickly down the street. As he went past the Hollybush his head throbbed in memory, then he realised he hadn't even had breakfast, just coffee. It slurped around his empty guts, but no matter, he doubted that he could keep anything else down.

The usual kids were about, the phone box their citadel. James saw a boy's hand stray down a girl's jeans and be slapped away, half-heartedly. They had no time for him today. Within minutes he was on the hillside. The man with the dog was coming back down and they passed each other.

It's raw up there, the man muttered, his face glowing a wind-whipped red.

Raw was what James wanted.

He started to climb, treading carefully on the rough sheep trail. He was determined to get to the ridge top today, no matter what. It was dry, with just enough sun for him to be aware of it on his face, but it did not fool him. It was just a soft yellow flicker passing behind the clouds.

Raw. The dog-walker was right about that. The wind was strong, it had an edge to it that picked him out, but James welcomed it. It went with the sense of renewal that had been building inside since Pete's funeral. Half an hour ago he'd been able to fight down temptation and each time it became a little easier.

James strode on upwards, ignoring his chest and the pain that was already present in the backs of the legs. Turf squelched underfoot. No matter what the weather, the landscape here would remain sodden until the spring. There were pockets of water all around him, tiny pools trapped in hollows, and a swollen stream ran past him, spilling over its banks to feed the pools. The sun found them, and the hillside was turned into a land of gleaming points.

James's body wanted him to stop, but his lungs were having their biggest fill of fresh air in a long time. He felt them wheezily try to respond to the challenge. The hangover was being wrung out of him, and he was starting to look forward to the evening.

James did stop, two-thirds of the way up. He leant against a dry stonewall and looked down on the hazy valley. Against his back was true masonry, stones that had been collected from the hillside, not quarried. Shaped by men, but held together by nothing more than skill and gravity. The wall had been weathered with generations of moss and lichen, now it ran down the mountainside in an uneven line, almost a living part of the landscape.

Pete's hanging tree was close by. James looked up at it. A young policeman had pointed out the tree at the time, it was just visible from the edge of the village. He was glad he couldn't see it from the hostel. Pete's face filled his mind, he saw him on the hostel doorstep with outstretched hand, anxious to make a friend before James even set foot in the place.

James walked over to the tree, his chest getting tighter. He rested a hand on its worn bark, and ran his fingers along its rough history, looking up just once at the high branches. A hawk chose this moment to glide over, noiseless as it worked the currents down to the lower slopes. It fixed James with its orange-yellow, impassive eye, and showed him the light brown of its rippled undercarriage as its wings fanned out. James waved a hand at the bird, and it veered away with the minimum of correction, leaving him with a single, high-pitched cry.

Like the hawk, Pete had been master of his own fate, at least at the end. He'd gone out on a show of guts and resignation. Not a bad combination. James touched Pete's tree one last time. He did not plan to come here again.

James tackled the last part of the climb, his calves complaining, his chest ever more breathless, but he reached the stony spine of the ridge top. As he gulped in air James felt a sense of belonging that was so strong he could almost touch it. This was his land now, he wanted to crush it up in his hands and mingle with it, dizzy, exhausted, but triumphant at the summit of his modest Everest.

James realised he was colliding with a kind of truth that he'd been working up to since Pete's death. Lies had protected him throughout his gambling years, but they had worn thin as each one chased the last. Pete had shocked him, jolted him back into real life. He sniffed at this new feeling cautiously, and hardly dared form the word in his mind, but perhaps it was hope, that essential arrangement of four letters from so long ago.

James was forty-eight years old, and a couple of hours. A time to reflect. He remembered his mother telling him he'd been a morning birth after *a very long night* and *difficult time*. As the elements attacked and James walked head down along the track he saw his parents sitting in their living room in a kind of grey unity. All the stuff that had been swept under the carpet demanded to be dragged back out now. Perhaps it needed to be. Once he'd left the family home, James realised how sterile it had been. What had been dread familiarity quickly became alien and he knew he wouldn't go back. He was glad he was nothing like *them*, he told himself. As he became the life and soul of every college party, he thought that maybe the Read gene pool had jumped a generation, that he was a throwback to warmer times, and more open people. Not that he did think about it that much at that time. Life was all about escape and forward motion then, laced with a modicum of success. Now it was too late to ask questions; the two other pieces of this jigsaw were long gone.

Now James thought the key to his self-destruction lay in his early childhood. His parents taught him to put himself first at all times. This was a powerful lesson, quite deadly, and life with Nina had always been clouded with it. Gambling was the result of selfish desire bursting out again, he saw that now. He'd made some attempt to keep it caged, when he became husband then father, but not enough. It had cost him.

James was glad it was downhill all the way back. The sun was long gone, and the clouds turned sooty black to settle over the hillside, in an echo of the coal that still lay below. At the edge of houses he turned for one last look at the ridge and saw the hawk tacking back up, checking each section of ground for its next meal. It was a small brown ripple against the darker sky, taking minutes when he'd taken an hour.

There was no one around in the hostel. For a moment James fantasised that the place was his own, a safe and private refuge. Billy would be back soon. He usually showed up for a few hours sleep, the half-time in his day of drinking. It amazed James how much alcohol a man could take, and for how many years. Billy walked a lot between watering holes, maybe that kept the inevitable at bay.

James made himself a meal in the kitchen and ate it quickly. Clare's card welcomed him back into his bedroom. She'd written *have a happy, peaceful birthday* on the back of a print of a Renoir cafe scene. He looked more closely at the envelope. It had been opened, quite clumsily, then re-sealed, but James was too tired to think much about this. He set his alarm clock for six o'clock and fell asleep almost immediately.

172

I had eight hours to come up with the kindest way to nip this in the bud but I doubt if there is one. Not that it's a bud for Adrian. For him it's a flourishing bloom, like his expensive out-of-season freesias that have come from Africa. I ran through all the usual suspects, *it's me, not you, I'm not ready yet, I made a mistake.* For a moment I didn't realise Clare is standing alongside me.

Having second thoughts, Mum? she says quietly.

What?

You know I've always been able to read you.

Have you finished in the bathroom?

I'm up the stairs before any more questions come my way.

Now Adrian drives us slowly through country lanes. We're on our way to a restaurant he knows in the Vale for an early evening meal. It's the only slot he could get but the time suits me. An hour ago I had it all clear in the bathroom, at least I thought I did. Telling myself I must finish it tonight, as neatly as I'm putting on this lipstick.

As I scan the chrome fittings and discreet strips of real wood in the car I realise many might think me foolish. Freedom is in the wallet, my father used to say, and it was only a short while ago that I was telling Clare that men didn't grow on trees for women of my age. Actually, they do. That singles joint was full of them, everything from battered, baggage-laden men, to hopeless, mother-pecked virgins recently bereft of mother, or just men on the make. Plenty of them. Plenty of quantity all round, it was quality which was sparse. I told myself this was a practical way for people of a certain age to meet, maybe it is, but not for me. That room was desperate, and it's made me question any feelings I have for Adrian. It seems ridiculous to think I'm not ready after three bloody years, but maybe I'm just not ready for Adrian, and never will be.

I've been to this place a few times, Adrian says. With work.

Good food?

Absolutely.

Christ, this is going to be difficult. I should have done it back at the house, not go out for a meal with the poor man, and then get rid. I'm putting it off and I'm not even sure that cowardice won't get the upper hand again. Adrian pulls onto the pub's forecourt.

Nina? Lost in your thoughts?

Sorry. It's been a long week. I don't usually do a full week now.

You're lucky.

I smile at him and wish to hell I was.

This place burnt down a while ago, Adrian says. They've rebuilt it and it's better than ever, they say.

The food is okay, but nothing as good as Adrian claims. I am served mediocre sea bass and stuffed peppers by two ageing and rather grumpy women who look like they ought to be stuffed themselves. They mirror my mood. A man more experienced than Adrian would pick up something was seriously amiss. I look for openings through all three courses but none come. Adrian talks on, about our trip north, his work, how well Clare is doing. The future. The man is happy, and it will be stripped from him very soon. I'm feeling worse and worse. A complete shit.

We finish the meal and go into the lounge to sit near an open fire. The night is cold and frosty outside and the logs burn bright.

I'm thinking of opening up one of the fireplaces at home, Adrian says. The chimneys are still alright.

That'll be nice.

Yes, I thought you'd like it.

I don't think we'll keep Clare for long, Adrian says. She'll be head-hunted by a bigger firm, that girl is going places, she has what it takes.

What's that?

Oh, innovation, fresh ideas, creative thinking, you need that, even in finance, believe it or not. Clare's got the lot, plus a hell of a good brain to boot. I know where she gets that from.

Adrian is wrong. These are all traits of James, not me. Traits he couldn't take forward, or make work for him. Clare can. She is. My ex-man is in my head again. I knew he'd wriggle in there before I can break the news to Adrian that *he's* going to be my new ex-man.

Suddenly I want to see what James looks like now. I couldn't press Clare too much on that score. It was a shock how much he changed in the months leading up to the divorce. I last saw him just after all the necessary paperwork had been signed. It looked as if some make-up artist had gone to work on him. Streaking the hair with grey, increasing the wear under his eyes, making his stubble distinctly un-designer-like. His clothes were already starting to look untidy and unloved. He never could iron.

I said I know where she gets that from, Adrian says. Nina, was the meal alright?

Yes. Fine.

You seem a bit distracted.

He's giving me the opening I need so I tell him before I can talk my way out of it. Adrian doesn't even interrupt. I come out with it being too soon, that I don't feel right, that it's me not him.

But we were fine in Scotland, he finally manages to say.

It was lovely, but we weren't fine.

You made me feel that we were.

I know. I wasn't thinking clearly. I'm sorry, Adrian.

You've been divorced for three years.

It's pathetic, isn't it, but things are still mixed up inside. I just didn't realise how much, until recently. I should never

have gone to that singles night. I don't think things out....
totally bloody stupid...

...Of course you aren't.

God, don't take it so well.

I feel my eyes welling up and fight to control them. I
had to be so bloody strong for the girls, pretend to be, then
wimp away after they'd gone to bed, idealising the early
days with James, hating him, wanting the love back,
bursting with rage and frustration. Once even smelling one
of his unwashed shirts he'd left behind. That was my lowest
moment.

I knew it was too good to be true, Adrian says. Meeting
someone like you.

I almost come out with *we can still be friends*, the
consolation prize that is no prize at all, but manage to bite
my tongue.

Don't sell yourself short, I answer.

Adrian is quiet for a moment, clasping his hands
together in what might have been mistaken for prayer. He
asks if I want him to take me home.

Yes, that would be best.

I shiver as we step outside. There's not much man-
made light around the pub, and stars are vivid tonight, hard,
blue-white points in a black sky. I feel their uncaring
vastness as Adrian drives us away, as carefully as ever.

The roads might be a bit icy tonight, he murmurs,
almost talking to himself. I sense he's done a lot of that
over the years. He knows his lonely life is about to come
flooding back. We pull up in front of my house and Adrian
puts a hand on my arm.

Is it alright if I keep in touch? he asks.

Of course, we'll have a link through Clare, anyway.

Yes. What shall I tell her?

That her mother is a bloody fool, though she probably
knows that anyway.

Do you think you might feel different about things after

a while? After a good while, I mean.

I don't know. Look, don't waste any more time on me, Adrian. Get on with your life.

A few hours ago I thought I was.

I squeeze his hand and get out of the car quickly and clumsily. It's hard to stop the tears now but I don't know who the hell they're for. It's a few minutes before Adrian drives off. I watch from a window as the rich man in the expensive car disappears. I'm back to square one. Husband gone. New man gone. Empty house.

*

James didn't want to get up. It took him a few minutes to realise it wasn't Sunday morning. A few more to remember it was his birthday and that he had a date. Another five to haul himself out of bed. His body creaked and muscles ached.

James re-examined the clothes he'd prepared. He fought to maintain what confidence he had as he shaved, showered and dressed with half an hour to spare. A half hour to avoid his hostel-mates and stay calm. Billy was out, called by Saturday night, and the Siren in a glass that controlled his life.

James felt as nervous as a school kid. He fidgeted with his clothes, thought about changing them, thought again, checked himself many times in the mirror, picked up a book and put it down, then stepped out into the street at ten to eight. His calves felt as if they were being slapped as he made his way to the pub. Meeting people outside the Hollybush was getting to be a habit. James stood a little away from its front doors, his overcoat up around his ears. It was spitting rain. Spots drifted out of the orange streetlights but he didn't have time to get wet, for Deborah was on time. At first she didn't see him in the gloom. He had to step out and raise a hand.

James had a moment's panic as he opened the car door. Its interior light seemed too bright, like a single spotlight on a stage. He felt like he was about to step out on one.

Say hello, then – birthday boy.

Sorry. Yes, hi.

You're not going to apologise all night, are you?

I'll try not to.

Where shall we go, then?

Uh, a pub somewhere other than here? I'm a bit out of touch, to be honest.

There's a new place further down the valley. Wine bar type of thing. Opened a year ago. I didn't think it would last, but it seems to be doing okay.

Not too posh?

Here? Don't be silly. Well, actually, I haven't been there. It's not really social workers' territory.

Less chance of prying eyes, eh?

Deborah smiled, but didn't answer.

James sank into his seat and tried to relax. This was another test. They were coming thick and fast. Pete's death, his public talk, Clare, now a date. A *date*. He rolled the word around in his head as if he'd just discovered it. He was excited, there was a buzz in him that had been missing for a long time. His hand closed on the money in his pocket, which he hoped would hold out.

Today I will be unafraid.

James changed the today to tonight. To this he added, I will not drink too much and will try not to make a total prat of myself.

Deborah looked great. She'd had her hair done, there was now a faint line of red amongst the black, and this was the first time he'd seen her with make-up. Her working day face had always been unadorned. James was flattered, and even more nervous.

What have you done today? Deborah asked.

I went for a walk. On the hillside. Got to the top of the

178

ridge.

Really? In this weather?

The weather was okay earlier. I'm trying to get fit.

That's good. I could do with some exercise myself. I want to lose a few pounds before Christmas, then I can put it back on and lose it all over again.

James managed to stop himself paying her some cheesy compliment about her figure and resolved to keep a tight rein on his tongue. It had been loose enough in the past. The night was turning wetter and the slap of the car's windscreen wipers took over from conversation. They were outside the wine bar in twenty minutes.

Looks quite imposing, James said.

Yes. Strange to see something like this appearing here. No expense spared on it, apparently.

Deborah was right, a lot of money had been spent. The place looked like it might have been sucked up from Surrey and set down in valley wilds. There weren't many customers, yet, just a few couples, and a group of older women standing near the bar who'd worked hard on their outfits. They glanced over at James, but only for a moment. There were a few American-style side booths, leather seats discreetly lit. Just right, James thought, as he guided Deborah towards one.

What can I get you? he asked.

Glass of house red will be okay. It's all the alcohol I'll be drinking. Losing my licence is not an option in my job.

Okay.

There was a mirror behind the bar that stretched along the whole length of it. James saw a man with a long way to go still. He was better than a few months ago, far better, but his furtive look had become ingrained. He needed to re-tune his features, calm down his street eyes, the ones he'd trained to watch out for all things at all times.

That's five forty sir.

Uh?

179

Guinness and red wine – five forty.

A fresh-faced kid took his twenty and made a point of staring at it. James looked at his change soberly. He took a quick sip at his beer and walked back to the booth very carefully. Whatever happened, this night had to be accident-free.

James, relax. You're wound up as tight as a corkscrew. I can almost feel the seat shaking. If I were Mae West I'd say you were excited to see me.

I used to be Snow White but I drifted.

What?

Oh, just another of her sayings. I'm surprised someone your age has even heard of her.

Deborah laughed.

My dad liked old films, but I haven't heard that one. Are you another film buff, then?

Used to be, not that Mae was ever in any classics.

Used to be. Everything is in past tense with you. Try thinking of the present. Even the future.

Is that the job talking?

No, the woman you've asked out for a drink.

Sorr…uh, right. Well, I am trying to.

Deborah raised a glass.

Happy birthday.

Cheers.

Mae West had broken the ice. Gradually, James did begin to relax, and the wine bar started to fill up. The conversation opened up. James found himself telling Deborah more than he ever would have in a formal situation.

Seeing your daughter was a big step forward, Deborah said. How old did you say she was?

He hadn't said.

Not long out of college. Shall I get us another drink?

My turn. Do you want the same?

He hesitated.

180

Well, okay, thanks, but two pints is my lot.

About ten less than last night, James thought, as he watched Deborah make her way through the now crowded bar. Older women were glancing over his way quite a lot now. Checking out the new face. He realised that this place must be a pick-up joint for people no longer fresh. Deborah was just about the youngest woman here. He was pleased and embarrassed by this in equal doses. She came back with the drinks on a small metal tray, threading her way through the crowd, with just enough undulation of her hips to keep James nervous. Not a speck of Irish froth had spilled.

Busy now, isn't it? Deborah said.Deborah added water to her glass of lemon and ice.

Yes, James answered, mainly people more my age though.

This must be the Saturday night crowd. The kids will be in Cardiff now, getting warmed up. So, are you glad you went to the GA meetings?

Yes. You were right about that. I was terrified, but just the fact that I got through it has helped a lot.

You did more than just get through it. Dave Connolly said they were all impressed.

For a moment James forgot about pacing himself and downed half the pint in one draught.

That disappeared quickly.

Old habits. I'll last the rest out now.

You don't have to. You don't have to behave in any special way with me.

Two women pushed into the booth. There was enough room for them and they took it.

Don't mind, do you? one of them said. We're too old to stand all night.

But they weren't old. Just a few years more than James. He jumped back into his shell, and the conversation became small talk again. He sensed the women weighing up ages and imagined their chat afterwards. *Must have been twenty*

181

years older than her, at least – maybe it was his daughter – don't be bloody stupid, bit on the side, more like – must be loaded – well, he certainly didn't look it.

When's the next meeting? Deborah said quietly, or at least as quietly as she could against the background chatter.

They're every two weeks.

Well, keep going.

I will.

It was turning formal again, James thought.

I'm going to the loo, he said.

It was full of fake marble, and pap was being piped through via invisible speakers. The Guinness was bringing back memories of last night. As he dashed some water into his face James knew he wanted to get back to the hostel. He'd come far enough this night. New-found confidence began to ebb away and suddenly his cheerless living place seemed safe, the refuge it was meant to be. When he went back to the bar and saw Deborah's face standing out amongst her worn peers he felt gratitude as much as longing.

The booth-sharers got up to leave and James gave silent thanks. He sat down again and leant towards Deborah.

I was feeling a bit crowded, he murmured.

I thought you were. Do you want to go?

Would you mind?

No, of course not.

The clock in Deborah's car showed that is was not yet ten o'clock. James Read, former ladies' man, felt his face redden.

Not much of an evening for you, he murmured.

Makes a change from going out with the girls, getting wrecked and losing Sunday. Not that there's many of *them* left.

What do you mean?

Well, my thirties crept up on me. At twenty-eight there were still lots of us single girls, then I blinked and they

182

were all hitched, or sorted in some way.

How come you're not?

There's been more than a few wrong choices along the way.

So, left with the likes of me, eh?

You're only at ease putting yourself down, aren't you?

Sorry… Christ, I've managed not to say that all night.

Deborah laughed, and then her hand was on his, the lightest of touches.

You've loosened up tonight, James. You can move on, you have something to move on to.

What would that be exactly?

Your daughters, for a start, and you could go back to teaching. I hear Comps are crying out for experienced teachers.

I don't think anyone would be crying out for me.

Once you get away from the hostel you could start off with supply teaching. Get back into it gradually.

That's where I left off and I didn't exactly cover myself with glory in my latter years.

Things change. People forget.

I've still got some way to go before I could do anything like that, Deb.

Deb! No one's called me that in years. I made it known I hated it.

She leant towards him and kissed him lightly. He responded. Lightly. So lightly he wasn't sure it had happened.

I really could do with an early Saturday night, Deborah said. I'm having to cover for someone and do my own work.

They drove back up the valley. Outside pubs people were being picked up by minibuses and taxis, to be taken to their second- stage watering holes. The night was awash with drink but all was quiet outside the hostel, the village road rain-slicked and empty as it curved away to the houses further down.

It's a bit bleak up here, Deborah muttered. So much life seems to be gone.

As you said, times change. I'm used to it, now.

Don't get too used to it. You're just passing through, remember.

There are plenty of good people here.

That's not the point.

James smiled as positively as he could and they brushed lips again.

I've got you this, Deborah said, reaching into a glove compartment. A birthday present.

She handed him a mobile phone.

Do you remember how to use one?

Just about. I can't take this, Deb.

It's one of my old ones. I've got a collection, believe me. This one just needed a new battery. I've put one in, so it's up and running. Oh, here's the instruction booklet, but it's dead easy to use, even for an old Luddite like you. You have five pounds credit, then you'll have to fund it yourself.

James looked at the device in his hand as if he was Stone Age man.

He fumbled in his pockets for money.

James, don't be silly. It's a gift and it will make it easier for me to get hold of you.

He looked at her dubiously.

Will you want to get hold of me?

We'll see.

Who else will I phone?

Start with your daughters, but you want to be texting. It's much cheaper. The book will tell you how.

Right.

James put his hand to his face as one of the dominoes players passed the car, humming tunelessly to himself.

Why did you come out with me tonight, Deborah? An old Luddite, as you say. Amongst other things.

Because you asked, and you're not that old. If you tamed your hair, cut it a bit shorter you'd look much younger. Besides, I've had enough experience with men my age – and younger – who didn't have a clue what they wanted or where they were going.

And I have?

Well, at least all your wrong moves might be behind you. Anyway, this was just a drink, remember.

Of course.

Use that mobile to get hold of me. No more lurking around phone boxes.

Right.

James got out of the car and watched her drive down the hill. He touched his lips thoughtfully, and looked up at the black outline of the mountain. His small piece of reality that he took in every night. He stood outside the hostel for a while, lost in his thoughts, moving the phone around in his hands, sucking in the night and enjoying the light rain on his face, his eyes almost closing. This was the best he'd felt in years.

As James turned to go in he sensed someone there before he felt the breath on the back of his neck. His hands tightened around the phone. It would be one of the spitting boys, after his new toy. He tried to turn but couldn't. Someone much stronger than him had a tight hold on him. An arm came up under his neck and it closed on his windpipe.

Hello, mate, a voice said. Been out enjoying yourself, with your lady friend? Keep still. Make a fuss and I'll break your neck – I've done it before. I'll take that phone.

James saw the tattoos on the bare forearm, the words on the fingers. *Love and Hate* came close to his eyes and the dragon pressed up close. Colin had been eating something rich in garlic.

Let's get you inside, Colin said. Billy's there already. I'm having a party.

I turn on the television, scan through channels and switch it off again. I'm edgy, but it's not Adrian that's making me so, he's just the catalyst. It's the ex-man of twenty-five years. I often thought that James saw me as just an extension of himself and I hope I'm not about to prove it, but things need to be resolved, not left to fester any longer. For the girls' sake, and my own. At least I must try to get him back for Clare and Zoe. I phone Clare's mobile.

Mum! You don't usually phone Saturday night. What? I can't hear you. Hang on, I'll go outside.

Where are you?

I'm in the Butchers, with some of the people from work. Aren't you with Adrian?

Not now.

It's early. What's happened?

Nothing's happened. He's gone home. Clare, I want to know where that hostel is.

What?

Where your father's staying.

Mum, have you been drinking?

Hardly.

I promised I wouldn't say.

Please, Clare. I just want to know where it is.

I don't know, Mum.

What does it matter?

You're not going to go up there, are you? He'll know I've told you if you turn up.

And I'll know you haven't told me.

It is blatant blackmail, which would never have worked with Zoe, but I sense the waver in Clare's voice.

Look, will you tell me if I promise not to see him?

What's the point, then?

I don't know what the bloody point is. Just tell me.

Clare relented. I know the village, even the street. Not far away from one of my Comps. A run-down place now, practically the last stop to nowhere. James being there brings home to me the reality of his situation.

My mobile bleeps. It's Adrian texting me goodnight. So typical of the man. I sense the desperation in his simple message. He hasn't been able to let it go for more than an hour.

Mum, you still there?

Yes, my mobile was ringing. Thanks Clare. Look, don't worry, it'll be okay. Go back to your friends. I'll talk to you tomorrow. Nite…

I cut her off. She'll be round Sunday, chasing the gossip over dinner. So, I have the address. Now what? Going to bed would be best. The sleep-on-it philosophy that never gets anything sorted, but at least puts off impulsive action. I'm thinking this as I look for the car keys.

I drive up to the valley slowly, giving myself plenty of time to change my mind. Furtive spying on an ex-husband won't do me any good, but I'm compelled. I'm pulling a James stroke. He was great at spur-of-the-moment stuff that didn't make sense. I don't even know what I'm looking for. Whilst there was no contact with James, what was unresolved gnawed away at me, but it became more passive as time passed. All it has taken to re-activate was another man.

I'm looking for excuses. Wild ideas pass through my head. Stories of people starting again. Even re-marrying. How sad is that? I tell myself I just want closure and shut my eyes for a moment, but long enough to move into the middle of the road. A small car blasts its horn as it speeds past, taking its pumped-up music with it. I see angry faces under baseball caps flash by, and a finger raised.

I'm used to getting home on a Friday afternoon, totally washed out, kicking off my shoes, opening a bottle of wine and savouring the peace of the house. Thinking about all the times it echoed with rows, and telling myself that I'm not lonely. I can do anything I want, when I want. I'm not lonely.

James is not the answer. With sudden clarity I know I could never get back with him, even if it *was* on the cards, any more than I could commit to Adrian. Any solution must lie in the future. This doesn't cause me to turn around however. I want to see him, and I want to sort it out.

There's not much traffic on the road and the rain increases the further up the valley I go. It's been ages since I've been up this way in the dark. I put Classic FM on the radio for support. They're playing Barber's Adagio. I used to love that piece but it has been discovered and done to death in recent years. Even so, the haunting music is just about right.

I'm nearing the village, slowing down on an empty, glistening road. A police car comes up behind me quickly and I'm thinking about my glass of restaurant wine but he's gone, speeding past with lights flashing. Another follows. I pull into the kerbside as a fire engine thunders past, then an ambulance and other support vehicles. I'm a little startled. It's as if I'm being warned. Perhaps I should turn around and go back, I'm not in the mood to come across some gruesome accident, but I go on.

I'm there, driving down the road that leads into the village, flanked by uneven terraces on either side. People are streaming out of a large public house that stands alone. At first I think it's just closing time, but some of the younger ones are running down the street. There's something burning up ahead, a blaze of colour in the dark street. It looks like a terraced house but I can't drive any further. A police car is blocking the road, and an officer stands in front of it, waving me towards the side of the road. Another policeman is trying to stop the crowd from passing him, but it's a hopeless task. I open the car window a little.

C'mon, Dai, someone shouts, le's get down there. It's

tha' hostel place. I bet one of them pissheads set it on fire. Bet they're fryin'.

*

Colin moved backwards and James was pulled inside the hostel.

You thought I hadn't recognised you, James, but I did. I knew who you were the first time I stepped into this shithole. Hello, I said to myself, it's that tosser from that squat. The one who ran away. The one who spurned me when I needed a friend. Must be a sign, I said. I'm always looking for signs. I knew you'd been put here for a purpose. My purpose. All the voices started to make sense again. Once I stopped the magic pills they started to make total sense.

Colin pushed James against the wall and locked and bolted the front door.

Don't want any interruptions, do we?

This is stupid, James managed to gasp, I don't know what you're talking about. He could hardly get his breath, and his legs thought they were going on another route march. Colin dragged him into the kitchen and pushed him down on a chair.

Put your hands on the table and keep them there, Colin said. Maybe you'll stay alive.

Colin stood over him, silhouetted against the strip lighting. He was in full regalia, battle fatigues, Doc Martins, and a freshly-shaven skull. Only the automatic rifle was missing. His face tattoo was even more lurid in the harsh light, it seemed to take on a life of its own, the eyes of the dragon alert, watching the action unfold.

Where's Billy? James asked.

He's around.

Colin paced the room, fingering some of his labelled possessions. He deliberately turned his back on James at one point, but James did not move from the chair. Colin came close and knelt behind him.

Gravity. Ever thought about it, James? It pulls you down. Sounds obvious, eh, Newton's apple and all that, but I mean it really pulls you down. Your thoughts, your life, your action, your everyfuckingthing, pulled down to the earth's core. That's in here, for me.

Colin tapped his head with a finger and put an imaginary telephone to his head.

Hello, anyone there? Yes, 'course you are. All of you. Don't worry, I will.

You're not well, Colin. You're just depressed. There's no need for this. It doesn't make any sense, man.

Sense? What the fuck's that? The world turned it back on sense from day one.

Colin's face came close to James, spraying him with pungent garlic again. His even, yellow teeth looked shark-like.

There's every need and don't *ever* put *just* and *depressed* together like that, Colin shouted. There's no *just* about it. You're like those in that fucking hospital. Take this, Colin, take that, Colin. Off you go, Colin. We've decided you're better now, but don't stop taking the pills, Colin, whatever you do. What kind of better is that, for fucksake.

Pull yourself together, soldier. I had that one alright, some Sandhurst twat who wouldn't know how to shit and shave at the same time. The type that let my mates hang around in that boat like sitting ducks. To get that stupid you need a lot of breeding, a lot of training. Army's good at that, training. Not so hot at thinking. I decked the bastard. One punch, all over. He crumbled like a house of cards. Bust his jaw. Would have been court-martialled if I hadn't been off my head…

Colin shut his eyes for a moment. James saw his hands clench into fists then open again.

190

I can still smell it now, James.

What?

Colin was silent for a moment, and then he began to whisper, his voice barely above a murmur, his lips pressed close to James's ear. James preferred him shouting.

Men burning, diesel slopping around... hard to fucking describe. Have you ever singed a piece of wool? That's the closest you can get to the smell of men burning. I saw one of the boys a few weeks ago in Cardiff. He survived, like me. Got a rebuilt face now. I avoided him, crossed to the other side of the road. What's the point in talking about it?

Why don't we calm down and talk about it now? James said.

I am calm. I'm perfectly calm. Fuck me, you must think I've climbed down from a tree – Jimbo. Isn't that what Billy boy here called you? Jimbo, the college boy. Humour the loony, keep him talking, while you think of a way to save your skin. I *am* crazy, but not stupid. *I* own your skin, now.

I've done nothing to you. I don't deserve this.

Deserve has nothing to do with it. There are no rules to this game. I'm off my head, remember, and it's full of fucking voices. I left off the tablets so I could hear them again. I *missed* them. Can you believe that? I fucking missed them. They were the only company I had... I *want* to do this. The gravity's become too strong. It's a way out.

Colin began to pace the room again. One hand became a fist that punched the palm of the other.

Where's Billy? James asked.

All in good time, Jimbo. Did you ever see that film *Easy Rider*? I saw it in Germany when I was a young squaddie. It had fucking German subtitles and the cinema was full of freaks. It was a film for freaks but I memorised that speech by Jack Nicholson by heart. Did you see it?

Colin flicked a hand against James's head.

I said did you see it?

Yes. A long time ago.

It *was* a long time ago. Aye, that speech by old Jack, well, he was young Jack then. Colin closed his eyes and started to recite. *What makes people angry is all that they don't understand. Then it makes them dangerous...* I've seen mobs all over the world, hooked on hate, and fuck knows what else. Out of control. Religious freaks, they're the worst of all. Inadequate bastards looking for excuses – excuses for the way their lives are, the way their wives are, their job, every fucking thing. I didn't fall for Jack's liberal bullshit. His speech made me realise I was one step further out there. I hated what I *did* understand. Now I'm looking for payback. A bit of fucking relief. Like you did with your gambling. Oh aye, I got all that out of Billy. He sang like a bird.

Is Billy here?

Colin chuckled.

Oh aye, he's here all right. Snivelling little shit. Coming in pissed every night, singing all that crap. *Whisky in the Jar*, be fucked. I wanted to put *him* in a jar the first night here, but the voices said cool it, Colin, check out the lie of the land. Do a bit of recce. They were just starting up again then, going through the gears. They got into top when they saw you.

It was easy fooling the so-called experts, the talking fucking heads. One of them stamped me safe and everyone accepted it. Bad mistake. That bird you fancy accepted it. Went out with her tonight, didn't you? I saw her car. Thought you were getting back on track, did you, Jimbo? Leaving all this shit behind you, forgetting about it. What were you before you fucked up? Office boy, some sort of pen pusher? Teacher? Something like that, I bet.

Teacher.

What subject?

English.

A waste of time teacher, eh? Bet you couldn't get them

192

to like Shakespeare. I read him, in the last hospital. The complete works. Haven't read much since. No need. He said it all. Took me a while to unlock the language, me being an uneducated squaddie, like, but I got into it. That guy knew everything about rottenness, about twisted people, tortured people. People like us, Jimbo. You and me. Take that Shylock, I had a lot of time for him. A pound of flesh makes sense to me. I'd like to cut out all the rotten flesh of the world, but there wouldn't be much left would there? Like those useless sods who sent us to those poxy islands, to fight a poxy war that meant fuck all, to please that mad tart. They're still doing it. They'll always fucking do it. Wog bashing. The world hasn't moved on at all.... people have always been rotten....

Colin subsided for a moment and rubbed at his head. He was swaying slightly, to the rhythm of his words. James glanced around. There was no sign that any struggle had taken place, not that it would have been much of a struggle with Billy. Colin could have done anything with him.

Looking for Billy? Why you worrying about him? Before you fucked up you wouldn't have looked twice at someone like that. You would have pulled your missus to the other side of the road, to avoid the *nasty* man. You *were* married, weren't you? 'Course you were. Kids too, I bet. You blew it all, didn't you?

No children.

Colin stepped behind James and put him in a headlock again.

I think that's a little porkie – Jimbo.

The forearm pressed, and James closed his eyes as the room swirled. He waited for the end and saw the girls running around the garden on a summer's day, the air alive with innocence as they squirted each other with water, and disturbed his hammock reading. The hammock was a present from Nina. He'd slung it up between two trees and spent most of the long summer holiday in it. Colin lessened the pressure.

Tell me, Colin said.

We couldn't have any. That's what started me drinking.

I can easily find out if that's right, Colin said.

Well, then you'll know I'm telling the truth.

Colin released him.

Who's this Clare, then? And Zoe?

James had forgotten the card.

My sisters.

How old were you, today?

Forty-eight.

Yeah? Well, tonight is my birthday present.

A few kids passed by the kitchen window, shouting, laughing, throwing cans. One hit the front door of the hostel. James heard it explode and spray out its froth.

Colin glared at the window. Like a feral cat his eyes were wild and full, then they narrowed to points. For a moment they closed. Colin was looking inwards, at whatever horrors lay there. He touched the dragon, letting a hand linger on it, and opened his eyes again, projecting his version of reality outwards.

Little wankers, he muttered. I'd like to mow all the fuckers down.

James wanted to rub at his neck but thought it best not to move.

Have *you* been married? James asked.

Still trying to get me to talk, eh?

Colin went to the fridge and came back with a bottle of Polish spirit.

The boys used to drink this down in Gib, he said. 90 per cent proof. Takes your head off like a meat slicer. Nah, talking's no good, Jimbo. Drinking's better.

Colin handed the bottle to James.

Have a good long pull.

Look, I…

Drink the fucker.

194

James took a small swallow. Liquid fire dripped down his throat.

More than that. I'll tell you when to stop.

James drank about four measures. He was instantly hot, and his face burned as the drink assaulted him.

Good, huh?

Colin began to hum to himself. James recognised Colonel Bogie as he tried to assess his chances. He'd escaped from Colin before, maybe he could again. He thought of smashing the bottle in his face and making a dash for the door, but knew this was fantasy. Better to wait, but for what James wasn't sure.

Have another drink, mate.

I don't think I can.

Oh, I think so. Drink, Jimbo, I'm doing you a favour.

James drank, and spluttered, Colin standing over him with hands flexing.

She fucked off sharpish when she saw what state I was in, Colin muttered.

What?

The wife. Couldn't handle it, could she? Shallow bitch. I went out fit and fancied and came back headshot and nuts. Last I heard she was in Portugal, with some club ponce. A singer, for fucksake. Where's yours?

I'm not sure, now.

You're better off. Well, you would be if I wasn't here.

Colin laughed, and his yellow teeth became part of the dragon. Colin's face was no longer the blank mask of a few days ago, it was alive, the outlet for all his secret mania. Colin picked up the bottle and finished it in one long draught. He smacked his lips.

First drink I've had in thirty years. So, you want to see Billy? Come on then.

James expected to be put in a headlock again but this time Colin pushed him along, prodding his back with iron fingers.

Up the stairs, Jimbo.

Colin was humming Bogie again, moving to the beat. James thought of trying to fall backwards in the hope of breaking away but was too fazed. One minute Deborah, re-establishing contact with his family, and a possible future, next minute Colin and a quick descent to hell. This man might be his nemesis, calling time on all his foolishness. It numbed him. He'd told Colin he didn't deserve this but perhaps he did. James had fallen down into the gutter, and nothing good was there.

Colin stopped James outside his bedroom door and told him to open it. It wouldn't, at first. Something was blocking it.

Push harder, Jimbo. That's it. Now squeeze in sideways, I'm right behind you.

Billy was blocking the door. His crumpled body lay behind it.

Thought I'd have us all in the one room together. Nice and cosy, like. Silly little sod caught me on my rawest edge, Colin said quietly. His bloody singing cut right through the voices and they didn't like it, they didn't like it at all. So I gave him a slap. He went down and cracked his head on the floor, smashed like a shell, as you can see. One punch dead. What do all the scum say when they have their day in court – *I didn't mean to do it, I didn't know I had the glass in my hand, I had a fucking awful childhood.* Well, I meant to. Didn't expect him to die though. He must have had a thin skull.

The voices said the dye is cast, now, Colin. Better go for it, all the way. One punch made up my mind for me. I'm a perfect killing machine, see, Jimbo. That's what some officer said, after we'd gone up them grassy fucking freezing slopes, wind blowing our arses off. Shot the shit out of kids in foxholes. I can see them now, spotty teenagers crying out for their mamies and Jesus. Neither was there for them. They were all in a rush to put their hands up but we gave them a few thousand bullets to catch. That worried me at the time but it doesn't now. War is all about murder. The voices made it cool. They liked it. That was when they really got going and when Billy's lights went out they were purring in here, Jimbo, fucking purring.

Colin made spider-like movements across his skull.

James didn't answer. He was transfixed by Billy's body. He lay like a crumpled rag doll behind the door, his mouth open, with a few teeth stumps showing. James recalled a childhood memory of a badger caught in a trap. The same expression of surprised and angry pain, registered instantly, then glazed over by death.

James turned and tried to hit Colin. He thought to push him out of the room and lock the door, then shout for help from the window. If he got lucky Colin might fall down the stairs. He didn't get lucky. It was an instant plan, instant and puny. Colin blocked the blow and James was on the floor. One side of his head pulsated and he felt searing pain in his left eye. It was already closing.

So, there's a little dog still barking away somewhere inside, eh Jimbo? That's good.

Colin dragged James along the floor, then yanked his hands behind his back and tied them with something he took from his pocket.

Just in case you get lucky, Colin murmured.

He propped James up against the bed. Colin stood by the window for a moment and scanned the street.

Quiet as a church out there. This place will love tonight. It'll put it on the map.

You have to stop this, Colin. It makes no sense.

You've already said that. One man's sense is another man's craziness. I can read you, James Read. You're stuck, can't believe what's happening, don't know what to say. How *do* you reason with a madman? You don't want to tell me I *am* mad in case it sets me off worse. You'll be thinking of a plea now, something to engage with my head,

197

something to get you out of this. It's hopeless trying to cut a deal with me, Jimbo. I have too many heads to deal with.

Colin sat beside him on the bed. He was calming, breathing slowly, flexing *Love and Hate*, the letters distorting amongst the hairs of his fingers. James prayed that one of the voices in Colin's head would break ranks and tell him to stop, to let him go.

So, how was it then? Colin asked.

He prodded James's shoulder.

Come on, don't go to sleep on me. It was only a tap.

How was what?

Your date. She's cute, yeah? Bit young for you though, isn't she? I reckon you're a dreamer, Jimbo, or a dirty old man. You dreamt your way down to the bottom didn't you? Wanker. You had no good reason to fuck-up. No good reason at all. You've thrown your life away – mine was taken from me.

Colin got up, and examined James's room. He picked up the gambling books, looked at Clare's card again. James thanked God she hadn't written *Dad* on it. The thought of Colin seeking out his family filled him with dread. Colin took another piece of cord from a pocket.

Put your feet out straight, he said.

He tied James's ankles together, a tight bond that allowed him little movement.

Are you cold, Jimbo? It's been a bitter winter so far, hasn't it? I like the cold myself. Kills all the bugs. Your chest doesn't sound too good, though. I noticed it straight off. I'll be back in a while. Be good.

With his hands tied behind his back and his legs immobile James could do very little, apart from roll on the floor. Many film images flashed through his head, all the old classics he'd once pored over. The countless times heroes had escaped from situations like this. Celluloid heroes. He should have left the hostel as soon as Colin arrived. His guts had told him to, but he'd ignored them.

That was the trouble when you had nowhere else to go.

Fallen teacher dies in crazed hell-hole. Tabloid heaven. Colin was right, the village would have its few weeks of fame. Colin's would last somewhat longer. James pulled at his bonds but they only cut into his hands. He could hear Colin moving around downstairs, then James heard him coming back up the stairs.

Alright, Jimbo? I'll be leaving you in a bit.

Colin knelt down besides James and tapped his shoulder, then, almost affectionately, brushed a hand over his head. James's spirits sunk even lower.

Yes, I think you're cold. Before Bluff Cove I always had a fascination for fires. I was the type of kid who was always lighting up the hillsides. I got a kick out of watching things burn, waiting for the engines to come, flashing lights, sirens. Made me feel like someone. Sometimes I think that burning ship was my punishment.

Colin stroked James's face this time, softly, with the backs of his fingers.

Never know, we might have been mates, if you hadn't rejected me back in that squat. I was desperate for someone, anyone, to be there for me then. I can still remember the disgust on your poncy face, but what goes around comes around. Are you a believer, James?

In what?

In God. The Almighty. A supreme being.

I don't know.

Don't you think it's make your mind up time? I believe. In something. Maybe in just purpose, the force that makes it all happen. From mad bastards like me to trapped bastards like you, to useless bastards like Billy here. You know what Tibetans think, people shouldn't have to work for some paradise in the next life, they should have it in the present, the here and now. That makes total sense to me.

And this is your way of attaining it?

Could be. The voices, maybe they are God, eh? That's

it. He's inside all of us. Then again, He might be dead. I started reading some philosophy stuff once. Some German geezer took that view. Said life was all about power.

It's been misquoted. Nietzsche said God is dead and we have killed him.

Did he now? College boy teacher talking, is he? Can't help it, can you, even when you're trussed up like a fucking chicken. Killed Him, eh? I like the sound of that, Jimbo. That means there's truly no hope. How right is that?

Untie me, Colin. We can talk. There's still time.

You're a trier, Jim, I'll give you that. No, there's no time. None at all.

Billy wasn't useless, James said quietly. His life made sense to him.

Colin shrugged.

It doesn't matter now, does it? It's over for him. I've done him a favour. I'm doing you a favour. Taking away the pain. The struggle...

Colin closed his eyes and rocked on his heels. He started up with his military humming again, then a snippet of *Whisky in the Jar*.

For a moment, James doubted that anyone else existed for Colin, then his face changed again, and he came back to the present, and the job in hand.

Go forward and faith will come to you. Maybe that's what I really believe, Colin said.

James looked at him blankly.

Here's some education for *you*. A guy called Gauss said that. Bet you don't know who he was, do you?

No.

German. Mathematician. Astronomer. Genius. When I was stationed in Germany I used to take off when I had leave. Just drive around. Anywhere where there wasn't any other squaddies around. Went to Brunswick once. Just liked the name. It reminded me of the old record label. Saw a statue of an old guy in a square there, you know the type of thing, solid Victorian gent with a book in his hand. Bit like those in Cardiff, the ones with traffic cones and pigeons' shit on their heads. I checked him out. His stuff was way over my head but that one sentence has stuck – go forward and the faith will come to you.

Do you call this going forward?

Absolutely. The voices love it. It all makes sense in here

Colin rubbed at his skull again with his hands, as if he was trying to tease out the voices, one by one.

I was fifty the other day, he muttered. Age, it's a bastard. Do you know what I think, James?

Nina had also passed fifty a few days ago. All the good stuff came back into James's head, their early days of passion and hope. He wanted to reach out and grab them back, but his fall was staring back at him sharper than ever. Maybe Colin was the endgame.

James was trying to fight off the drink, stay alert, and come up with another plan, but it was getting harder by the minute. He just wanted to sleep, then wake up from this nightmare. He didn't answer and received a sharp kick in the thigh.

I said do you know what I think?

What?

That nothing matters. None of it matters. A man scratches away, busts a gut to get on, to get money, then thinks he's got it made. He hasn't. One day he gets up, looks in the mirror and thinks he's old, and nothing he's done is worth it.

James tried to think of an answer that was safe, but Colin did not need one. As they continued to rub at his shaven head, Colin's fingers began to work a bloody furrow. He was creating another tattoo and a thin line of blood ran down his head to seep into the dragon. Its eyes became redder.

The army was a place to run to, Colin continued,

armies always have been. Before, I was just running for the sake of it. I was a headless chicken kid at first, but by the time I was twelve I'd worked out that running was the best way to fight back. Against *her* and all the fucking Daddies. To disappear is like a continual punishment. They don't know if you're dead. They don't know how you died. They go through horror stories in their mind. Nothing like vanishing to stir up guilt. Even my old girl was capable of that, if it was washed down by a couple of lagers. They'd get me back, and she'd promise the earth. Say she'd get a job, get us a bit more, get rid of the latest tosser. Then it would start again, until I was old enough to get out for good.

Is your mother still alive?

Maybe. I went back once. When I was nineteen. Some weasel she had there nearly shit himself when he saw the size of me. Rolled off the sofa and spilt his can. I didn't stay around much longer than him. I just wanted her to see...

Colin's words tailed off and he stopped moving around the room. He stood in its centre and noticed the blood on his fingers.

Blood on my hands – that's kinda right, don't you think? Like that Macbeth guy. The voices started when I left home. Didn't notice them too much at first. I always did have an overactive mind, thinking all the time, and I thought it was just the glue, I was into that at the time. Then they began to talk, and I began to listen. Later they started to think for me, suggest things. I tried to keep them under control, said nothing about it. The blokes in my squad just thought I was weird and they let me be. Safer for them.

They really got going in Ireland, and by the time The Falklands came along they were well settled. You know when you hear that bunch of wasters in parliament, when they show them on the news, all jabbering on, that's how it was in my head. Bluff Cove was the final push they needed. They seemed to burst out then, and afterwards they were rampant. They have been ever since, apart from a few months in that hospital, and even then they learned to work around any treatment I got. I don't know if they're talking now, or me… they are me…

Colin punched at the sides of his head with both fists, and almost stumbled. For a moment his mask dropped and anguish passed across his face. James sensed that some part of him was trying to fight back, a pocket of sanity trying to burst its chains and cast off his potted fragments of knowledge, his cracked philosophy funded by madness. The moment passed.

Like the ape house in here, Jimbo. Crazy chatter all the time. My own private parliament. Not to worry anyway. We're all going up soon. You know about the caldera in Yellowstone Park, in the US of fucking A? The super volcano. It's long overdue to blow. The world will be covered in ash. It'll die a slow, grey death, and the people in it. Even the rich won't escape. Then something else might crawl out of the sea and start it all again. Make less of a mess of it.

Colin examined James a final time, pushing back the hair that was worrying James's wounded eye, and resting a hand on his shoulder for a moment.

Make less of a mess of it, he repeated in a whisper.

Colin left the room, turning to offer a salute as he did so

Dont worry, he said, the things we fear the most have already happened to us… death is something we all manage. Bye then, James Read. See you in hell, if there is one.

Maybe this is a preview of it, James thought. He heard Colin rattle a key in the lock. James tried to get up but could only roll on the floor. Out on the streets in the last few years he'd realised life was capable of doing anything to you, but this topped it all. His brief glimpse of better things in the last few weeks had been a false dawn, all part of the torture.

There'd been many times when James had thought it would be better for his life to end. Better for him, better for Nina, better for the girls. He'd stood on bridges, stared at pill bottles, once balanced on a high cliff whipped by the wind, destiny tugging at him, mesmerized by the rhythm of waves striking the rocks below, but had always pulled back.

Now James wanted to live. He wanted it so much he could smell it. To be alive like he'd been just hours ago on the ridge top. To move on to better times and deny this man.

He rolled onto his back, and stared at his room. He'd hardly noticed it before but now he registered every detail. Its cracked and flaking paint, its undulations of wear and patterns of nicotine stains, the central light in its cheap, pink plastic shade. The colour of flesh. He saw a dead spider in a corner, encased in its own web, the task of living through the winter abandoned. His eye turned to the window and the shabby curtains that framed it, whorls of faded red and black, then his meagre collection of books on its sill, dog-eared and faded by the sun. James took in the fake mahogany world of his tall wardrobe and his few other pieces of equally worn furniture. For a moment, despite his wounded eye, pounding head and semi-drunk state, all was pin-sharp, as if his system was sucking in a final series of images.

James pushed his way to the door to check that it was locked. It was and he only succeeded in punishing his punched head. He heard Colin leave the hostel, closing the front door quietly. His heavy footsteps echoed on the pavement of the deserted street. They stopped outside the bedroom window. James sensed the man was looking up, then Colin walked on, his steps fading away into the night. James tracked each one.

James's clear-sighted vision was short-lived. Things were blurring again, it was difficult to see out of his right eye, impossible to see out of the left. It had bunched into bruised flesh, and felt like Colin's fist was still in his face. He had rainbow vision and was seeing in colours, mainly reds, and something wet was running into his eyes. He shook his head and drops of blood showered him. More pain followed, it pressed against the side of his head like another blow and the rainbow danced around.

Billy had no trouble with either eye. They were both open and they looked through James from their weird angle on the floor. Billy had been a small man, now he looked like a boy, his arm jutting out at an angle, like a warning heeded too late. A red island was forming around his head, getting darker all the time. It merged with the design on the Wilton. It had been a good carpet, once, now its fading patterns had taken on new life. New blood.

James's breath came in short gasps now, but this time something other than asthma was affecting his chest. He sniffed the air. Sniffed again. Smoke. It was beginning to seep through the gap under the door. James tugged at the cords again. They cut at his wrists. Colin had tied him well but this time there was a slight movement, just enough to rotate a hand a little. Just enough to rub away skin, and dig into his flesh.

Downstairs must be well alight. Colin must have set a fire below so that the flames could work their way up to the hapless creature above. Locking the bedroom door to stretch out James's fate. Very symbolic.

The man would be out in the darkness somewhere, maybe in a place where he could watch the scene he'd created unfold. A devil watching his hellish fire, proud of his handiwork, content that he'd taken his childhood arsons to what was for him a logical conclusion. German mathematics, Celtic myths, Roman poetry, and Christ knows what else joining with the voices to bang away at his head. The mad bastard.

Something small exploded downstairs but there was no

205

one around to hear it. If only the house next door wasn't empty, if only the hostel wasn't on the end of a row, if only he'd followed his instincts with Colin and got out of the hostel. *If only*. The story of his life. If only always meant it was too late.

There would still be people in the Hollybush, there always were. It just needed one straggling drunk, or a spitting boy to appear and overdose on the scene then shout excitedly into his mobile. At least Colin hadn't taken Deborah. James tried to hang onto this thought as he felt the heat increase.

He tried shouting as smoke started to collect in his chest, shouting and coughing alternately, but his voice was soon hoarse and losing power. A car went past in the street, but it didn't stop. James tried to stay alert but the alcohol was steadily working on him and he knew he did not have much time. A few minutes at best.

He worked at the cords again, clenching his teeth as his wrists were bloodied. Pain was a spur as his bonds moved further, despite being half-blinded and his lungs starting to fill up with smoke, James's mind fixed on a glimmer of hope. He managed to wriggle out a few fingers this time, and tried to heave himself up. He lunged at the window recess, and tried to catch his tied hands on the windowsill but fell back, striking the floor hard with a shoulder. James spun over and came face to face with Billy. Billy's blue eyes looked like they knew where they were going, and liked it. He was out of it for ever more, sleeping the big sleep, dead and about to be cremated in one. For one deranged moment James envied him.

Colin had made a better job of his ankles, they wouldn't move at all, he was essentially crippled, but James had reached crisis point. In a few moments he'd be joining Billy, but his death would be far worse than a one-punch end. James rolled around again on the floor and this time managed to get up onto his knees. Lurching up at the

windowsill a second time he knew there'd be no chance of a
third. He managed to grab an end of it. For a few long
seconds he thought his fingertips would slip off but they
held. James gave thanks for the sill's cracked and rotting
frame and the hold it gave him. He gave thanks for the lack
of double-glazing, something he'd moaned about when he
first fetched up at the hostel. Shutting his eyes tightly,
James charged at the window with head and shoulder. If he
fell back now it was all over.

*

An ambulance pushes past me. Its flashing light fills the car
for a few seconds and I feel very cold. I get out of the car.
The fire is clearly visible now, a terraced house a hundred
yards ahead is burning. Yellow-orange flames burst through
the roof, vivid in the dark night. People are being drawn to
it, running down the street to where the action is. Police are
trying to keep the crowd away, and make a path for the
ambulance. There's also a lot of activity in the middle of
the road outside the hostel. People are bending over
something, and police trying to make a cordon. A
policewoman beckons the ambulance towards this as I walk
forward. Perhaps it isn't the hostel. Anyway, it's Saturday
night, James would surely be out.

As I push closer I'm seeing his face that first time we
met, James holding court in the union bar. I'm seeing it
again as I'm stopped by a policewoman's arm. Seeing it
now. Barely recognisable, it's so battered, but it is James.
Lying twisted on the ground.

You can't go any further, the policewoman tells me.

That's my husband, I answer.

Her grip slackens.

Your husband?

Is he alive?

Yes.

The paramedics arrive. There's activity all around James. Fire-fighters are trying to quell the fire, unfurling hoses and aiming them at the hostel, which is now an inferno. The terrace next to it is alight too. Flames leap roofs and start to devour.

An excited crowd is milling around and I'm milling around with it. The police girl, for she's barely twenty-one, looks at me anxiously. She is still holding my arm.

I'll go and get the sergeant, she says.

There was three dossers living there, a voice shouts, where's the other two?

They go' no chance if they're still in there, shouts another.

'Course they ain't in there. They'll be out on the piss.

Tha' one who fell out the window was tied up. Hand an' foot 'e was.

Nah.

I'm telling 'u. I saw 'im fall out. We was running down from the Bush when we saw them flames. Out he come. Like 'e was shot out of a rocket. Smack on the bloody road. Lucky a car wasn't coming.

I feel my rubber legs giving way. This can't be happening. I'm part of a scene I can barely comprehend. Perhaps if I shut my eyes tight I'll wake up in my bed. James has given me plenty of nightmares before, God knows. Someone is talking to me, a tall man with a red face.

You're saying this man is your husband?

Uh, yes. James. James Read. I'm Mrs Read.

The paramedics have James on a stretcher now. He is close to me for the first time in nearly four years. I put a hand on a stretcher and the medics pause.

James, it's Nina. Can you hear me?

One side of his face is a badly cut mess but his right eye seems okay. He's looking at me with it.

James, it's Nina.

Under the blanket I see him move a hand slightly. I try

to hold it but am stopped.

Best not do that, love. We're not sure what exactly he's broken yet. Let us do our job, eh?

Will he…?

… the quicker we get him to hospital the better off he'll be.

Can I go with him?

Yes, of course.

An officer will follow on down, Mrs Read, the sergeant says. There are questions we'll need to ask.

I don't answer. There's nothing to say for I don't know anything.

I will have to tell the girls about this. I imagine Zoe's reaction all too well. She's just settling down in college, coming to terms with the last few years. For a moment I feel so angry with James. I don't know what's happened tonight but he's at the centre of it – he always is. I recognise the old mix of frustration, anger and despair then look at James's battered body again, and feel other things. I put a hand on his shoulder, very lightly and the eye steadies on me. He's trying to say something. I put my head close to his.

Is it you? he whispers.

Yes.

Nina. Are you dead too?

You're not dead, James. You're not going to die.

How are you here?

Never mind about that.

James tries to say something else but it doesn't get through his lips. The words end in a bloody dribble and the eye closes. The medic puts an oxygen mask over James's face and I hear his struggle to breathe. It reminds me of the nights when his asthma was bad. James standing by the bedroom window, wheezing, looking out at the night sky for answers when it was all going wrong. James moans over every bump in the road but we are in casualty very quickly.

It's a quiet Saturday night for them, apparently, but it still seems like bedlam to me. Walking wounded stumble around the war zone they have created. Some dazed, others loud, a few angry and loud. James is rushed through. I rush with him. People are very kind. They think I'm still his wife. I'm showered in *he'll be alrights* and *we'll look after him* from nurses and young doctors. One of these looks at James and quickly asks for the consultant.

As James is being assessed that sergeant arrives.

Mrs Read, we are trying to piece together what's happened tonight.

Is it true? Was James tied up?

Yes, he was. From what I can gather at this point he was thrown or fell from a bedroom window.

I feel the floor moving under me and the sergeant's steadying hand.

Look, let's sit down over there, he says.

He guides me to a chair in the corridor outside the treatment room. I can sense his thoughts. He's looking at the way I'm dressed and thinking of James living in the hostel.

We are divorced, I say quickly. I haven't seen James for three years.

Ah, I see.

Look, I want to be with my … with James.

Alright, Mrs Read, but CID will be along shortly. They'll want to know what you were doing outside that hostel at that time of night, if you hadn't seen your husband for three years.

I'd only just found out where he was living. James has been going through a bad patch. He's had problems.

So, you were going to see him?

No ….I don't know. I just wanted to see where he was living.

Late on a Saturday night?

Yes. Look, I really don't know anything about James's

current life.

We are interrupted by the consultant.

Mrs Read?

I feel like I'm in one of the hospital soaps Zoe so loves. The handsome consultant, the anxious wife, the dysfunctional family. Make-believe drama but tonight it's all real.

Will he be alright. He's not going to...?

The consultant holds up a calming hand. I notice his face is grey with tiredness and it looks as if he's lived in his suit for some time.

Mr Read is stable. He's got a number of broken bones. Left ankle, right leg, a few ribs, dislocated shoulder, and lots of glass cuts, but somehow his head kept away from the road. He must have bounced off it with his shoulder. In that respect he's been lucky, very lucky. None of the injuries are that serious on their own, but with this many it's the accumulation that's the problem. He'll be going up to theatre as soon as the team are ready for him.

Can I see him?

I'm offered a hopeful smile and am ushered through. James is festooned in wires and drips, but he's not alone. This is a place of sudden and unexpected suffering. A young girl is sobbing, almost noiselessly, her body trembling as she holds the hand of a boy who looks as if he's gone through a car windscreen. They are no older than Zoe.

James seems to be breathing calmly, the beats of his life counted out by the machine alongside him. He's even harder to recognise now, as his misshapen face takes on a life of its own. One side is a lurid bruise with little sign of his eye, the other lacerated with cuts from window glass.

He's not really conscious, a nurse says quietly, but all the signs are good.

I touch his hand and his eyes flutter slightly. His good one seems to focus on me for a moment and I feel his hand flex against mine. Then James is gone, wheeled away to theatre.

I'm standing in the corridor again, wondering what to do. I should phone the girls but don't feel up to it yet. I doubt if either will be too sober this time on a Saturday night. A man approaches, a plain-clothes policeman. He wants to talk to me.

*

James was being sliced but he sucked in fresh air. He could still see out of the one eye and he saw the black night, felt the slashes of rain. Orange lights revolved, he heard noises, voices, a woman screaming *Oh My God.* Other shouts. Maybe sirens. Maybe it was all in his head. Voices.

He pushed at the window again with head and shoulder, and the rotten frame gave way. James was through it and falling, and the books on the windowsill fell with him, each one a marker of his life. He tried to twist his head away from the ground as it rushed up to meet him in a black wave. It all seemed to take such a long time, but he passed through the wave, down many layers, to the darkness beneath.

It was his strangest dream. The usual casino, but everything had been altered. The fittings were more opulent, the pile of the carpets a deeper ruby red, the staff perfect as they smiled out invitations. James wasn't playing. He floated around, taking it all in, but not taking part. That was what was so strange. The scene was like a favourite painting, familiar, comfortable, but no longer a vital part of him. He watched a man win big. The man was his father, happy in a way he'd never been in life, throwing the chips up in the air as his eyes sparkled. James wanted to reach out for him but couldn't. He was leaving the casino behind without a glance back.

The dream was changing. He could smell the fire. Lots of images and noises were in his head. Colin's whisper was there, the quietest and clearest sound. James saw *Love and Hate* coming towards him but he floated away. Colin disappeared, his face getting smaller and smaller until it vanished. The pinprick of a shaven head was the last he saw of him.

James was on the hillside, on the land that had become his. Checking that each familiar marker was in place, and sucking in freedom in big gulps. Nina and the girls were approaching him. He blinked as they stepped out of the sunlight, all smiles.

James … James?

James tried to open his eyes. He wasn't sure where he was. He heard his name again, and vaguely felt a slight pressure on his arm. One eye began to work. He saw shapes clustered around him.

He's coming round, a voice said.

Wherever he was, it wasn't a casino. Suddenly the dream was very far away. A place in the distant past.

James …?

He recognised Nina's voice. Then he recognised her face. Then Clare's and Zoe's. Blinking hard, he wasn't sure if this was another dream, but the touch was real, Nina's hand on his arm, and they weren't on any hillside.

His brain managed to engage with his voice.

It is you?

Yes. We are all here.

The girls smiled encouragingly.

You've been very ill, James, Nina said.

Have I?

A man appeared in his vision. He talked slowly and explained about the many broken bones, the various operations that had taken place, but James didn't really take it in. He was more interested that he was in the presence of the entire Read family for the first time in an age. Then came pain. It was all over him but not sharp, more a dulled sense that he was hurting.

The worst is over now, Nina added. It will take time, but you *will* get better.

It was coming back to him. The hostel, the fire, dead Billy. Then Colin. James tensed and the pain surged through him.

Where's Colin? he managed to ask.

Don't worry about that, now, Nina answered.

Do the police know about him? Have they caught him?

Yes, it's all been dealt with.

The reply puzzled him. Dealing wasn't catching, James thought, as his family faded away again.

Colin watched the fire from his outpost on the hillside. He'd prepared it a week ago, when the voices had made the decision and was pleased in the way he'd camouflaged the tent, making it blend into the landscape, even in winter. It was brown and olive, like his battle dress. Sitting in front of it, on his rock, he looked down on the fiery scene, at the hostel that was now a funeral pyre. The police were coming. Their blue lights worked their way up the valley road, followed by the rest of the cavalry. They noisily announced their arrival but it was too late for any of them to do much, other than tidy up. Colin leant his head to one side to listen to the main voice.

Its not hate, Colin. It's love. Remember the poem, your favourite. Yes, that's the one, hate and love... and the pain is crucifixion. No, you're not mad. Don't go there. You are right. It was a necessary action. You had to make a statement. Yes, a quest.

Time passed, but Colin did not move. He sat still as a statue, impervious to the weather. The action in the village was calming and flames no longer came from the hostel. Fires die, like people.

James and Billy would be found. What was left of

214

them. The rope he'd used to tie James might have been burned completely away, it might not. Colin didn't care. The thoughts of the police would turn towards him either way. No matter. They did not exist. Nothing existed outside his head. Not any more. It was just faces, colours, smells.

Colin sat with his knees hunched up against his chest. He began to sway slightly from side to side. He was many different places in his head. Bits of a former life came to him. He saw himself joining up, bursting with pride at achieving his goal, getting his ticket out from his wretched estate life and his mother's whining hopelessness. He loved it all, at first. The routine, the bullshit of order and polish, the purpose that was no purpose at all. He liked the other boys looking up to him, recognising his power. It was crazy, but it all made sense to the young Colin.

He grabbed at these memories, and the voices were stilled for a moment, as old bits of happiness were paraded in front of them. There had been some, even for him. Early army life, meeting the wife in Aldershot. She'd been a looker, a barmaid in one of the local pubs there. He loved to show her photos to the boys, but it didn't last long. Colin found that out well before the Falklands. Things had already changed when he came back from his first Irish tour and that fucking war put an end to it. She moved on to other, more promising situations. There were no kids.

Colin rubbed at his eyes with a muscular arm, and felt the cold night for the first time. Things were settling down, the village quieting, with just the vague residue of smoke in the main street. He realised it had stopped raining and was much colder and he was being buffeted by a keen wind. It made him think he was back on that bastard island, bent under the weight of his pack as wind howled down off those grassy slopes. His hands flexed around an invisible weapon. It was a shame Wales wasn't the States, he would have liked to build up an arsenal. It would have possibilities. The voices would like it.

The nightmares that had haunted him as a kid had become real in the south Atlantic. Now he lived them every day. Those images had become part of him, kept alive by the voices. They were experts on the war. They'd made a film of it, which they showed him all the time. His head was one great big cinema, but he was the only one watching the show. The junk they gave him in the hospital dimmed the screen but the film never stopped running. He just told the shrinks that it had.

Colin remembered Read coming to that squat. A middle-class tosser who'd fucked up, and thrown everything away. A self-pitying bugger. They were the ones who usually got all the help. All they had to do was bleat. It was a time when he was outside the system. Outside everything. His head almost shaking apart. Read was different to the usual street shit. Colin thought he might be able to talk to him. Even make a friend, but the guy was true to his class. He'd lost it big time after that and had gone inside again. There was no way Read didn't have kids. The guy must have thought he was taking to a moron, like that runt Billy. It would be easy to find them.

Yes, the voices said. *Very easy, for a man like you.* The night grew blacker, and more bitter, but he managed to fall into a light sleep. He'd learned to do this in any conditions, it was a trick of his old trade.

Colin came to with a start. He knew that sound so well. The heavy drone and thump of blades pushing air. At first he thought it was in his head, but the chopper was going over above him, quite low. He looked up and saw its searchlight probing the hillside. They were looking for him already. Colin wondered if Read had survived, lived to tell the tale. No, that was impossible.

He was so tired. Suddenly a lassitude was crushing him, making it hard to think. Hard to listen. He pushed at the sides of his head with his fists, making his scratches bleed again. It felt like someone had a buzz-saw in there, working away. Colin wanted out. It wasn't a decision, it certainly wasn't a message from inside. It was instinct and he knew all about that. His life had been saved by it more than once. He hadn't turned a corner one time in Ireland, when everything was kicking off there. He'd felt the hairs on the back of his neck prickle and come to life on what should have been a routine patrol. They'd become his antennae of danger. The young kid in front of him had no such awareness. He took a rifle round to the top of his head. Bits of his brain and helmet spattered Colin but he lived on

He stood up suddenly, arms outstretched, willing the searchlight to find him. It didn't. The helicopter was further along the ridge, spraying out its light blindly. He'd surprised the voices. They were struck dumb as Colin left the tent and walked upwards. His head seemed to be clearing, the buzz-saw calming down, like it did when he popped the pills, the ones he hadn't taken in weeks.

He wanted to go back. Start again. A fair start. Colin wasn't sure if he was talking to himself out loud. The rain was back. His eyes were wet with it, or maybe something else. It was turning stormy. Stuff was clashing overhead, a touch of thunder. He saw Billy crumpling under his fist, dying so easily. He hadn't meant to kill, but the voices had cheered. It was a result. They told him to deal with Read, make him the next target. It was necessary. *Go on Colin, he's the one who spurned you. He made things worse. Put you in hospital.*

Faces of the dead floated through his mind. So many faces. He saw his mates burning in the hold of that ship, the snivelling, wind-pinched faces of Argy kids as they thrust their hands up. Read slowly roasting. Colin tried to shake his head free of them. He needed the voices back; he was glad they had gone.

He skimmed over a broken wall, and pushed on to the top of the ridge. The helicopter would turn and come back down the valley. They'd have night vision, and the machine would see him even if men didn't. He was scrabbling over shale and loose rock now, nearing the summit.

Colin walked along the ridge top until something told him to stop. A long time ago a gash had been cleaved in the rock face here and a small cliff created. He peered down into the darkness, shielding his face from the driving rain. Then it was not so dark. The helicopter's searchlight picked out the rocks below. About sixty feet below. Colin stood near the edge and raised his arms again. This time they had to see him. They did. He was caught in the beam.

White noise in his head. Hard to distinguish anything. Voices talking, but amongst themselves. A babble that no longer needed him. He'd been excluded, a final betrayal that he'd been waiting for all his life. Colin was slipping outside it all. Outside his head. Drifting away. Drifting away was good.

The searchlight steadied on him. He was centre stage. A star at last. He felt the air pushed into his face as the craft got nearer. Colin steadied himself on the cliff edge, heavy body on light feet. His life balanced.

There were no more voices. Then no more noise. He could see but not hear. Everything was shut off. No past. No future. Just now. Life was always just now. Calm. Peace. A peace he'd never known before, so intense he felt he could sink into it. All the anger was gone, it had drained away to another place. Colin felt tenderness for those he'd killed. He wanted to join with them, to find out if any of it made sense, if there really was a better world. He saw his mother in the kitchen of their ramshackle house, saw her how he'd wanted her to be. His hands wanted to touch her, and they stretched out. Love and Hate probed the night.

Feet took him forward. Colin slipped away, a gentle glide into the void. Caught by the light his fall seemed to take for ever, and he savoured every stretched out moment.

*

James has been unconscious for three days. We thought we'd lost him a few times. They even asked if I wanted a priest. I didn't know. Three years ago that would have made James, the dedicated atheist, laugh, but I don't know what he believes in now. Religion wasn't necessary, for James rallied and the danger passed but this showed me how final our parting was. It shouldn't have been like that. I should not have allowed him to disappear, that was *his* weakness, but a weakness that was contagious.

He didn't say anything to me, Zoe mutters.

He was barely conscious, love.

Rest will be paramount now, the consultant says. It will be a long haul back.

Zoe scowls at him for stating the obvious, but manages to keep quiet.

Get some rest, I tell the girls, and something to eat. I'll stay here.

I want to stay, Zoe said.

Nothing is going to happen. Dad will sleep now.

Dad. It sounds odd. The most I've been able to manage since the divorce is *your father.* How remarkable life is. James always had the ability to bring down destruction on his head, but for it to happen the night when I was ending my first new relationship in twenty-five years, is so bizarre. I added to it by going up there. Perhaps there is such a thing as fate.

The papers have been full of what's happened, full of James, the local ones especially. I've been hiding from reporters for days. I can't blame them, it's a riveting story. They've picked up on James's past, what he was, what he became. They've pestered me and the girls for details of our lives together but have got nowhere. The national tabloids have concentrated more on this Colin Childs creature. He seems to be the monster of their dreams. They've done low life, and deprivation, in that odious, righteous, and dishonest way they thrive on. The valley has copped it, very unfairly. Someone wants to start a campaign to close all hostels. The people who live in other worlds and know least about it have the most to say, as always. Talking heads talk and rarely think, but it's quieting down now. I try not to think too much about that night, how horrific it must have been. Police check on James every so often, waiting for the chance to talk to him. It will be at least a few more days before they can do this.

Adrian has phoned, all genuine concern, asking if there's anything he can do. There's nothing, apart from giving Clare all the time off she needs. He should be glad he's out of all this but I doubt that he is. Adrian is a born helper, or would be if he had the chance. He thought he had one with me and I hope he gets another, but I don't think about it that much. With James fighting for his life I've become selfish for the Read family.

I wonder if we can all function in a more normal fashion when James gets better. That might be the good that comes out of all this but I have no idea how it will work out. Whether James will even want me around when he convalesces. I can accept that, as long as he wants the girls. This has been a huge shock to us all, and it has taken something away from me. I've fought for years to keep the lid on the hurt James caused, but now it seems much more distant. Our minds have focused on James's survival, and we are all better for it. Only James could salve in such a extreme way.

There's been so much time to think in the hours I've sat besides him. I keep going back to how it must have been for him as a child. His strange and distant parents, James as a youngster washing up against their stunted emotions. I don't think he really knew who he was by the time we met, he'd built up a fantasy world which he tried to break out of but never quite made it. Perhaps he will now.

The police have been trying to piece together what happened that night but James is the only one who really knows. I'm trying not to read the tabloids but Zoe pours over them. She's been all over the place since the news broke. She does peaks and troughs as well as her father but is calmer now that she can see him visibly improving. Zoe insists on sitting with him for long periods, holding his hand, talking to him, making up for lost time. At last she has the captive father she always craved.

Zoe fills me in on psychopaths, schizophrenics, alcoholic gamblers, all the troubled histories of people gone wrong. James's world of the last three years. Maybe all his dreams, out-of-step ideas, and stubborn diffidence collided that night in the hostel, but he's still here.

*

The bleep was far away, like a signal barely heard. It was calling James, but he didn't want to go there. He wanted to stay with the dream, which came back to him easily as he slept. He'd left the casino, feeling light, airy, and released. His father was also outside and had been joined by his mother, larger than they'd ever been in life. James could hear himself talking to them, but could still look on. He tried to explain how it had all gone wrong, why he'd gambled. He told them each bet was a plea, a compensation for what they hadn't given him, a desperate attempt to change things, to inject purpose into a life they'd made a sham. They looked at him with a kind blankness, his father fussing with his pipe, his mother continuously knitting, but it didn't matter. Not any more. James felt a sense of freedom, for the first time in his life. His parents faded away.

Nina was talking to him. The girls were with her. They were children, then not so young, then almost grown-up. He saw a life with them without any major wrong turns, the life he should have had. Colin was standing behind them. James wanted to shout out a warning but there was no need. Colin was smiling, a genuine smile, and waving good-bye with a hand. James could not see the tattoos, the dragon was gone, *Love and Hate* were gone. The bleep was closer now, louder, more insistent. This time he responded to it.

He tried to focus. Blurred images and soft colours were becoming clearer but he wasn't sure if he was awake or not. Probably not.

Dad? Can you hear me? Can you see us?

It had been so long since he'd heard Zoe's voice. The sweet sharpness of it, the way it rose and fell so easily. James opened his eyes fully, both of them.

Do you know where you are, James? Nina said.

No, he didn't. Not at first. He could barely move, something was pressing in on him, a tight band around his chest.

You're in hospital, Dad, Clare said.

James blinked. Zoe was very close to him. He saw the young child he'd known shine through, then was amazed by how much she'd changed.

Hello, Dad, Zoe said, long time no see. Fancy meeting in a place like this.

You've grown up on me, he managed to murmur

Zoe touched his hand lightly, then her grip became firmer as she felt him respond. It was one of the few parts of him that was unhurt. James turned his head, very slowly. He was in a private room. As his brain turned itself back on, memory was activated.

Colin? Where is he? Not still on the loose?

Don't worry about that now, Nina said. It's over, James.

They've caught him?

Yes.

Clare smiled at him and held his other hand.

They found Billy? James asked.

Yes, Nina said. Poor soul.

A doctor entered the room and told them James should

get some more rest. Nina left with the girls, Zoe the most reluctant to go. James had thoughts about everything, that crazy last night in the hostel, the crazy last few years, crazy Colin, but he felt his eyes closing again, still scarcely believing the Read family had been in his presence.

In the corridor Deborah watched the Reads leave. The last week had been very difficult. Press everywhere, questions asked, and a torrid time in work. The tabloids hadn't taken long to build up a hysterical picture of Colin. They dragged up all the stuff from the Falklands, and James's history was another gift. Billy added to the mix and Colin's suicide iced the cake. You couldn't make this up, a London hack told her, it's got the lot. All the *why was he let out* stuff was being aired. Shrinks and social workers were being kicked again. At least only her professional opinion had been sought. There were so many juicy bits to the tale that her evening with James had been overlooked by everyone other than the police.

Deborah had tried twice to see James, but his family was always there. She'd witnessed his old life. She did not want to get into a conversation with Nina Read for maybe James and his wife would be re-born after this, and his marriage with it. It went like that sometimes and might be a good ending, she told herself, best for everyone, but there was not much conviction in the thought. She'd seen more than a few colleagues develop relationships with clients before, and had always disapproved, to the point of incredulity, but there was something about James that had got to her from the start, if she was honest. By the time she'd dropped him off that night, she'd already made the decision to see where it led. A liaison with a scruffy, ageing little-boy-lost who'd ruined his life and had zero prospects. Good choice, Deborah. There was no sense to it at all, but she'd been around long enough to know that life didn't rarely offered sensible choices. She'd thought she'd made a few of them before but they'd ended in chaos. Why not start with chaos this time, she thought, and see what happened. Then came that night, their first night. How weird was that?

Deborah hung around, and stopped the consultant as he left James's room. The doctor thought she was there in some official capacity and told her that James had regained consciousness and was on the mend. That was enough for her for now, and Deborah followed Nina and the girls out of the hospital, keeping a discreet distance. His daughters were very attractive, and his wife, ex-wife, had aged well, too, all things considered. Seeing them made James's downfall all the more tragic.

*

The fuss about that hostel night has died down. Fortunately, for us, new horrors come along very quickly for the newspapers.

Clare's back in work, and Zoe's just about managing to stay in college, though she's down every weekend. As James mends, he goes over that night with the police more than once. He was told the full story as soon as he was well enough. Colin's suicide surprised him at first. I felt relief at the news, but James has told me he feels more sympathy than hatred for the man. I ask him why on a visit alone.

I don't have the energy to hate, James tells me, or the need. The devils eating away at Colin's head came spilling out that night. He should have got more help. What were my problems compared to his?

We've got something back through all this. We are talking again, and you are talking to your daughters. Maybe that would not have happened without that night. Don't live in the past any more, James. You always have, you know.

No one will ever know me like you, Nina.

That's some poor soul saved, then.

James attempts a smile, more a wince of pain, and

dozes off again. He's been spared the sharp end of media attention by his recuperation. It will take many weeks. Lots of pain, of all kinds, and many bridges to rebuild. For us all to rebuild. Zoe wants the most reassurance. It's quite sweet the way she guards her own space with James. She wants to make sure she's got him back and that he'll stay back. I think he will.

It is a few weeks before James asks me about Adrian. On a day when snow presses at his hospital window, and sticks on the outside sill.

He's no longer on the scene, I tell him,

Didn't last long, James mutters.

No … he was a nice man, but not right for me.

Oh.

James stares at me. His eye is quite healed now, both of them are brighter than they've been since that night. His hand reaches out and touches my face.

You still look young, despite me. I probably look more like your father than an ex-husband now.

Don't be silly. James, you won't disappear again?

No.

You've done a great job with the girls, Nina.

You were around for most of that time.

I was hardly a hands-on father, was I?

You were as hands-on as you ever could be. What do you think you will do, when you are better?

Good question. I don't think I could ever go back to schools. The kids will have too much on me now. Maybe adult learning, something like that. At least I won't be going back to another hostel.

James holds a letter up with his good arm.

They've allocated me a housing association flat. That's what fame does for you, I suppose. Look, about this Adrian chap, you haven't cut off your nose to spite your face, have you?

I smile inwardly, and am glad that James retains some

vanity. He would not be James otherwise.

What do you mean?

Well, after all that's happened.

No. That was the strange thing. We'd gone out for a meal, that night. I finished it then. It was something I drifted into. I should have thought it out more, but too much has happened for me to feel guilty about it.

James does not look convinced. He's improving each day, the ingrained tiredness on his face is fading, and now that he's started shaving again, he doesn't look half so old as he seems to think. I have a glimpse of the younger man, but that pretend-extrovert seems long gone. There is a seriousness and substance to James now that might be his salvation, if it sticks. It might be just the reaction to what has happened to him but it would be ironic if his character could change at this late stage. Ironic and vital. They say people never change but I don't believe that. I never have.

Neither of us has asked the other to start again. I can never be sure what was really in my mind that night, what might have happened if it had been just another Saturday night and I'd seen James in that hostel, or fished him out of the local pub. Perhaps it was an echo of the past that I needed to get out of my system, or a moment of panic brought on by the experience of Adrian. I think each of us knows that we can never go back. There is a mutual realisation that that particular bridge will never be re-built; too much water has passed under it. It's a realisation so strong neither of us has to voice it. It would be better not to try. James has the girls to consider, or re-consider, and I don't want him to lose sight of them again. That is a plus. A huge plus. I'm more positive about Zoe's future than I've been since the divorce. She's caught up with all her college work. In a way what has happened to James has freed all of us up. It has taken something this big to move us on. The Read family's personal cataclysm. Now James and I might maintain a kind of friendship. It won't be easy, it never was, but I think we'll manage it, now.

*

It was a warm day in early May which spoke of renewal, and soft, fleece-like clouds did not threaten a pale blue sky. Even the bare hillside ridge was softened by new growth, clusters of shoots pushing their way through the shale like green fists. James had taken his time. There was still some stiffness in one leg, and pain in a hip when he climbed, but he had reached the top. Again. He sat on a large slab of stone, amongst sheep that kept one eye on him and the other on their grazing. He was on the far side of the valley to Pete's hanging tree. The far side to Colin's drop. That was a place of dramatic ends, he wanted this side to be of new beginnings.

James looked down on a valley half-hidden in a wispy haze. He had the best of the sun. It sprayed down on him, gradually clearing the haze. Lambs ran at him sideways, veering away at the last moment. They were still young enough to have a lack of suspicion of man. He savoured the peace.

James tried to read the regional paper he'd brought with him, though the wind interfered. They were still talking about a super casino in Cardiff. He'd first heard of this when he'd been at his lowest, glancing through a scrap of some of Glasgow Paul's newspaper bedding. James had read about gleaming flagships coming to town, and the cold had gone away for a while. People wanted to support him, build him a huge church, a place where he could worship at the foot of the Wheel. Then he'd prayed he'd be able to get in, enter his paradise, and was lost in these prayers until Glasgow Paul snatched the page out of his hand, spraying him with bits of red wine as he shouted in James's face — *thas ma fookin' bed you're readin', Jimm*y.

James read about it again in hospital. It was a few

227

weeks after Christmas. The girls had inundated him with papers and magazines, Zoe even digging out some of his old novels. He'd been amazed Nina still had them, and equally amazed that he was able to read a few. James looked at an artist's impression of the casino. Local dignitaries were excited. They talked with fervour about *this great opportunity.* He wondered if the world really was going mad, or just confirming that it always had been. The rich falling into shiny vacuums, the poor desperate to join them.

Convalescence was the best thing that could have happened to him. It gave him a quality of time he'd never had before. At first his daughters were shadowy figures at the edge of his bed. Then they became clearer, and began to become part of him again.

It was three weeks before he had the full picture of what had happened that night. Colin's suicide was the final piece of a dreaded jigsaw. For Pete, Billy and Colin, the hostel had proved a place of savage ends, but James had another chance. Fate, or luck, had given it to him. Colin would like to think that insanity could be positive.

James took a photograph from his wallet, taken by Nina. He was standing outside the hospital, Zoe and Clare either side of him, Zoe with a proprietary hand on his shoulder. Three people staring into a shared future. He stretched out on the ground. It was hard, but still comforting to him. James closed his eyes and felt the sun's heat on his eyelids as he gently turned the photograph around in his hands. The lambs lost interest in him and moved away. James was alone and it was very quiet. The ridge top was too high for road noise to carry up, breeze sifting through the shale made the only sound.

Colin's night- he'd always think of it as that- was six months ago, and James had come back to the village for the first time since then. He felt it was necessary. All was peaceful as he walked past the Hollybush, down the street to the hostel, his legs getting more reluctant as he neared it. It had been boarded up whilst they considered rebuilding it.

He stopped outside and breathed in hard. It still smelt of the fire, there was an acridity in the blackened stone that might never leave it. Grey corrugated sheets had been nailed to its windows and front door, but what was left of the roof was exposed to the sky. James measured his fall from window to road with his eyes and wondered how he was still alive. The sheets were free of graffiti, which surprised him. Perhaps the memory was too raw for everyone.

As he stood on the hostel steps James saw Pete's welcoming hand, heard Billy's fractured singing, and Colin's voice of that night came to him. The twisted hatred, pain and ultimately fear that fused his words. James felt no bitterness. Six months of healing had left only relief, and gratitude for life.

Oi butt!

James looked across the road to the phone box. There was a gathering of boys there that he hadn't noticed appear, so lost was he in his thoughts. He remembered some, others were new. They crossed the street and approached him. The lankiest one came up close, walking in a way that brought back memories of Colin, long strides in regulation striped bottoms. James wondered if hell had a coda.

He could read the boy's tattoos, count his eyebrow piercings and note the ripples on his cropped head. James tensed, feeling the pain in his leg. A hand was stuck out.

Put it there, mate.

Even the hand was tattooed, but not with *Love and Hate*. This hand liked *Mam and Jade*, and a motif of moon and stars.

James took the hand hesitantly and shook it. The others came over, all talking at once. One tapped him on the back.

Nice one, buttie, Lanky said.

Seen it all on the telly, another added. You're 'im, an'

you.

I seen 'u dive out tha' fuckin' window, Lanky said. As if 'u were shot from a bloody gun. I was the first one there, like.

'E must 'ave nine lives', another added.

James wondered if he was now a celebrity, in this place that had so little, and the boys wanted to share in it, to have a piece of it rub off on them. He was offered smiles, a cigarette, a half drunk bottle of Coke. It was as if he was looking at the boys for the first time. Looking at them without bias or quick value judgements. At the faces behind the regulation uniform of the poor. That was all they were. Poor, born in the wrong place at the wrong time. The poor always had been.

Even in a new millennium, it seemed to James that society was arranged on much the same lines. He'd lost sight of this when he'd first come to the village, supported by his dislocation, and fall from grace. Now he looked at the boys closely, and saw a mix of guile, boredom, and even innocence, already tinged with the buds of despair, but these kids *were* together, like the old domino players in the pub. The village was still together, despite everything that had been done to it. It was like an old prize-fighter, bruised, battered, but still on its feet. In the years he'd lived with Nina and the girls, in a new-build cul-de-sac, they'd gained just a fleeting knowledge of their neighbours. It was a place where people watched but rarely connected, each house locked into the rituals of advancement. The sterility of the place had once gnawed away at him, but as time passed so did the feeling. Now he'd escaped, and he wanted to keep it that way.

James stayed on the ridge top until the weather grew fresher. As he made his way down, he fixed the village in his head, perhaps for the last time. At this distance bright brickwork looked like dabs of paint from an artist's brush. Terraces curved in rows against the hillside, sprouting unison grey satellite dishes as they took in the new world. All colliding in a crazy geometry that defined the whole valley. A design that spoke of hurried need but had led to massive collective spirit. Dissipated now, but not vanquished. James hoped it would always remain, despite the decay that was all around him. He thought it would.

His old friends the pigeons were out again, full of joie-de-vivre as they hurtled past him, turning in a sharp angle to come back for another look. Their usual arrow formation sped low over his head, as a dozen sets of eyes looked ahead. James heard their wings working the air, and felt some of their energy settle on himself. He breathed easy today, despite the climb, and felt a lightness of being that was new to him. Gambling was still in his gut, it always would be, a permanent regret that could never be undone, but it felt a long time ago. Between now and Colin's night lay reunion with his daughters, understanding with Nina, and a convalescence of mind as much as body.

It seemed all too neat. Part of James waited for this new man to crash and burn, to wake up in the street again, in the hostel looking up at Colin, or, worst of all, in a school facing a class. This was his weak, addictive part telling him it would always be around, but at least he knew it now, by God he did.

James passed the Hollybush. He smelt the ale, heard the low murmur of voices but did not go in. Old commandments passed through his head but he did not call one up. He did not need it.

Deborah was waiting for him. She was standing by the side of her car, taking in the sunshine. Her long hair streamed down the back of her light blue dress, and James stood and watched her for a moment, still not quite believing it.

You're late, Deborah said, and you've switched your mobile off – again.

James smiled and tapped his pocket guiltily.

Sorry.

Did you get to the top? Deborah asked.

Yes. Took a bit longer than I thought.

But you did it, though.

Yes.

Deborah turned and glanced down the road to the burnt out hostel, then met his eyes.

Seen enough?

I think so.

Come on, then. I'll buy you lunch, if you play your cards right.

About The Author

Roger Granelli has published five novels and has been the recipient of three writing awards from the Welsh Arts Council He was a prize Winner in the 1999 Rhys Davies Short Story Competition and has had numerous short stories published in literary magazines, some of which have been broadcast on BBC Radio.

He has recently been selected to be part of the Quick Reads programme and his novel *Losing It* will be published, also by Accent Press, in March 2008

Roger is also a professional musician and composer, working in the UK, Europe and America for many years. He is currently teaching music in his home town of Pontypridd.